Praise
for
SUNNY GALE

"A moving, memorable, and fully realized rodeo saga. In Forbes's historical novel, a woman fights for the right to compete in rodeos—and becomes a star in the process.

"When Hannah Brandt, who comes from a hardscrabble background in Ohio and Nebraska, first gets to ride a horse in 1895 at the age of 14, she realizes that there is no going back to the way things were.... She wins first place in a race at the Cheyenne Frontier Day rodeo at 18, and soon she's known by a new name: Sunny Gale....

"This is a story of rodeos, marriages, sexism, and social mores—all churned together. In a wonderful afterword, Forbes offers a little-known real-life account of when women competed in the roughest of rodeo events from the very end of the 19th century to the early 1930s. In fact, Sunny Gale is modeled on the real-life Prairie Rose Henderson, and her rival, Ruth Pickering, is inspired by Bonnie McCarroll....

"Forbes is an experienced author, and her latest novel is beautifully, even poetically, written with well-developed characters."—*Kirkus Reviews* (starred)

"As a retired professional rodeo cowboy and rodeo announcer the wild West genre has been a major part of my personal life for years. I thoroughly enjoyed reading Sunny Gale and constantly found myself reluctant to put it down. Forbes captures an accurate picture of the relentless drive to compete along with a fascinating story of the earliest women in rodeo."—Abe Morris, author of *My Cowboy Hat Still Fits*

"Powerful, poignant, and authentic, Sunny Gale reveals how women once ruled rodeo, a story long hidden from history. Jamie Forbes brings these women into the light in a novel you won't forget."—Lynn Downey, author of the award-winning *Dudes Rush In*, Book #1 of the H Double Bar Dude Ranch series and *Dude Or Die*

"…a wonderfully written story that is filled with action and wonderful family moments along the way as well as historical accuracy of the time period. Sunny is a very strong and interesting protagonist and shows that strength throughout the story in the losses that she suffers and her ability and determination to never give up on her dreams….

"The descriptive writing makes one feel that they are really in the wilderness trying to survive or in the rodeo ring trying to win, right alongside Sunny and the others.

"*Sunny Gale* is exciting, well-written and developed, and will make the reader laugh and cry throughout.… I would highly recommend the story to all.

"*Quill* says: Sunny Gale is a wonderful example of a story that will pull readers into a new world, in this case, one of rodeo riding and the entrance of women into the sport. With its wonderfully descriptive writing and historical accuracy, I am sure that it will be a great success and of interest to many."—Kathy Stickles for *Feathered Quill Book Reviews*

Full reviews of all titles are available at:
jamielisaforbes.com

Praise for Other Books
by
Jamie Lisa Forbes

EDEN

"The author details 1950s small-town North Carolina in a way that makes readers feel like they're sweltering in the heat of the courtroom and shivering amidst the coldness of racial and class prejudices. To be able to communicate to the audience different relationship dynamics—friendships that break racial barriers, family ties, or the relationship an individual has with themself—in such a heartbreaking and realistic way shows her dedication to understanding diverse backgrounds and what it meant to have grown up in the south during such emotionally charged times. This book is the perfect reminder for readers that life would be much less colorful if not for the people we meet along the way."—Nellie Calanni for *The Feathered Quill*

Quill says: "Unexpected relationships can be the most rewarding, and award-winning author Jamie Lisa Forbes details them beautifully throughout *Eden*."

"*Eden* is a compelling read with unforgettable characters and an insightful look at our culture in a time and place where the color of one's skin tainted every aspect of life." —Virginia Campbell, *Amazon*

"I am pleased to recommend Forbes to family and friends. Her prose rides right up there with the classic southern novelists. This is a story to savor."—Bonnye Reed Fry, *NetGalley*

"Forbes really captured not only the time period but the atmosphere of the American South in such a beautiful, fulfilling way."—BettyBee306, *Goodreads*

"...very touching novel. I enjoyed the depth of characters and fell in love with them. The story moved at a good pace and I stayed engaged with the story throughout the book. It is a very thought provoking novel and days after finishing I find myself still thinking about the characters and the choices they made."—Hillary Swiers, *NetGalley*

"A powerful absorbing book right from the first page. I felt as though I was part of the story right along with the characters."—Erin Stetler, *NetGalley*

"Forbes has a deft hand at crafting space, time and character."—Deborah Cleaves, *NetGalley*

THE WIDOW SMALLS AND OTHER STORIES
2015 High Plains Book Award Winner

"Wonderful read. Showed compassion yet strength of character development."—J.E.B., *Amazon*

"Forbes's people have real hearts and battle real, sometimes subtle, problems. She is particularly skillful in portraying the helplessness of the individual pitted against a social system that makes little room for idiosyncrasies. And it is her understanding of the intensity that characterizes small-town life and family relationships that makes Forbes so effective"—Cara Chamberlain, *The Billings Gazette*

UNBROKEN
2011 WILLA Winner
for
Contemporary Fiction

"Forbes's debut novel is powerful and she presents a host of characters who are all complex, emotionally flawed beings. The plot's emphasis on two strong women struggling to maintain a relationship is unique against a dramatic background of infidelity, single motherhood, poverty and small town isolation."—WILLA Judge

"What an amazing story about strength and weakness and about how grinding disappointment and endless hard work plays out in people's lives."—WILLA Judge

"The writing is realistic and true to the nature of life in rural Wyoming. Harsh winters, endless wind, and dependence on neighbors to survive form the backdrop of this novel. Ms. Forbes writes with a sparseness of prose to match the landscape. This book is one that opens a window onto a way of life few people experience."—Suzanne Lilly, *The Teacher Writer* Blog

SUNNY GALE

A Novel

JAMIE LISA FORBES

Cover Design: Antelope Design
After an early photograph of the grounds and crowd
at Cheyenne Frontier Days

This is a work of fiction. Any references to places,
events or people living or dead
are intended to add to a sense of authenticity
and to give life to the story.
Names, characters and incidents
are products of the author's imagination
and their resemblance to any real-life counterparts
is entirely coincidental.

Pronghorn Press
pronghornpress.org

For Addison and Carter

*I have never tired of rodeo in my life.
I have never seen one show too many,
be it good, bad or middlin'. I hope there's
an arena in Heaven...that's where
you'll find me.*

Fanny Sperry Steele
Champion Saddle Bronc Rider

SUNNY GALE

1

The shed door drags on the snow. She wrenches it open, grimaces at the dwindling piles of coal. The fall of '29—that was the last time she and Clem had filled this shed. Now snow filters down through gaps in the roof, dusting the coal that remains.

Maybe there's a month left there if she burns it for just a few hours a day.

Heavy snows fell in December stranding her on this ranch. She crossed the last day of 1931 off the wall calendar. By her count, it's now February 2, 1932.

Any day now—maybe today—a warm wind will come and melt the snow, open the roads. Then she can go for help.

Old friends—time and chance. They'd been her steady—if fickle—partners in the profession she had crafted.

Back when she was a girl, her stepfather, Tremain, would send her to collect dried manure to burn for fuel. The chore turned her stomach and though no one was watching, she felt ashamed as she trundled along with her wheelbarrow. She'd happily haul a wheelbarrow out now if only there were bare ground anywhere.

Hannah Brandt—that was the name she'd had when her family settled in the Sand Hills. Her given name. Fourteen years old when her first winter began on the Plains. In 1895, she'd been bounced in a wagon all the way from Homer, Ohio because her widowed mother, Francine, had deluded herself into believing that the new bridegroom by her side—her errant former brother-in-law—would become a man while building them a homestead in new country. Tremain, who, long past the storied age of sowing his wild oats, had no prospects. Never mind. Francine had squared her shoulders and faced the horizon, determined to set the facts at odds with her presumptions miles behind. That was the kind of woman she'd always been.

Hannah left Nebraska with a name of her own choosing, "Sunny Gale." Tremain and Francine didn't fare so well. Of the three, it was Hannah who was transformed, not by the rigors of pioneer life, but by passion. The passion that engulfed her that winter when she found the wild filly she called "Zephira."

SUNNY GALE

Day after day the winter wind had rampaged over their rickety homestead, making Tremain grind his teeth and Francine hold her hands over her ears. It roared from hunger. An unabated hunger meant to drive all living things into the earth. Strip hide and flesh. She sensed it was after her, too. That's what she heard when she listened to it.

Hannah had found the wild filly—she believed it was hers even if she'd never laid a hand on it—during a late winter thaw. Sun and wind had cleared the snow from the land, except for crusty lumps pocketed here and there. When she'd balked at Tremain's orders to go collect cattle manure for fuel, he'd barked, "You were quick to feed that stove at the least chill! You've frittered away our coal as if we were still back in Homer. Look out over those hills! Do you see the deliveryman approaching with your weekly haul of coal? You'll get off your plump heinie and hunt for fuel. It's nothing to me if you're cold."

Tears streaming down her face at Tremain's taunts, she rolled the wheelbarrow down the hill. To pass the time, and to distract herself from her disgust at the task, she imagined the stories of the Greek gods. She had a picture book of them. Zeus, Hera, Athena, Apollo. She loved the illustrations: the men's corded muscles, the women's flowing robes. Some of the women carried weapons: Artemis, a bow and arrow and Athena, a spear. Nowhere had she ever seen a girl toting a spear. Here's what she loved about the god family: they could be angry, jealous, even sad, but never crushed, never broken, never made to feel as if they were worthless. As if they were a clumsy human oaf trudging over the prairie in long skirts. Goddesses didn't have to yield to male tyrants. Goddesses never had to pick up cow manure with a pitchfork.

She could pretend her pitchfork was a spear.

After an hour, she parked the wheelbarrow, climbed a slope, and slowly rotated as the wind whipped her skirts against her legs. She'd spent so many days indoors hating it here that she'd never realized how grand this land was. So grand her senses couldn't absorb it all. She felt rooted in place yet transported to the farthest reaches of the horizon all at the same time. Smudges of green spread in the depressions where the snow had melted. Hope, for the end of winter, flushed through her, warm as the sun on her face. She took her hat off and shook her hair free.

And that's when she spotted the runt filly watching from a half-mile off. It looked thin and ragged. She began to descend the hill toward it, but the filly wheeled away and ran.

Feed, that's what Hannah knew she needed to get close to that horse. She hustled for the house with the cow patties bouncing in her wheelbarrow. If only she could get in the barn before Tremain returned from checking his cows. His calves should be coming any day, he'd said. She should be able to sneak out a bucket of feed while he was gone. But as she pushed the wheelbarrow up toward the buildings, there was Greta, their draft horse, in the barn doorway. There, too, was Tremain, rising from the ground. At his feet lay a half-skinned dead cow.

He glanced at the wheelbarrow. "That's not even half full," he said.

She gagged again, this time at the sight of glistening pink flesh.

"You can drop your delicacy, Hannah. There's no place for it here. We've all had to get used to new ways, harder ways. It's simple. We have to survive. You've got to learn to work like a man and not faint away at a homestead's tasks. This isn't the first time you've seen a dead cow. If the grass doesn't grow soon, you're going to see a lot more of them."

Hannah shifted to avoid the smell. "Are you going to take the hide to town?" A trip to town would give her half a day or more to sneak feed out to the wild horse.

"You're no brighter than a cow yourself. Why would I waste a whole day's trip for one hide?"

He squatted back down to his labor.

"I was hungry," she said, to explain her half finished task. Not a complete falsehood. A creature she cared for was hungry.

"Hungry? As if your mother's got a full larder to bake you cakes and cookies at your whim like you were used to. You haven't done near enough work to be hungry. You'll eat when that wheelbarrow's full."

It was Hannah's father, Henry, who'd proposed the homestead in Nebraska. All the men talked about it at the lumber mill, he had said. Plots of land for nothing, or next to nothing. The work would be hard, but with land of their own, secure, they'd build a better life. The savages had been rounded up or killed. Endless grass for grazing, alfalfa tall as a man, that's what the advertisements told him. Fresh air and sunshine for Hannah to grow on, too.

Back then, her Uncle Tremain had been her treasured companion. He'd burst through the front door, pockets full of sweets for her to dig out. He'd bend to kiss her forehead and she'd knock his cap off to watch his thick hair fall over his eyes.

With Hannah in tow, he'd stride to the kitchen and bellow, "Francine, what will we be having for supper?"

Francine would straighten from kneading dough or rolling pie crusts, flour on her apron, tiny beads of sweat along her nose.

"Nothing for layabouts such as you, Tremain. Henry's hauled lumber to the mill all day and his supper is on the stove. You know very well that he's said if you're having a plate here, you're to work for it."

The sparkle in her eyes didn't match her words. Oh, yes, she liked Tremain. Very much.

Tremain broke the heel off a loaf of bread and bit into it. "Fullerton let me go at the blacksmith shop. You know that."

"He expects his employees to be there before midafternoon."

"I am offended at your exaggeration. His specific complaint was about my gambling. His laborers wouldn't have to play chuck-a-luck until dawn if he paid them a decent wage.

"Hmmm. You've put fresh rosemary in this. You grew it yourself, didn't you? Henry doesn't know how lucky he is."

"You can take that ladle now and wash it."

He set the ladle down on the stovetop, winked at Hannah and sidled to the door.

"Tremain..."

He wasn't done teasing, even if Francine

was. He grabbed Hannah by her shoulders, pushed her in front of him and whispered in her ear. "Save me, my sweet princess."

"Stop using her. I won't have her swayed by your indolence, no matter how charming its veneer."

"Spare a plate, won't you?"

"Only if I can tell Henry in truth that you stopped by but couldn't stay because you were looking for work."

Tremain took a deep bow that made Hannah laugh. "So it shall be, m'lady. As soon as I savor this repast, out I shall go to seek my advancement through honest industry."

Tremain's jokes had failed to move her father. "There's no sufferance in the world for a man who won't be employed," he had said.

The wagon and horses had been paid for and the house was half-packed when her father complained of a toothache. They all believed he'd heal quickly once the tooth was pulled. Instead, within days he collapsed in a fever and died of blood poisoning.

Two months after the funeral, Hannah had been ecstatic when her mother told her she was going to marry Tremain. There would be laughter in the house again after all the gloom and tears.

"What do you think, Hannah?" said Tremain. "Your mother wants me to pick up Henry's plan and see it through." He shrugged. "I guess it's as good as anything else. It's tedious how they all look down their noses at me here. No farmer would have me at harvest-time. Your mother's right. We have to make a new life. No matter what hardships we find, at least we'll all be together."

Now there was no trace left of her companion, Uncle Tremain, in the grizzled man bent over the cow carcass. The hardships had scoured away the charm, leaving this ogre who took his rage out on Hannah...as if she'd had anything to do with it. She'd lost her father and her uncle both. But there was the promise out there of a creature she could care for, one that would become her own.

"The clods just fall through this pitchfork you gave me. I could pick up more if I had the spade. I'll just run in the barn and get it."

All he did was grunt and when he didn't look up, she lifted a bucket from the grain bin, filled it and hid it behind her skirts.

"Good day, Tremain!" she called as she started down the slope. *Who was the stupid one now?*

The next morning she found the bucket empty. Had the filly eaten the grain, or had other wild animals come along? She searched the horizon. Her heart jumped when she spotted the filly. Sure enough.

After a week of sneaking buckets of oats out from under Tremain's nose, Hannah had been able to get close enough to count the knots in the filly's mane, but no closer. The filly was cocoa-colored with white stockings and a white blaze. Hannah could count her ribs, too, so she must have lost her mother. As soon as she licked the bucket clean, she would knock it over, snort and run away. She'd look back, as if she were teasing. *Come catch me.* And if Hannah tried to follow, she would buck and then thunder away. Hannah would plead, "Please come back," but the hoofbeats stubbornly pounded into the distance.

She wished she were back in Homer so she could tell her best friend, Thea, of her new secret. Thea would be envious since the only animal she had was a fat old cat who wouldn't play and who lounged on pillows all day long. Back home, it would still be cold enough for ice skating. Hours and hours of circling round the pond, trying to catch the boys' eyes and ignoring them when they called out. When she and Thea were tired, there was the warming hut with hot chocolate and hot cross buns. Warm huts, warm food. None of this rampaging wind.

Wind rustled the grass husks. The filly was nowhere in sight.

How would it feel to be on that filly's back with her fingers woven through her mane? How puny Tremain would look as they ran away, leaving him behind.

Every day she would leave the bucket a bit closer to home.

It wasn't spring, after all. Snow rode in on the wind with a fury. The first day of the blizzard nothing could be seen from the house. No ground below, no sky above, only frothing blasts of white.

For the first few hours after dawn, the three of them sat at the table while the wind rattled the door, and snow sifted through cracks in the chinking. Francine's hands shook as she bent over her sewing.

Tremain sucked on his pipe as he watched her. "What do you think this weather will do to our calves, Francine?"

The storm unnerved Hannah. The wind was so strong she was afraid it would peel the roof off their heads. But the tremor in her mother's voice frightened her even more. No doubt about it. Their very lives were in danger.

"You mustn't think of going out. You wouldn't be able to see your hands out there. You could get lost in an instant. And don't you make Hannah go out either."

Tremain reached across the table, pulled Francine's hand to his mouth, and kissed it. "We both know that a calf born in this storm will never survive. Not to mention what might be happening to the ones we already have, defenseless. Can we afford to lose what we've put into our venture? And what will we do then? We've gambled everything."

"What about our lives? If you are lost, what about Hannah and me? Alone, fodder for thieves, vagrants, beasts?"

"If anything were to happen, you've got the Winchester."

"But I don't know how to use it. I don't want to know how to use it! The cruelty in this wasteland—it's unending. We should have taken a house in town until we'd had a chance to see what this place was like before we invested anything."

"And gone through our money at the hotel, waiting and waiting?"

"I know how to use the Winchester," Hannah said. "Tremain showed me how."

"Hush. Young ladies do not fire weapons."

"Francine, there's no other way," said Tremain, "If I don't go out to try to save what we have, we could lose it all." He pulled on his overcoat, picked up his boots by the stove.

"Tremain!"

He opened the door and Francine shrieked as the snow whooshed in. Snow was already drifted knee-deep at the threshold. Her mother grabbed his arm. "Don't go out there!"

He gripped her shoulders and pushed her away. "You used to scold me for how I behaved in front of the child. Will your hysteria help her now?"

He might as well have tried to soothe the raging wind itself. The moment the door closed Francine broke out in sobs.

"We've made such a terrible mistake. All this way to nowhere and we shall lose our lives here. Oh, Hannah, I've failed you so."

Hannah looked past her mother toward the door. Somewhere in this storm was her filly waiting for its bucket of feed.

Two days, three, passed before the skies cleared. And when her mother had finally allowed her out, she'd had to break a trail through the snow until she found the filly again.

Tremain saved one calf, lost three. More hides were draped on the corral rails.

Tremain cursed, her mother cried, while every day Hannah moved her feed bucket closer. A mile from the corral, a half-mile, a hundred yards. At last, inside the gate.

Wrapped in a horse blanket, Hannah waited by the rails while the runt filly stood tensed outside. The wind sliced right through the blanket, and she shivered. *Please come, Zephira.*

Zephira. That was the name she'd chosen for her filly. In her book, one story told of how Zephyr, the spring wind, had fallen in love with a dancing white mare and, in time, their offspring became the foundation of all the great and fast horses that roamed the globe. In the illustration, Zephyr and his mare watched as their plump colts galloped away in all directions.

Here was one of the lost daughters: Zephira. A demigoddess.

Hannah didn't dare move, though she was turning numb from cold. Blown sand collected around the bucket. The filly's mane lifted and fell. She wouldn't budge. Too many unfamiliar sounds around the house and barn, the banging of loose boards, the blades rattling on the windmill. She stamped and whinnied.

Hannah understood.

Bring the bucket out here, where it's safe. That's what Zephira demanded.

Hannah knew the filly had no fondness for her; the bucket was their only connection. As unendurable as these moments were, she knew time was running out. If she didn't catch that filly within the next few days before the grass came up, she'd never see her again. Zephira would drift off beyond this homeplace in search of her brothers and sisters and never return.

Hunger. Hunger was Hannah's helper. Hunger called to the filly better than Hannah could. Zephira took two steps to the gate, then stopped. Hannah's pulse pounded in her ears. *Five paces more.* The wind gusted, again. The filly listened. And just like that she walked far enough into the enclosure where the gate could be swung shut behind her. She sniffed at Hannah. Hannah nodded back. *Yes, you know me, you can come in.*

The filly snorted once before plunging her muzzle into the bucket. Hannah slipped the blanket off, crept around to the gate, and latched it.

Now what will you do, Hannah?

All her energies had been channeled into this one moment. She hadn't thought of what would come next.

Tremain would come and she wouldn't be able to hide the filly from him. Another mouth to feed, he would say.

Howling, pleading, throwing herself on the ground—that would do the trick. Please let her stay. I will care for her, then you can sell her and get your money back for the feed. Surely, he would agree when he saw how much it meant to her. For all his rants, she still believed he loved her.

The bucket overturned. The filly was done. She wheeled, walked back to the gate and found her way barred. She nosed along the corral, probing for the way out, every step quicker, more panicked. She broke into a dead run and slammed into the corner so hard she nearly fell over backwards. She wheeled and tore the other way, slamming into the next corner. Then she was running blindly, all the while blasting her alarm, a racket heard over the wind.

Hannah didn't know what to do. Something had to be done before the horse hurt herself. She tried walking toward her. *Please, please stop.* Zephira was too terrified by the enclosure to even know that Hannah was there. Already, the skin on her chest was bloody where she'd hit the rails. Another slam and her injuries could get even worse.

With tears burning her eyes, Hannah unlatched the gate, and the wind swung it wide open. The filly found the open space and was gone.

"What in the hell?"

Hannah heard Tremain's voice behind her. She turned. Tremain had the Winchester with him.

"You heard me. What are you doing?"

"Nothing."

"You've been feeding that mustang, haven't you? I see the bucket there."

"I thought I could tame her. I thought I'd have a horse to ride."

"You don't even know how to ride, and that's not any kind of horse. All that is is a wild animal."

"I've seen people ride. I can learn."

"We don't need you to ride. Better you tend to your mother and see to her needs. This winter is about to kill her, too." He nodded to where the filly had stopped to look back at them. "That animal is starving. It's kinder to end its misery."

"No!"

"You've been teaching her to eat our feed, feed for our cattle and horse. They don't have enough as it is. We could all die out here if this weather doesn't break. Don't you see that? Your foolish mind is still lost in some fairyland. When will you grow up?"

Hannah dropped to her knees. "I won't feed her again, Tremain, I promise."

"It's too late. She already knows to come here for food. She'll come back, maybe even break into the barn. Look, she's not leaving now."

And it was true. The filly hadn't moved.

Tremain raised the Winchester to his shoulder and took aim.

"No, please, I'll do anything. Just please... *please* don't."

He fired and the filly crumpled.

Hannah ran out the gate, stumbling and falling through the drifts, and when she reached the filly and saw it was dead, she threw her head into its neck. The touch of warm fur at last. She sank her fingers into the filly's mane and sobbed and sobbed. She didn't know how long she laid there, but when she sat up, all that met her were empty hills fanning out to the horizons and up above, a sky where clouds raced blind.

The loss of the filly had happened only to her. The world had moved on.

2

February 3rd

Dawn blazes through the ice on the cabin windows. Droplets run off the sill, but it's not warm. Sunny can see her breath.

She can't get up for the pain that radiates down her neck and through both shoulders. Pain she's borne since her accident in 1918. It always worsens during the winter. If she didn't have livestock left to care for, she'd just lie in bed, like a bear waiting for spring.

She pushes herself up. Only remedy for the pain is caring for those animals. Abiding with them moment by moment gives her hope, makes her think that they will survive this winter together.

SUNNY GALE

On her bed are two packets of letters. She had re-read them and thought to burn them for fuel this morning. One packet is from Francine. The smaller packet is from her first husband, Luke Mangum. She was sixteen when they married. What had he looked like anyway? She closes her eyes to conjure his image. Slim as a pole. Straight whitish-blond hair. Ice-blue eyes.

The first time she'd seen him in Alliance, Nebraska, she had ached to jump off her parents' wagon and chase after him.

In the packet are their divorce papers and letters and postcards he had sent her for a few years after she'd left Nebraska. He'd write a page or two and conclude by asking about their daughter, Mollie.

Sunny never responded. Their marriage had faltered from the start. Luke's idea of love was to treat her as one of his possessions, like a horse or cow. Use her when and as he wished. He couldn't tolerate the notion that she craved a destiny of her own making. She'd hoped her lack of response hurt him. She wanted him to grapple with the fact that he'd never have any kind of hold over her again. Not even through the child they shared.

Well, she was a rotten mother to both her children. Everyone thought so. Francine thought so though she never said it to Sunny's face. After the fiasco with Tremain, she would never have dared. But remorse for keeping Mollie from her real father? Hell, no! Luke had had the means all along to come see Mollie if he'd wanted. She wouldn't have tried to stop him if he'd come. She suspects he never tried to come because he couldn't face her again. All the days he must have spent in miles and miles of open range, it gets easy to set people aside.

Silly this sourness about him now. After all, they'd been children themselves.

The last letter was dated 1901. He had written to tell her that he'd remarried, that he was happy, and he hoped she was happy, too. "Give my love to Mollie." There was a wedding photograph. He'd grown a little stout.

Sunny rises with a groan, steps over to the coal stove, and dumps the packet inside. She looks back at Francine's packet. No, she couldn't burn those even if her life depended upon it.

In Alliance, a mirror wide as a barn door hung in the Overland Bar. Hannah noticed that the first thing every man did when he entered was to look at his image. It didn't matter if they came in laughing with their companions, exhausted, frozen, and alone. It didn't matter whether they were landowners or cowhands, trappers, homesteaders, or just filthy drifters. Like arrows, their eyes shot to the glass. Some of them were startled by their reflections, as if they hadn't seen themselves in months. No doubt about it, the mirror drew them every bit as much as the liquor. Why else would the place need a mirror, much less one that big? Certainly not to reflect brawn or beauty. The customers were nothing to look at, nearly all of them hairy as bears and smelly as carcasses.

Watching them and their reflections, it seemed to Hannah that they sought reassurance—

I'm still here. Once their glasses were in front of them, they never looked up again.

The mirror reflected the glitter from the gas chandelier and the liquor bottles on the shelves and counter. Glittery light, even in the middle of the afternoon, because the shades at the Overland were always drawn.

The mirror wasn't intended for women's use because Hannah never saw other women there, although she looked for them. Whores, that's who they'd be if they were there. Hannah was dying to see a real whore. What did it feel like to be a whore? In filched pictures she'd seen at school, they wore lacy corsets and bloomers. They were always smiling, unlike women in regular family portraits where everyone stared straight at the camera, expressionless. Maybe they felt pretty. That would be nice...to feel pretty.

Hannah gazed in the mirror, too, not to confirm her existence, but to look for the tiniest sign indicating her forthcoming transformation into graceful splendor worthy of a goddess. Surely beauty awaited at the end of this process of developing a bosom, sprouting hair and bleeding between her legs once a month. What good did it do to become a woman if she couldn't be beautiful?

Hope fluttered in her chest every time she walked into the Overland only to be dashed, as it was now. The mirror reflected a lumpy clod, shoulders too broad, hair too kinky, buck teeth too noticeable. Before she averted her gaze and searched for Tremain—which is why her mother had sent her there—she chafed at this image and wondered what her future would be. How would she find a man who would even notice her, much less marry her? And if she couldn't get married, what kind of a life would she have? A nasty, mean spinster who all the children hated—that's what happened to women who weren't pretty. Worse than a whore.

"What are you staring in that mirror for?" Tremain grabbed her arm. "There's nothing for you there to look at."

"Mama's getting cold sitting in the wagon waiting for you. She sent me to get you."

Before Zephira, she used to want Tremain's attitude toward her to change. She had hoped that if she complied with his demands, he'd transform back into the teasing companion he used to be. But after he had killed the filly, she realized there would be no going back. She no longer cared what he thought.

They stepped outside and the blinding sunlight made her blink away the image of that ugly girl in the mirror.

"Tremain."

"What?"

"I never see any girls in that bar."

"Of course, you don't. That's no place for women and girls to be."

"Do you ever see girls there?"

He stopped. "What are you asking me?"

"I'm just asking, that's all."

"Stop asking. Stop thinking about it. The life in there is no life for a girl like you. You have a path to follow. You are to help me and your mother. One day you'll marry and be a comfort to your husband. Someday maybe you'll own our place. Maybe you'll get a bigger place. And you'll have means to an income off land that no one can take away from you. You have nothing more to think about than that path straight ahead of you."

So he had seen whores there.

Her mother called from the wagon. "Tremain, what took you so long?"

"Getting advice about planting. Trying to pick up what everyone else here knows."

"Look at how low the sun is. We'll be traveling in the dark."

"I'll put Greta in a trot."

"And bounce us right out of the wagon? And our supplies, too."

Greta hadn't traveled twenty feet when they were overtaken by a stream of bawling cows and calves and forced to stop. Cowboys on either side of the street hustled the cattle along with ropes and bullwhips. Hannah's homestead didn't have more than twenty cows and here were dozens, maybe hundreds. The cowboys were all lean and unshaven. A young one with a few blond hairs on his lip rode up alongside the wagon and tipped his hat. Hannah smiled. She was sure he had intended it just for her.

"What's your name?" she called out.

"Hush, Hannah," her mother said.

The cowboy smiled back. "Luke Mangum. What's yours?"

"Hannah," she started to say before Francine pinched her arm and said loudly, "You are not to speak to that boy."

Hannah waved and the young man waved back as he trotted ahead to turn the cattle. Her heart sank as he disappeared around the corner. Not likely that she'd ever see him again. Not him or any other boy out in the dirt patch where they lived.

"Mangum," said Tremain. "I heard they are the biggest landowners around. They must be moving those cattle off to summer pasture."

Cattle streamed around them until all that was left were straggling calves. Half a dozen cowboys brought up the rear, talking loudly and joking with one another. She liked their ease in the saddles. She liked their rangy horses, all different sizes and colors. She longed to be on a horse with them, waving at the people gawking on the sidewalks and then easing on into a trot and not looking back.

"I could be a cowhand," she said.

"You'll do no such thing, Hannah. I spoke to a Mrs. Ida Hepworth over at the store today. She's a widow. She's just filed on land two miles away from ours. She's going to be your teacher and you'll go back to having lessons. We may live among the uneducated and uncivilized, but you will not become one of them."

"I want to learn to ride."

"No proper gentleman will be interested in a horseback rider. We can hope that soon, proper gentlemen will migrate here, just as we have, and will be looking for educated girls to make a proper home for them."

"It would be a help if she learned to ride, Francine. If something were to happen and us so far out..."

"I thought we agreed that raising Hannah was my responsibility."

Tremain looked off beyond Greta to the ruts ahead. "So it is."

SUNNY GALE

After Hannah had helped Tremain with planting oats and alfalfa, she walked the two miles twice a week to the Hepworth property. It was June and the hills were dotted with tiny blossoms—purples, lemon yellows, bridal whites. She knelt every few steps to study the details of the petals, delicate as if they had been sculpted by fairy hands. Just two months ago, it had seemed as if nothing would survive on these plains. Yet life had sprung back as if those miserable days had never been. So much color and motion around her, so many voices of birds and frogs. Every few steps she heard a different swirl of sounds. Was it possible that there was too much of life to hold on to? One had to parcel it out in slices to be savored, a slice such as just one petal of purple phlox.

Mrs. Hepworth spread her lessons on a table outside her cabin. Studying outdoors had its hindrances. Hannah had to find stones to hold the books and tablets down so they wouldn't blow away and, in the brief moments when the breeze stalled, mosquitoes swarmed over them, an unwelcome seasonal manifestation.

"It's finally summer and we still can't roll up our sleeves, or our flesh will be sucked dry by these pests," said Mrs. Hepworth. "Are you sure you'd rather not study inside? It's cooler and we can have some nice tea without worrying about insects befouling it."

"It feels so warm after being cold for so long. I don't want to miss a moment of it. And it's lovely watching the scenery change from one moment to the next, how the light and shadows shift."

"All very distracting from Mr. Dickens and *The Tale of Two Cities*. Plus, your face is turning beet-red from the sun. Put on your bonnet, please."

"I don't want the bonnet. It's too warm."

"That settles it. We will have to move indoors." Mrs. Hepworth rose, collecting the books.

"Wait, there's a cowboy coming."

"He's just passing by, Hannah. He has no business here."

"What if he does? What if he wants directions? Or food and water?"

"Oh, Hannah." Mrs. Hepworth was annoyed by Hannah's diversion.

He was riding toward them. And with a jolt of pleasure, Hannah realized it was the young man she'd seen in town, the one who had ridden up next to the wagon. She waved her bonnet frantically to make sure he saw them.

"Howdy," he called out.

"Howdy to you," Hannah answered.

Mrs. Hepworth squeezed her arm. "Hannah! You don't know this man."

He was almost upon them, too close to be able to tell Mrs. Hepworth that she did know him. He jumped off a tall buckskin.

"You all must be newcomers. I don't remember a homestead here before."

Mrs. Hepworth curtsied, as did Hannah.

"I am Ida Hepworth. I did just arrive here last fall, as did my young student here, Miss Hannah Brandt."

"Luke Mangum. Nice to meet you both."

"You met me two weeks ago in town," said Hannah, "Don't you remember?"

"Can't say that I do."

"You were coming through with your cattle, and I was in the wagon." Her spirits rose when she saw the recognition in his face.

"You were with some folks."

"My parents. We were on our way home."

"Do they live here, too?"

"No, we're a couple of miles west."

"The place on the hilltop with the big corral?"

"That's it."

"Mr. Mangum, can you tell me if these mosquitoes will be bedeviling us all summer?" asked Mrs. Hepworth.

"No, ma'am, they'll die off when the water dries up, then come the horseflies and you'll find they're even worse."

"I wonder that you're not swatting at yourself the way we are."

"Just used to them, I guess."

"We were just about to move indoors. Would you like a cup of tea with us? And I have some biscuits as well."

"I'd like some water, please. I can't stop long. I'm looking for a missing bull."

"Let's stay outside," said Hannah. "Please."

"If we must, but only if you put on that bonnet. And please continue reading while I get some refreshment for Mr. Mangum. I'm sure our visitor would enjoy your reading. Mr. Mangum, have you read *A Tale of Two Cities*?"

"I don't read too well."

"Then, Hannah, your reading will illumine this young mind as well as your own."

"Yes, ma'am."

She looked down at the page. "'A wonderful fact to reflect upon, that every human creature is constituted to be that profound secret and mystery to every other,'" she read. "Hey, Luke, how far do you live from here?"

"About eight mile. Our homeplace is along Jumping Creek. So how do you get over here for these lessons?"

"I walk."

"You walk four miles a day? Where's your horse? Can't you ride?"

"No, I don't have a horse."

"It's not safe to be out here without a horse. You don't know the country. You've got to be ready to go somewhere fast. Like if you got snakebit. Or overtaken by a storm."

His slender hands were folded in front of him, elbows resting on the table. Blond hair, damp with sweat, stuck out from under his cowboy hat. His gaze was so earnest, so fastened on her.

"The storms are all gone now. And I can watch out for snakes."

"You can watch all you want, but you're likely to step on one before you even see it. It happens to fellers all the time. And you might not think it on a day like today, but storms are never gone. Never. They can blow up over you in a moment. Me and my dad feel sorry for you 'steaders. You're not equipped at all to be able to survive out here. You're all likely to get killed or blown away."

Mrs. Hepworth set a pitcher of water and glasses on the table.

"Luke says we're all likely to get killed or blown away, Mrs. Hepworth."

"And why is that?"

"My dad says it's because the government and money-hungry grubbers misled you. They sold this to you like it was Garden of Eden and it's not anything like that."

"Thank you for your words of wisdom. And how old are you, Mr. Mangum? Eighteen?"

"Nineteen, ma'am."

"Nineteen. And unread. May I share with you that in just a century, immigrants from many countries and all walks of life have settled half of this continent. Which was wilderness when we found it. What it takes, Mr. Mangum, is character and hard work. That is what we have learned. With our industry, this wilderness will become a breadbasket to the world, and there will be bustling, prosperous habitations, just as exist back east."

Luke downed his glass of water. "If you say so, ma'am." His spur jingled as he threw his leg over the seat and stood up. "As you say, I don't have book learning to speak of. But character and hard work won't get you very far without a horse. Miss Hannah, we'll lend you one, if you want."

"You would do that for me? What about your parents? What will they say?"

"It's just my dad. My mother's passed on. I'll work it out if it's what you want."

"I almost had a horse."

"What happened to it?"

It still stung. She didn't want this boy to see her pain. Or her shame at the mistakes she'd made that had cost Zephira her life. She looked down at the rough splintered wood.

"She didn't make it."

"Well, here's a new chance. Are you going to be home tomorrow?"

"Yes, I only have lessons twice a week."

"I'll stop by tomorrow."

"Thanks."

"You've made a new friend," Mrs. Hepworth said flatly as Luke trotted away.

Hannah noted the gray in her hair—she wasn't young anymore. She'd come out here without a husband. He must have been gone for a long time. That's why she couldn't share in Hannah's joy. By the pucker of her mouth, Hannah could see she'd forgotten what it might feel like if a boy sat across from her, folded his hands on the table and talked to her as if she were the only girl in the world. Mrs. Hepworth no longer remembered how the blood would pulse right up a girl's chest into her cheeks.

"Yes, ma'am."

"It seems as if Dickens will suffer. And long division as well."

"He's doing it to help me," Hannah said.

"Young men don't know altruism, Hannah."

The next morning, Hannah raced through her chores. Light the stove, draw water for the house, feed the chickens, milk the cow, slop the pigs, all of it done by the time sun launched off the horizon.

"What's got into you?" Tremain asked. "Never seen you up before daylight before."

Hannah didn't look at him. She leaned against the corral, her eyes scanning the green hilltops and following the deep shadows still in the gullies.

"Nothing."

"With all that energy you can come help me put up more fence."

"I want to stay with Mama today."

"Suit yourself."

To Hannah's relief, Tremain soon left. She didn't want him around when Luke came. But what would she say when he came home?

Well, he couldn't complain about feed now. It was summertime—wasn't it—and grass was everywhere. And this wouldn't be a wild horse. It was a tame horse, ready to ride. By fall, when he'd seen how useful it was to have another horse, he'd be all right with it.

The hours crawled. Her mother sat her down to sew a new blouse for herself. She'd been allowed to pick her own cloth, but it was the last thing she was interested in now. She popped out of her seat every few minutes to go outside. Francine scolded her for opening the door and letting even more mosquitoes in.

"What's the matter with you today, Hannah? Are you sick?"

"I just want to be outside. It's boring in here."

Her mother put the back of her hand against Hannah's forehead. "No fever. All right. You're driving me mad. Go outside then."

A hot wind bent the grasses. Clouds massed overhead, then tore apart and dissipated. There would be no rain today. The sun tipped at the zenith and the barn's shadow lengthened across the corral. Hannah sat in the shade and wrapped her arms around her knees. She closed her eyes and willed him to appear. When she opened them again, the shadows had traveled a smidge further. A cottontail hopped by. She had kept so still he hadn't seen her. A swallow flitted from post to post. Maybe he wouldn't come. Maybe he had forgotten. She couldn't pick herself up and go back inside the house. Her mother would read her disappointment.

Shadows had swallowed the corral whole when she spotted him in the distance at last. Yes, he was leading a horse. She leapt to her feet. How slow he was. He couldn't feel how her heart was yanking him toward her. It was too much to stand in one place any longer. She flew down the hill and still it seemed that she ran for miles before she was close enough to shout, "Luke, you came!" She was out of breath.

"Hold off, you about scared my horse. Is there a fire or something?"

"I didn't know where you were."

"Working. We're putting in some windbreaks. I couldn't get over here until I was done for the day. I brought you your horse. I figured you'd need a saddle, too, and I brought that. Truth is, you can ride your horse from here."

She looked at the horse he led, a mahogany color with a black mane and tail.

"He's beautiful!"

"He's got some age on him but he's yours. Name him what you want. You need to grab a hold of him quick. My horse is jumpy at your skirts flapping in the wind."

She took the lead rope and stroked the horse's face. His head dropped at the pressure of her hand.

"Atlas."

"Atlas! We usually name 'em something we can remember, like Blaze or Pepper. Why Atlas?"

"Because I like the stories of the Greek gods. There's something divine in a horse, don't you think?"

"No. But you can't get any work done without them."

"Look how he's dropping his head, so sweet and kind."

"Well, you better get on him."

"Luke, I have to tell you something. I don't know how to ride."

"You start by getting on."

"How?"

Luke dismounted. He looked below her waist and frowned. "You're going to have to hitch up that skirt. You got something on underneath?"

"Bloomers."

"That'll work for now until you come up with something better. Pick up your left leg there and put it in the stirrup. Now I'm going to boost you up. Ready?"

"Yes."

He grabbed her hips and pushed her up so that her right leg swung over the horse and down the other side to the stirrup.

"Now put your feet in those."

She felt thrilled at her new height, amazed at how much more expansive her view was. The view brought a new sense of freedom. Luke had been right. Now a person could really get somewhere...if they could bust loose from their parents. Her gaze shot toward her house and, yes, Greta was there at the barn. No time to plan. She was going to have to take Tremain head on.

"Pick up the reins."

"I don't know how."

He took her fingers and curled them through. "Like that. You got it? Give Old Atlas a nudge with your feet and take off."

She bumped her feet against Atlas' sides, but he didn't budge.

"He's too used to the other horse. I guess he'll follow me up to your place."

Luke started to move off and Atlas followed. Even at a plod, Hannah had the sensation of gliding over the ground. It seemed her head would explode at so many feelings all at the same time—ecstasy

43

at these new sensations of height and motion. And dread as the homestead and Tremain grew closer.

Through their slow ascent, Hannah watched Tremain chewing on his pipe, mulling over all the rules of modesty she had violated. First one would be that she was setting astride a horse with her bloomers showing.

It served them right, didn't it? How absurd it had been of Tremain and Francine to think they could haul out to this wind-blasted land and sprinkle it with all the trappings of civilized life. Couldn't they see this land would slough it all off?

When the horses pulled up in front of him, Tremain growled, "Just what do you think you're doing Hannah?"

Her hands curled around the saddle horn. She decided she was not getting off. "You remember Luke, don't you?"

Luke held out his hand but Tremain didn't take it.

"I remember him but I can't think why he's here today."

Luke spoke up. "I saw her the other day at her teacher's. I offered to lend her the horse. Until she could get her own."

"I thank you. I know you meant well. But that's not a saddle for a young woman to sit in."

"Side saddles aren't used out here. I've seen plenty of girls and women, ride just like this. We don't ride for a hobby. People ride for work. Or to get somewhere. She'll be a lot more comfortable— and safer, too—in this saddle."

Tremain rocked back and forth on his heels as he considered. If those words had come from Hannah, he would have unleashed a torrent of ridicule. But filtered through this young stranger who seemed so at ease in the land, they wore the mantle of authority. Hannah looked down to hide her grin. She was going to get to keep Atlas after all.

"What if she falls off?" Tremain asked.

"Then she'll learn to get back on."

"We'll see what her mother says," said Tremain, and he turned toward the house.

"That was wonderful, Luke. I couldn't believe all those things you said. They've got to let me keep 'im now."

"You're welcome. But you do need to learn to ride. Think you want to learn some now?"

"If you'll teach me."

He dismounted and opened the corral gate. "Get Atlas in here."

Once again, she couldn't make Atlas move.

"I'm not helping you this time. Take the bottom half of your reins and slap his rump."

"But that'll hurt him."

"He'll be fine. You've got to let him know you're his boss. You can't let him decide when he's going."

She slapped Atlas with the reins, and he took one step.

"Harder."

"I don't want to hurt you, Atlas," she said and slapped him again. It worked this time. She glowed at the forward movement she'd produced on her own.

"You do that a couple more times and you won't need to do it anymore."

Luke shut the gate behind her, made her tie up the reins and attached his rope to the horse's halter. He wanted her to know how to sit when the horse walked, trotted, loped. Shoulders back, heels down, gaze forward over the horse's ears. She suffered through trot. Too bouncy.

"Hold on to the horn, grab with your thighs," he shouted.

She couldn't seem to coordinate it all. But then Luke launched her into a lope and her heart felt as if it had sprouted wings. Round and round they circled to motion that felt like soaring. She threw her head back to laugh, but what came out sounded more like a cry of joy, the same cry the falcons made as they glided on the updrafts high above. To move this way was to feel the wildness of the land pulse up from the ground, through the horse's hooves, up through the saddle to her core and then up and out her throat.

"Do you want to stop?"

"No!"

Round and round they went—she couldn't get enough of it—until Luke let the horse slow to a trot and Hannah's exhilaration drained away into awareness that the day was closing, the first star already poking out from the dusk. The cessation of motion brought her back to herself, to the corral, to Luke, to Tremain and her mother at the rail. Francine looked as if she'd been hit by a bolt of lightning.

SUNNY GALE

3

Past midnight, February 4th

Sunny and the full moon eye each other through the window, the moon's expression frozen at her plight. She has too much pain to sleep lying down, so she's made herself a bed in the rocking chair, covered herself with an elk hide. She can see her breath in the chilled cabin. Outside, there's nothing the moonlight hasn't touched. Light shimmers on the snow. Almost as clearly as in daylight, Sunny sees the pastures, the livestock huddled for warmth, the low hills beyond.

Snow so dazzling white.

She found one of her yearling heifers dead this morning. Coyotes had ripped open the carcass, sullied the snow with blood and entrails.

Tomorrow all of it will all be covered by blowing snow.

Will she end that way, too? Where will the moon find her then?

The cracks in her thumbs throb, reminding her that she is very much alive. She gets them every winter. She hears Clem's voice. "Hold them out. Nothing a little bear grease won't fix." She closes her eyes. She sees him taking her hands in his, warmth spreading down her forearms. He used to rub the salve in her hands for longer than what was needed, then look up, his eyes shining. "Better?"

She opens her eyes, tilts her face back toward the moon. Clem's eyes, the trace of his mouth, fade into the moon's fixed gaze.

Jars of Chief McGowan's Bear Grease were stacked on a table outside a tent in Alliance. What had made Hannah pause to study them on that summer's day was that the skin on her inner thighs had been rubbed bloody by saddle leather.

Chief McGowan emerged from his tent, mounted a soapbox, and beckoned the passersby to stop and hear the tale of his amazing product. He began with how his Irish mother had been kidnapped from her camp by the Sioux and then wedded to a most fearsome brave, how he had been born of this union and had been tutored, since infancy, by medicine men in the secrets and mysteries of the inscrutable Indian nation. He was now prepared to share one of these secrets with the world for mere pennies. Mind you, he confessed, it was not his own fortune that he pursued, but rather the ascension of the Red Man to his rightful and most noble seat among civilized nations.

Sitting behind crates of bear grease was his "squaw," so he said, and although she was dressed in buckskin, it appeared her face had been browned with shoe polish.

Hannah was stinging with both pain and shame. Her mother didn't know that she'd taken to skipping lessons at Mrs. Hepworth's so she could ride with Luke. They would meet at a little creek bed midway to Mrs. Hepworth's and off they'd go. Lessons done for the day. At first, the thrill of riding with Luke had made it easy to ignore her discomfort, but now Tremain was asking why she walked so oddly.

She had no money to buy the bear grease. She picked up can after can under the hawk eye of the "squaw." No chance of snatching one. She could leave it, pretend she wasn't interested, mosey away as if she didn't have a care in the world. Only the pain would still be there, pain she couldn't confess to anyone.

"Will you trade for it?" she asked Chief McGowan.

"What'd ya got?"

She hobbled as quickly as she could back to their wagon already loaded for the trip home. Francine and Tremain were at the bank. A bolt of grey wool lay wrapped in brown paper. Francine had meant to start sewing winter clothes. If Hannah rearranged the other purchases, stacked other items on top, maybe they would not notice it was missing before they left town.

Chief McGowan sucked on his pipe. "A whole bolt of cloth? My dear, I am not a knave. What do you say, a yard of your cloth for two cans?"

"Yes, sir."

He measured off a yard and slashed it with his pocketknife. Hannah hid her grease in her pockets and quickly replaced the bolt before Francine and Tremain returned. And so, the shame of prevarication supplanted the shame of theft, even as Francine's eyes swept over the wagon contents finding nothing amiss. Later, as Hannah hid in the barn and smeared the concoction on her thighs she thought at least her skin was soothed, if not her conscience. And her conscience would quit clamoring in a day or two. After all, she'd gotten past lying about Mrs. Hepworth.

The bear grease worked as a remedy, but Hannah knew it was not a solution. She needed clothes, an outer covering like the chaps Luke wore. Where could she get them or how could she make them? In spite of her theft, she thought of asking her mother. She had some cover as Luke visited every Sunday afternoon and she was allowed to ride with him then, although it was a grudging permission. Horseback riding was a habit that Francine hoped Hannah would tire of. Francine stared in horror every time as Hannah stepped in the stirrup and threw her leg over the cantle. It was as if she was seeing a woman hoist her skirts above her knees.

If Hannah had a pair of chaps, she could wear them under her skirts and over her bloomers. There was no other choice than to ask Luke if he had another pair. The more she thought about it the more it seemed rude that he hadn't anticipated her condition. Had he considered that she wore only bloomers between her skin and the leather? Maybe he hadn't. Maybe he was too embarrassed to mention it, as Hannah herself had been. For all the hours they'd spent in the saddle together, some topics were beyond the limits of decorum, like Hannah's legs.

She'd worn holes in her bloomers anyhow. She tried to plot the conversation with her mother when, inevitably, she'd have to patch them.

"Why are there holes in your bloomers, Hannah?"

"The flannel's too thin, Mama. If you'd buy some thicker cloth, they'd last a little longer. You know I'm riding to Mrs. Hepworth's twice a week. For my lessons."

Instead of her mother shaming her, she'd make Francine feel guilty. Hannah glowed at the leverage she would wield with that ploy.

But then a miracle happened, like one of those miracles out of the Bible where what people most desire appears right before their eyes. It was her own sign from Heaven: a deerskin riding skirt.

It came from Luke's mother's wardrobe. Now that the weather had grown hot, they'd begun stopping at Luke's house at midday, a two-story, white-washed house plunked in an ocean of waving grass. A mile or more off, when the heat began to weigh her down, she could see the air shimmering off the roof and anticipate relief on its shady porch. All the doors and windows had been thrown open on the main floor, and even if that meant the floors were strewn with dead flies, there was always a breeze pushing through.

Jax, the cook, would bring them a pitcher of cool water. He'd nearly frightened her out of her skin when she'd first met him—short, gruff, and missing every last one of his teeth. He was a Frenchman from Quebec, Luke said, but he looked more like an Indian, or at least what Hannah imagined an Indian would look like.

According to Luke, Jax had retired to the house kitchen because he was too old to be a cowhand anymore. Come fall roundup, he would go back out with the "boys," but he'd be manning the chuckwagon and keeping them all fed.

"Fall roundup?"

"That's when we ride out for a few weeks to gather all the cattle."

"Can I go on the roundup?" she'd asked.

Luke blew through his teeth, a shushing sound he made when he was exasperated with her.

"Two hours in the saddle a day and you're already whining that you're thirsty or too hot. Roundup's not a picnic social. It's all day in the saddle no matter if it's raining, hailing, snowing. Makes no difference how miserable it gets. And then camping out every night. What's your mama going to think about you sleeping on the ground?

"And even if the cowhands didn't all quit when they saw you coming, you don't have any kind of gear to ride in. Hail would rip that flimsy skirt. The little bonnet you wear would be shredded in two hours' time. With all the looking after you'd require, you'd be more trouble than help."

Hannah paused. Those words had burned. Once again, she'd run head on into another bar of exclusion, same as at the Overland Bar. All around the globe men had been bestowed with the right and the privilege to declare where women would or would not go. Improper, inappropriate, immodest, too rough. If a woman could carry a baby in her belly and then, all by herself, push it out through a keyhole, well, she ought to be able to make up her own mind on just what her limits would be.

"If all you are concerned about is clothes, then you could help me so I could go. You could share some of your own clothes. If that's the only reason you're saying I can't go."

She cringed at the harshness in her tone. She didn't want to do or say anything to push him away. How could she find the balance between keeping his interest while still asserting what she thought and felt?

Luke looked over the porch railing. His jaw twitched, but otherwise nothing in his face gave away whether he wanted her to go or not.

"Mama used to ride. There might be some riding clothes in her wardrobe."

"Can we see?"

"Go on up there and take a look."

"It's your daddy's room, too, isn't it? I don't want to go up there by myself."

"Why? He's not here."

"It's not proper, a girl in a man's room."

"You think he's going to jump out of the wardrobe?"

"Would you come up with me, please?"

Their steps rang hollow on the stairs. Jax came out of the kitchen, wiping his hands on his dirty apron and staring at them. The scowl underneath his bushy eyebrows unnerved her. It occurred to her that she'd never before been in a home without other women, and she felt exposed, threatened, like Little Red Riding Hood closeted with a wolf.

Luke called back down the stairs. "I'm just going to let her go through Mama's things, Jax. We'll only be up there a minute."

Luke had to shoulder the bedroom door before it would open. Unlike the main floor, the windows were closed, and the air reeked of sweat and leather. The bed was covered with a bear hide and an assortment of pipes cluttered the small table beside it.

Luke pointed to the wardrobe. "There."

She hesitated.

"Go on. This is what you said you want."

She turned the latch, and the door released a waft of pent-up odors: cedar, dried sweat, horsehair, a whiff of campfire smoke and lavender from a few moldering sachets. She closed her eyes for a moment and tried to conjure the life of the departed woman. Whoever she had been, Hannah was sure she had loved being out of doors on a horse. When she opened her eyes, she found blouses so petite and pretty a doll could have worn them. But there it was, a riding skirt of the softest deerskin.

She pulled it out. "Oh, Luke, it's beautiful, but it's so tiny. It will never fit me."

"Maybe you can add some material to it. I don't know."

"Can I take it?"

"I don't guess Dad will know it's gone. He's not using it."

On her ride home, she fretted over how the skirt could be altered. It was a level of sewing far beyond her skill. And even if she could do it, she had no way to hide the work from her mother. Why did gaining the freedoms of life come with so many complications? In order to ride with Luke, she was forced to seek her mother's help, which could end in punishment and the loss of both Luke and horseback riding.

If only there were some other way.

At least Tremain was not lurking around. It would be easier with her mother one on one.

Francine sat outside the cabin fanning herself. "It's hot, Hannah. I believe we'll have supper outside this evening. Did you have a good day today?"

No point trying to hide behind a lot of useless words. Might as well just blurt it out.

"I haven't been going to lessons, Mama. I haven't seen Mrs. Hepworth in weeks. I haven't seen her in so long that I don't know how she's doing and couldn't tell you if you asked."

Hannah held out the deerskin skirt. "This riding skirt belonged to Luke's mother. I need it. I ride with Luke every day and I can't wear skirts and bloomers any longer. The bloomers are so thin, and they've worn out. Luke says a hailstorm would rip this skirt to shreds."

Francine's fan dropped in the dirt. "You've defied me? And all because Tremain shot your horse? I've told you I believed he was rash and thoughtless. But you were wrong, too, Hannah. You brought the creature here without asking. And now this? I don't recognize you."

"And I've told you I'll never forgive Tremain. Ever. You weren't there. You didn't see him. It wasn't just thoughtless. It was the most extreme, deliberate cruelty.

"But this has nothing to do with Zephira. You brought me out here. To Nebraska. This was your doing. Yet you act as if you're molding me for the debutante ball. Look around. Emptiness all around us. There isn't going to be a ball. There's never going to be one. You want me to perch on

55

a shelf inside that cabin and wait for things that aren't ever coming while life happens out here. There's wild horses and antelope fast as the wind and mountain lions and eagles. There's new hills and valleys to explore every day. I love to ride, Mama. I don't ever want to get off a horse. Luke's talking about..."

On second thought, she'd better not mention the fall roundup.

"Hand me the skirt, Hannah."

Francine was appalled. "This is leather from savages!"

"Mama, please help me. Please let me ride."

"It's pants really, just pants made to look like a skirt."

Hannah hesitated. She couldn't tell what Francine was thinking as she studied the fringes, the tarnished silver buttons down the front.

At last, Francine held the garment up by the waist. "That a proper wife wore such a garment. Scandalous." She set the skirt in her lap and looked back up at Hannah. "I cannot fix it for you. There's no room in the seams to let it out."

The pressures of the day exploded, and Hannah couldn't stop herself from blubbering. "But what can I ride in, Mama?"

"Lies and more lies. And you had no shame in telling them. Are you trying to get back at me? Is that what you're trying to do?"

"If I had told you from the beginning, you wouldn't have let me go. And I would have gone no matter what you said. Even if you'd had Tremain take a cane to me." But she knew her mother would never have allowed that.

"There's one more lie in all this. It's about

more than horses and beasts and birds. It's Luke as well, isn't it? You want him."

"Yes, ma'am."

"You think you'll win him by being his saddle companion? It won't work that way, Hannah. That's not what a man wants. A man looks for a woman to provide comfort and freedom from cares. In the end, he will pick a woman like that, or someone will pick such a bride for him, and it will break your heart."

Wrong, everything Francine was saying was wrong. She didn't know Luke at all! That's how Hannah wanted to respond. So why was she crying even harder? She snatched the riding skirt from her mother's lap. "Don't mind, Mama, I'll find a way to do it myself."

"If you are doing it yourself, I worry that the result will be more shaming than what you've already confessed to. How are we to make up your deceptions to Mrs. Hepworth?"

"I could go to her and say I'm sorry."

"You will do that. And resume your lessons. I will confront Luke myself on Sunday.

"And in return for you resuming your lessons and limiting your rides with Luke to Sunday afternoon, I will make you a split riding skirt like this one. Not out of savages' cloth. Out of proper cotton twill."

Hannah fell on her knees and hugged her mother around the waist.

Francine twined her fingers through Hannah's hair. "I worry about what kind of life you are about to start," she said gently. "But I am not strong enough to hold you in this house. And I won't have Tremain cane you. You already knew that. Having Atlas has made you happy. I do want you to be happy."

"I will make you proud of me, Mama. One way or another, I will."

4

February 4th

    Francine's hope chest, a whale-sized domed trunk, sits at the back of the cabin, next to Sunny's bed. Tremain had complained about hauling "Pandora's Box," as he called it, from Ohio. There was no room for it in the wagon. It had to be shipped to Sidney by train. And Tremain had had to haul it the last ninety miles by wagon.

    Since then, "Pandora's Box" has traveled so many miles that the pastoral scene etched on it is scratched and chipped.

    Now it contains mementos from Sunny's rodeo career, mostly scrapbooks that Francine had compiled. When Sunny thinks of how much Francine objected to her lifestyle in the beginning, the loving care Francine put into this project touches her still, years after Francine's passing. Each of the pages are separated by tissue paper. And although there are newspaper articles, photographs, programs from all Sunny's exhibitions and rodeos, there are no photographs of Francine.

The more determined Sunny had become to deviate from the life her mother had envisioned for her, the more Francine tried to counter it by emphasizing the proper role of a woman: submission and subservience. One's joy was to be found, if at all, in raising loving and obedient children—ideas that to Sunny merely resembled buzzing mosquitoes. She longed to swat them out of her way. Ride through them hard and fast as she could until they were well behind her.

All the clothes and costumes Francine sewed for her...hand-sewed. There were no machines back then. And this box. Signs of the devotion that Sunny had taken for granted.

For her part, Sunny had dragged Francine to places she didn't want to go, places she didn't deserve to be in. In the end, she had left her behind. Not abandonment, exactly. She told herself her mother wasn't meant for the traveling life. She couldn't have lived in a barn, as Sunny had done when she worked for Laroche in New Mexico. And she couldn't have withstood one more attempt at pioneer life on yet another wind-blasted outpost, this God-forsaken ranch.

Sunny had done the best she could for Francine. In the end, they just have to make up their minds to make peace with one another. She tells herself there's still time, even if she can't be sure

*Francine will hear. She touches the top of the hope
chest and says it out loud. "Mama, I wish you were
still here."*

*And the wind answers, shrieking around
the cabin.*

Hannah stood on the corral rail, grinning at
the spectacle in front of her.

All the three-year olds wheeling, prancing,
loping, weaving through one another and breaking
away—it looked like a dance. Chestnuts and
blacks, a palomino, a grey, a roan. Morning light
splitting through the rails glanced off their hides.
Steam rolled off their backs. They'd pause and prick
their ears, then they were off again, some bucking,
kicking. The odors of hide, sweat and manure
rode the clouds of dust they churned. No one was
hazing them. Nothing was frightening them. It was
movement for no other reason than the passion
for motion. All spontaneous yet all in harmony.
All of them individuals and in all, a collective joy
at their power.

These were the young horses that Luke and
the rest of the cowhands were breaking to ride
for fall roundup. September had come and gone
leaving the grass blanched and the ocean of hills
silent, all the birds flown. Mornings were chilly now.
Hannah kept talking about the roundup as if it
was understood that she was going with them. She
was outfitted; she had riding pants—full, blowsy
pants made to look like a skirt that buttoned mid-
calf, like boys' breeches. And she had a new wool
vest, wool coat and a ten-gallon hat. Luke couldn't
say that she wasn't ready to ride. There was the

problem of placating her mother and Tremain. But she'd done as they'd asked all summer. She'd gone to lessons at Mrs. Hepworth's. She hadn't run off with Luke without permission. They couldn't say no. They wouldn't.

Luke joined her at the rail and asked, "What do you think?"

"They're beautiful! I love them all!"

"See that palomino filly on the far side over there. I've been thinking about her for you. She's real gentle, eager to please. She's never bucked. I believe you need a replacement for Atlas. That'd be a good one over there."

"She's pretty, but she's not my favorite. I like that tall one with the four white stockings. Look how he's stopped to listen to us. He knows I'm talking about him."

"That's not a horse for a girl. He's got a mind of his own. We've tacked him up and some of the boys have ridden him. He's a smart one, I'll give you that. He'll bide his time, play along with a rider for thirty minutes or so, then out of the blue he'll just blow up. It's going to take thirty days or more of hard riding to turn his head around."

"I can ride him."

"You can't go from Atlas to that cannonball."

"Luke, it's very sweet that you want me to have a horse for the roundup and I don't want to seem ungrateful. How about this? If I can ride that horse, will you let me have him?"

"You never give up. Even when I told you months back that you can't go with us."

"I have all the clothes, just like you said."

"I never said the clothes were the only thing."

"Luke, you...."

"You'd like to believe you're as sly as those

fat raccoons that slip in and out of the grain box. Every time I've talked about the roundup, I've told you you're not going."

"I won't see you for months and months."

"A month and a half, maybe."

"But I thought you wanted me with you. All the time."

"You're fourteen. I'm a man already and you're just a kid."

"I'll be fifteen first of November."

"Look, it doesn't matter because you're not going with us. That's it. Don't ask me again. Aw, c'mon Hannah. I knew that fat lip of yours was going to pooch out. That's why I thought I'd give you another horse. You know how to ride. You don't need me to help you anymore. You can ride on your own, go anywhere you'd like. Except on the roundup."

The horses had played out now. Their heads dropped. They snorted, coughed, sniffed the dirt. Luke could be just as dogged as his Hereford bulls. Like them, once his mind had hardened, he couldn't be pushed. But she was not nearly so dismayed as she had let on, because now she knew his feelings for her had to be more than what he'd admitted to. He wouldn't be giving a horse to a girl he just liked a little.

"I forgive you about the roundup," she said.

"I didn't say I was sorry."

"Just give me a chance with the cannonball. Right now."

"I told you. I got that pretty filly picked out for you."

"Well, if you're going to give me a horse anyway, what do you have to lose? If I get on him and he throws me, then I'll say I'm wrong and that you know best."

"Those are words to look forward to."

"But if I ride him and stay on, I'll have shown you that I'm a better rider than you think I am."

"You haven't listened to anything I've just said. Sure you might do fine in the corral, but he'll outsmart you once you go outside and all hell will break loose."

"Give me thirty minutes inside the corral and thirty minutes outside. On my own. If I'm still in the saddle when I come back, he's mine."

His jaw closed and he ground his teeth. But he wasn't saying "no." He wouldn't say what he was really feeling, either, that her drive to try what no other girl would do piqued his interest.

"Francine's a real nice lady and she's always kind to me. I wouldn't be able to forgive myself if I had to haul you back home all busted up."

"What are we all standing here for?"

Luke's father, Ollie Mangum, pushed between the two of them. This was only the second time she'd seen him. The first time he'd surprised her family by coming over with Luke on a Sunday in August. Tremain had fretted at what the county's biggest rancher would have to say about a homestead one loose nail away from being blown into splinters, but Ollie had acted as if their little place was the pearl of the Sandhills. He'd complimented Tremain on his calves, admired the riding wear Francine had fashioned for Hannah and commented that while he didn't see Hannah mastering her mother's expertise in the domestic arts, they ought to take comfort at what a fine horsewoman she was becoming. Even so, Francine's brittle smile had made it obvious that she was not at all comforted.

"You and the boys should have been through sorting these horses by now," he said to Luke, "and penned the ones we're going to sell."

Luke gestured to Hannah as if the delay was all her fault. "She won't take the horse I was about to give her."

"Why not?"

"She thinks she's going to ride that gelding I've been telling you about."

"I thought you wanted that horse."

Luke glanced at Hannah. "I do. He's fast, that's what I like about him. But it doesn't matter what I want, or whether you want him, or whether anyone else wants him because he'll never be a ladies' horse."

"Mr. Mangum, all I asked was for Luke to let me try him out."

"The hell you say."

"I don't want you to think I'm ungrateful. If Luke was going to give me a horse, that's the same thing as saying you were willing to give me one, and I know that's a special gift. I liked that gelding. I told Luke if I could ride him thirty minutes in the corral and thirty minutes outside, with no one helping me, that he should let me have him."

Mr. Mangum looked over the horses. The brim of his cowboy hat shaded his face to where she couldn't guess what his thoughts were. He shoved his hands in the pockets of his coat.

"Let her try."

"What if she gets thrown off?"

He shrugged. "Whatever happens will be an education for them both."

All the other horses were shuttled to smaller pens. The gelding was quickly caught and saddled. Hannah's heart thumped so hard that she thought everyone could hear it. It would have been a relief if Ollie had refused to let her ride. It would have given her a way out. She'd have nothing to be ashamed of. Now there was only empty space between her and the horse, who shifted quietly to face her. She looked him in the eye, put one foot in front of the other and tried to scrape together the willpower to carry her to an end she couldn't begin to foresee.

The cowhands were finding excuses to dawdle by the corral. Jax had come out of the house to lean against the porch post. Luke looked scared. Ollie Mangum showed no expression at all—there wasn't even the slightest twitch in his handlebar mustache.

Luke grasped the headstall. As she picked up her foot, he said, "Are you sure about this?"

All these past months had been consumed with either being in Luke's company or longing to be with him. She had believed she wanted to share every thought with him. With her foot in the stirrup and his question hanging between them, she realized how childish her preconceptions had been. Being fond of someone meant that you selected what you shared, even more so than with her parents.

"I'm sure," she lied.

She settled herself in the saddle and looked over the men around her. They expected her to fail. In their eyes, she was already flying through the air. She nudged the horse's sides and he launched into a jog. No one made a sound. She pushed him on to a trot and was surprised at a thrust of power so strong it forced her back into her seat. This was no Atlas.

The horse tossed his head, tried a crow-hop. She halted him, started again. Again, he crow-hopped, once, twice. She kicked him harder and yanked his head around to the side. Her onlookers gasped. Off they trotted again and this time the cannonball obliged her, making a complete circuit around the corral. They traveled so fast that the faces at the rail blurred. The horse broke into a gallop, ploughed into the corner, then braked to throw her off, but she braced against the saddle horn. So this was what it meant for a horse to have its own mind!

Okay, you want to run? You run! She let the reins loose and when he tried to steamroll her into the next corner, she yanked him inside off the rail and kicked him again. He spurted forward but didn't try to bash her in the corners again. Two or three more circuits and he dropped back down into a trot. She halted. She hadn't lost her seat and yet now that she was no longer in motion, she shook so hard that she thought she might fall at last.

Luke walked up. "More than you expected, wasn't it? Ready to give up?"

"No, I'm not."

Ollie Mangum ambled across the corral, his eyes down the whole time, and Hannah began to fear what he would say. But once he was next to her, he looked up and said, "Nothing to be ashamed of in that ride. You showed us all. Now you choose one a little less headstrong and no one will think the worse."

"I want this one."

Luke and his father exchanged glances.

"It'll be a lengthy number of days before you can ride him out of this corral. I'm pretty sure if we let you out now, we might never see you again. Tell you what, you can ride him in here while we're gone. By the time we get back maybe you'll have him sanded down to where you can ride out with Luke."

No sense defying Mr. Mangum. Better to grin and say, "Yes, thank you, sir." Getting to ride the cannonball in the corral was better than losing him altogether. And with them all heading out on their precious roundup, there would be no one around to stop her from doing whatever she wanted to do.

Next morning, she rode Atlas over to the Mangum place before dawn. She thought she had started early enough to catch one more moment with Luke before they left, but she was too late. House, bunkhouses, and barn were all deserted. Only the cannonball was left in a pen next to the corral, pacing at the fence, whinnying in rage at being left alone.

"You're just hungry, that's all," she called to him. "We'll fill up your belly and then things won't seem so bad." She brought out a bucket of oats from the barn. As he sucked them down, she stroked his neck, pulled the knots out of his mane. "No wonder you're hungry. Hardly a blade of grass left in this little pasture. We're going to have to move you out of here no matter what.

"And what are we going to call you, anyway? You've got to have a name. Cannonball is no name for you." The ends of his mane were sand-colored but the color toward the base was crimson like the last light bleeding out at sunset.

"How about I name you Helios? The sun god come to earth."

Blanket, saddle, bridle. He did pull away from her when she tried to mount. No problem. Luke had taught her the remedy to that trick. She grabbed the headstall, pulled him in toward her as she stepped on, and then she was settled with both their noses pointed to the open gate.

Release, Hannah thought as the gate eased out of her vision. Released in body, released in spirit, the same lift a caged bird would feel the second the door was flung open. Their shadow stretched long over the bent grasses. The sky ran wide and open, windswept as the land before her. If she nudged Helios faster, she felt that his next stride would carry them into that blue ether above. How magnificent it would be to watch these plains and hills expand underneath them.

The sun's warmth radiated down on her shoulders, burning away the chill. The air, so sharp and clear, seemed to magnify sound. It was if she were hearing for the first time. The rhythmic shush of the horse's hooves in the sand. The last grasshoppers buzzing as they warmed. An eagle's bark above her on the ridge as they ascended it. Her thoughts spilled out of her like so many tufted seeds to float and spin in the sunbeams.

All these months when she'd ridden, she'd had Luke beside her, and it was the ebb and flow of words between them that had absorbed her. Now without him, her soul eased with gratitude into the dome of sky, becoming one with God's breath.

Was this what dying felt like, this letting go? It didn't feel frightening at all. It felt as if she had just now started to live.

And then the pheasant flew up from the

grass. At first, it was a flapping blur of scarlet and cinnamon feathers so wondrous that she caught her breath, but Helios jumped and before she'd had time to gather her reins, he sprang forward into a murderous run.

The sense of self that she'd released came back to her screaming in pure terror as Helios bolted to the top of the ridge and then over the flat open ground, wild as the first horse ever to run and just as unstoppable. When she tried to pull back on the reins, he only stretched his neck out longer to run harder. She cried out as if that would stop him, but he'd forgotten her, forgotten everything other than the single-mindedness of blind speed. One more desperate grasp to pull him in and when that failed all she could do was grip the saddle horn and plead with God.

Just ahead, the bluff was ending and though she shouted again, over it they went, plunging toward a gulch below. Her feet had come out of the stirrups so that she was barely in the saddle, but the fear that she might fall underneath him spurred her to cling on. Just yards short of one last headlong drop into the gulch, Helios whirled to the side, throwing Hannah hard into the sand.

She struggled for breath, gasped once, twice, three times, before she choked and spat out sand. Everything hurt: her ribs, back, arms and legs. She looked for the horse, terrified that he'd fallen and hurt himself, or that he'd run away where he'd never be found. She was surprised to see him standing on the ledge above her. The sight of his hooves, level with her gaze, conveyed an odd serenity. He hadn't abandoned her.

Before he could run again, she lunged for the reins. She scrambled up the bank until she was next to him inhaling the odor of his sweat. Then she leaned against his withers and sobbed. How had she been so wrong? No wonder Luke treated her like a silly fool. She'd never have a place among these cowboys. Like Luke, they'd always be polite, humor her, dole out little compliments, but they'd know, just like she now knew, that she was just an impostor.

Yet how could that be true when just yesterday she had ridden this horse and watched their jaws drop. All of them. Had they been there this morning, they would have seen her ride out with her head held high. She'd been fine. Up until the pheasant. She had failed in that one moment, not in all moments. The shock of the horse's explosion, that's what had caught her by surprise. Her shortcoming hadn't been a want of skill, it had been a lack of imagining—knowing in that way—what was possible and being prepared for it. Now that she knew and had felt what he was capable of, she wouldn't be taken by surprise again.

She would visit him every day. Feed him, ride him. She'd stay in the corral until she'd learned all his tricks and figured out how to counter them. And then they'd ride out here again.

Two weeks after her mishap, she had saddled Helios in the corral and was getting ready to mount when the front door of the house slammed and there was Jax with his hands shoved in his pockets. He was several yards away, yet she felt the same fear that she'd felt that day on the stairs. It was the scowl on his face, she decided, and the coldness in his eyes. Like a wolf. What did he want?

"Hello, Jax. I thought you'd gone with the men on the roundup."

"They sent me home. Too old. Too slow."

"They didn't want me, either."

"If a woman wants to do as a man does, he will be hard on her. Try to chase her away. He fears she will be better than him, and if she is, it makes him mad. Makes him crazy."

She stared at him. She'd never heard him speak so many words, much less words like these.

He nodded toward Helios. "This horse you are trying to tame, he ran off with you, didn't he?"

His comments had invited her confidence. The promise was there that he was on her side, that he would keep what she told him to himself.

"Yes."

While she mounted, he walked to the rail and stood there, tobacco juice running down the corners of his mouth. Had he only come out to watch? She felt uncomfortable under his scrutiny.

"Is there something you want to say to me?"

"Pick up a rein. Right, left, it doesn't matter. Now pull his head 'round to your knee. Make him walk like that, tight little circle. Tighter. Round and round."

Helios fought it for a few seconds, then surrendered into the turning.

"Now other rein. Other side."

"I'm getting dizzy."

"You need to do it every day. Hundred times. Until you so dizzy you puke. You do that until when you pull his head, he knows to turn inside and that's how you'll stop him. When you want to stop."

And with that, Jax pivoted and walked straight back to the house.

But she knew he'd given her a gift. A secret strategy. And she would learn to use it.

When Luke returned, she didn't tell him what had happened. The first words out of his mouth were, "His name is Hell-what?"

"Helios. God of the sun."

"Is this that Greek thing again? I didn't know the sun had a god. I thought we all had one god who was god of everything. You mean the Greeks think the sun's got its own special god?"

He was watching her from the corral rail. Hannah and Helios moved past him at an extended trot. She shouted back to him. "The ancient Romans and Greeks had gods for everything. Ancient, that means it was a long time ago. Before the Bible. Now they're all Christians, like us."

"So their sun god was a horse?"

"Yes, strong and fast as this one."

"I bet that god didn't have as pretty of a girl on top of him."

She stopped in front of him. "I turned fifteen while you were gone."

He reached through the rails and rubbed the horse's neck with the back of his hand. "I know."

Not long after the fall roundup ended, the first snow came. No wind. Just flakes hurtling straight down and landing in a soft *shsshh* until a white mound buried the grass and flower husks.

At the Mangum ranch, the cowboys were all cheery even though winter was coming. They were packing to leave, heading to points south to wait the winter out. Some were pleased at the money they'd managed to save. Others rued all the money they'd wasted in town. Either way, all were itching to move on.

At Hannah's house, Tremain paid her no mind. He sat in front of the barn door, brooding, watching the snow, saying nothing. Drought had desiccated his oat crop. What was left of the alfalfa had been too short to harvest. The cows were on it now and there'd be nothing left to feed them through the winter. He'd sold the calves for what he could get. Prices were rock bottom because of the drought and what pennies they'd brought didn't cover payment on the bank loan.

Hannah had nothing to say to him, either, even if she did feel pity for his fate. But there wasn't anything she could do for him, she thought, as she saddled up Helios and rode off to Luke's. Neither Tremain nor her mother asked her where she was going anymore. She trotted down the hillside and when she'd gone a mile or more, she glanced behind at the white landscape broken only by the horse's tracks. Up on the hill, there was the lonesome corral and barn topped with snow. Tremain was no longer visible at all.

Two days later, all the snow melted. Though the sun had tracked far to the south, the day was warm, more like autumn than winter. At Luke's, five of the cowboys remained, young men, though all older than Hannah. They dawdled on the bunkhouse porch, too comfortable in the unexpected warmth to want to move on. When they saw her ride up, one of them called,

"We've been wonderin' how you ever got that horse broke, Miss."

She remembered Jax's comments about men and women and suppressed a grin. "Not much to it. Just rode him every day. That's all."

"He's never run away with you?"

She leaned over and patted the horse's neck. "No, never had any trouble like that."

"He can run, you know that, don't you?"

"Sure he can run. He can outrun those nags you broke."

The cowboy whistled. "Big words for a kid."

Luke walked up to her. "What's going on?"

"Kid says she's got a horse that can run."

"Stew, if you don't clear out of here, another storm'll come along and you're gonna cry like a girl yourself if you're stuck here another six weeks."

"Aw, he's all right," said Hannah. "They can lay around the bunkhouse if they want. Or they can put up some of their money and we'll have a race."

"Hannah!"

"What?"

"Francine will skin me alive!"

"Who's gonna tell her? Helios can outrun your pony, as well."

In five minutes, everyone was saddled up. The men anted up their coins in a coffee tin. All of them bet against Hannah. Hannah had no money and the men complained so Luke lent her two bits. A course was plotted, starting at the dirt track out of the ranch, turning west over the hills, circling around to the north and then down across the dry creek bed, up the butte to the east and south along its top, and then down once more on the track back to the ranch.

Luke fired the starting shot. All the horses jumped. One reared back and threw off his rider.

The rest thundered down the track and veered up the first slope, Hannah and Luke in the lead. She let her reins loose. In the past two months, the experience and thrill of speed had helped her to forget her fears. She had come to crave that sensation of ripping through the air and feeling hooves pound the miles away.

Luke lunged past her up the first hill, but she caught him on the level and passed him. As she came down the other side, the rest of the cowboys caught her, and they swept down the slope neck and neck. She could hear the chuffing of every horse beside her. All the horses flew over the creek bed at the same time.

Starting up the next slope, Stew, the cowboy who had taunted her, passed her, slapping his horse with a quirt. Never mind. He was all hot air and nothing more. She knew she had plenty of speed left. She let him run his horse out as they crested the next slope, and then she passed him in two more strides. On top of the butte, Luke and the other riders started to catch her. She was only a length ahead of them as they came down in the final loop back toward the ranch. Luke closed in. His horse's nose was just near her knee. She took up the slack in her reins as if she was going to pop Helios, but he anticipated her and sprang forward, stretching the distance once more between her and Luke. She tore through the gate ahead of them and fearing that Helios might run smack into the corral rail, she pulled him in a circle to stop.

Just as Jax had taught her.

The others piled in behind her. Stew shouted to Luke, "You chose the wrong horse, Boss."

Luke looked over at Hannah. The thrill at seeing the wonder in his eyes was as great as her thrill in the race itself. She was more than just a chum now and his new-found appreciation of her tingled down her spine.

"My God, Hannah!"

5

February 5th

In the morning, there had been a hint of a thaw. The sun blazed as it crossed the horizon, striking the icicles on the eaves. Slowly droplets formed. By midmorning there was a wet sheen on the snow. She yanked off Clem's coat when she fed the livestock. Not that it was balmy, mind you. Just that the sun burning through the chill felt so welcome on the back of her neck. Warmth. And hope.

But by the afternoon, the east wind returned, freezing the top layer of snow. Clouds massed low and thick. Now the snow was swirling, riding the updrafts, swirling again.

SUNNY GALE

She turns away from the window and back to the scrapbooks she's removed from "Pandora's Box." The life recorded in those books doesn't quite square with life as she's lived it. To look at those photographs, Sunny Gale was never unhappy, lonely, broken, aching. Never cold. Whatever fate might befall her in a rodeo arena, the thrill of being there had made her glow.

First photograph: Cheyenne Rodeo, 1898. The contestants for the Ladies' Relay Race. After that year, they called it "Cheyenne Frontier Days." There she is in the center with her toothy horse grin and her arm around Eleanor Lefever, who would become her best friend. Eleanor's braids hung clear down to her leather belt. She'd never had her photograph taken before that day and it was only because Sunny had hung an arm over her shoulder that she'd relaxed, and a flicker of a smile broke over her smooth complexion.

All of them so unaware of where the years would carry them.

There's Ruth Pickering, who became her sister-in-law, eventually. A Western version of regal Artemis with her arched eyebrows and long tapering hand on her thigh. Sunny remembers that her blouse was grey-blue. How she had envied Ruth's pearl buttons that day. Right before the flash, Ruth had straightened her silk scarf, brushed the curls on her forehead to the side.

Ruth had had her photograph taken before.

Even after all this time, she can feel the excitement that she sees reflected in her own face. Nothing there of the unhappiness in her marriage to Luke. He had been her riding companion, her teacher. She had hung on every word he uttered. She had wanted him so badly, but none of it had come out as she had expected. It had all taken a sour turn. Instead of the longed-for marital bliss following candles and vows, she'd been deflowered before he'd even proposed. Instead of a marriage bed, she'd been violated on a cowhide rug.

That summer of 1897 they'd taken to sneaking away for a few hours a day in the barn. Nothing about it had seemed threatening to her. An hour or more of sweet kisses to where it almost hurt to stop. Every moment of it had been intoxicating, from pegging Jax's whereabouts and insuring he was occupied, to the pressure of Luke's body against hers.

Until the day he had rolled over on her and pushed her legs apart with his. She knew at that instant that they'd gone too far, and she pleaded for him to stop. But he had treated her no differently than if she'd been a calf to be hog-tied and branded. That was exactly what it felt like.

She had slapped his face after he had rolled off her. She had sobbed with outrage and pain. If he could do something so vile, who was he? Had she really known him at all?

He had the gall to act as if he had been the one who was hurt.

"Why are you so worked up?" he'd said. "I'm going to marry you. Not because of this. Because I want to. You've got to know that by now, don't you? Isn't this what you wanted?"

Yes. No.

A shabby, deflated sort of wedding followed. She had submitted to it out of shame mostly. It had seemed to her that if she was married, she could hide the shame, sweep it out of sight, at least to where Francine wouldn't know. Then, too, she'd hoped that somehow in marriage, a spark could be rekindled.

The sunburnt man there at the altar was the one she had once adored. Surely when she'd crossed the bridge of wedding vows, the feelings of betrayal would shrivel and die.

Instead, resentment at his arrogance smoldered. And then one day in Alliance the two of them had seen posters advertising a cowboy and cowgirl competition—a rodeo—first of its kind in Cheyenne, Wyoming. They'd grasped hands, looked at one another and grinned.

This would be the path at last to union with her young husband.

Mr. and Mrs. Luke Mangum drove to Cheyenne in a wagon with Helios and a second horse tied to the back. When Hannah saw the Cheyenne lights flare across the prairie, she'd grabbed Luke's arm and squeezed it. They were alive to share this moment together. Hannah was in love again.

Down the main thoroughfare, at least ten bars were lit, open, and overflowing. Music poured out into the street: a cacophony of reels, cakewalks, polkas, waltzes. Knots of cowboys jostled one another under the streetlights. One was trying to ride his horse into a bar while others cheered him on. Even the women were loud. Many of them smoked cigarettes as they hung onto their men's arms. Hannah poked Luke.

"Are those whores?"

"Most likely."

She wondered if he really knew. "Most likely," he'd been with one. The Mangum cowhands would have taken him with them. Before he'd met her, of course. She wondered, how many times had that happened? She was sure he wouldn't have visited a whore after he had met her. Then, remembering the barn and cowhide rug, she wasn't so sure.

There were Indians, too. Dozens of them. No women. Just men with long, coarse hair drinking at the street corners. A handsome one sauntered down the street arm in arm with a black woman, the first Negro she'd seen in the West. They leaned into one another, both happy, laughing. What could they have in common? They might have met this evening for the very first time, but there wasn't the slightest awkwardness in their manners. Their familiarity seemed so easy and natural. They weren't bothered by the doubts she harbored about the husband sitting right next to her.

Luke had agreed to get a hotel room, the first time she'd slept in a bed since they'd left the ranch a week ago. Sounds from outside flooded the room: the music, dogs barking, horses and wagons, glass breaking. It was already well past midnight, and she knew she would never sleep. Her nerves were on fire over how she would do in the Ladies' Relay Race the next day.

They'd entered ahead of time by mail and studied the rules together. A two-mile race, horses to be substituted after one mile. Riders had to dismount, switch their tack onto the second horse. One assistant was allowed to hold the second horse. Helios would be the second horse. No worries that he would dominate the field so the only thing to practice was the stop midway. Bringing a horse at full charge to a hard stop, changing the tack to the second horse and bolting again. If she could master that much, Helios could do the rest.

She closed her eyes and imagined it over and over, plopping her backside hard against the cantle for the halt, vaulting to the ground, releasing the cinch, lifting saddle and blanket in one swoop, and throwing both on the second horse, tightening the cinch, vaulting back on, and quirting Helios' rump just once. That's all it would take. Over and over, she saw the first mile marker approach and Luke there holding Helios.

In her dreams, Helios pulled ahead, stride after stride away from the other horses, away from the crowds, away from Luke. Just Hannah and Helios and the ground flowing away like water beneath them.

In the morning, the hotel lobby smelled of coffee and bacon. Hannah was too jumpy to eat. She watched impatiently while Luke devoured his breakfast. She was anxious to move on to the grounds, get familiar with how the layout looked and smelled, and warm up the two horses. When they stepped out, the street was more subdued than it had been at night, but still crowded, and the excitement she felt buzzed in the throng, too.

Indian women were out now, selling merchandise at the corners. She meant to keep on walking, but a piece of clothing caught her eye: a soft leather tunic with beaded diamond patterns on both shoulders and a thong around the waist to tie it. She looked down at her own outfit, red bandana, white blouse, and the brown blowsy riding knickers her mother had made. If she had that tunic, she'd stand out, she'd be different, someone everyone would notice.

She stopped in front of the Indian woman. "How much?"

The Indian woman was sitting on a barrel smoking a pipe. She looked up at Hannah from under the brim of her hat. "Pretty girl like you," she said. "You in the rodeo?"

"Yes, I'm in the relay race."

The woman nodded, as if she knew exactly what Hannah was thinking.

"Seven dollars," she said.

"Seven dollars!" said Luke, "That's more than the hotel room and breakfast together. You don't need that, do you?"

Hannah felt the leather. "It's perfect, Luke, it really is. Can I have it?"

Luke turned to the woman. "Three."

"Seven," she answered.

Luke took out his wallet and pulled out some money. "Here you go," he said. "C'mon, Honey."

She took the tunic and Luke hustled her down the street away from the woman. "Luke, why are you going so fast? You're hurting me."

"I only gave her three. We got to get away before she sends the war party to scalp us."

"Luke!"

"It didn't take her nothing to make that thing, Hannah. They tan the hides themselves and the beads are just a few pennies."

"It's not right. We owe her the money!"

Luke pinched her arm, hard. "We can't get cheated by Indians, Hannah. That's not what we come here for."

The rodeo grounds had been erected west of the town on the prairie and consisted of an elongated pole arena, a dirt racetrack encircling the arena, a grandstand, and holding pens. The arena was long, maybe as much as a half-mile. The covered grandstand, on the western side of the arena, seemed so distant from the opposite side where they had arrived that the crowds blurred. Spectators in buggies and wagons started to line up along the outer rails of the racetrack. The wind blew so hard that Hannah had to tie her cowboy hat down to keep from losing it, but even with the wind, the sun beat down hot.

More cowgirls arrived with strings of horses. Cowboys as well. Drovers herded horses and steers into holding pens. People who had come up on the train from Denver were ferried to the grounds in buggies. Soldiers and cavalry rode in from Fort Russell. A team pulled a cannon. All these people— cowboys, cowgirls, spectators, soldiers, Indians— congregating on this barren strip of ground. For Hannah it was as fantastical as a dream. She couldn't tear herself away from the pure spectacle of it all.

An hour later, the festivities began with a parade inside the arena, announced by a man who stood in the center with a speaking trumpet. First the dignitaries rode in: the governor, the secretary of state, the mayor, the sheriff. A tall man followed them on a dancing palomino stallion with a thick silver mane and tail. He spurred it into a canter and circled around, tipping his hat to the crowd. He came to a sliding stop in front of the grandstand and, to the crowd's delight, the horse reared up.

It was Sam Pickering, Cheyenne's own native son, the announcer said, impresario of Wild West shows, local rancher, and the stockman who had provided the rodeo stock. He handed the speaking trumpet to Pickering.

"On behalf of myself and my extraordinary family, my wife, Ethel, my children, Tad and Ruth, both of whom you will see perform here today, and on behalf of Cheyenne, our Magic City, and the Great State of Wyoming, the Equality State, where every man and woman is free and equal under this sun and has the right to vote, I welcome you to this premier spectacle showcasing the triumph of our pioneers over this imposing and magnificent frontier. God bless Wyoming and keep it wild. God bless you all."

The horse reared again, and Pickering then joined the line of dignitaries while their wives filled the ring in buggies festooned with red, white, and blue ribbons.

Indians paraded in next. Only the chiefs, on horseback, were introduced. At the tail end came a cavalry detail followed by a team with the cannon. The cavalry cantered once around, their flags snapping smartly. The cannon team stopped in the center in front of the dignitaries.

While a snare drum rolled, the announcer warned the crowd that the cavalry would now fire the cannon to start this grandest affair in the history of the West, the first ever Cheyenne Rodeo. Ladies must not take a fright. Horses must be secured. Then, while a second and third drum joined in, he strode back to the grandstand and the crowd grew silent.

Boom! went the cannon and even Hannah jumped. Sure enough, horses across the panorama reared, bucked, jerked in terror, and bolted. One team overturned a wagon.

With the crowd aroused, the arena was cleared, and the rodeo launched straight into saddle bronc riding, which Luke had entered. Teams of men wrestled blindfolded broncs out to the center. The broncs were a spectacle in themselves, each screaming, straining against their ropes and pawing the air. Each was subdued and saddled. Next, the rider was boosted into the saddle, the blindfold undone, the ropes released and off the horse lunged and bucked. The cowboy had to stay aboard for ten seconds with one arm raised and one hand on the lead rope.

One after another, cowboys were pitched off before the ten-second bell. The more the horses twisted, reared, and plunged, the more the crowd cheered. It was a ten second embodiment of life in the West: savage, murderous, unforgiving.

A team dragged out Luke's horse, a white stallion, "Grand Teton." Grand Teton fought his ropes so hard that a couple of men were thrown aside, and a third was kicked and lay motionless in the dirt. Others flooded the ring, then contained the horse long enough for Luke to climb on. As the ropes fell away, the horse reared straight up.

"C'mon Luke," Hannah shouted. "Hold on!"

Luke had stayed on but hadn't raised his arm. The horse landed hard, jarring him. Another second and he was off and Grand Teton continued bucking on his own around the ring. Luke picked himself up. At least, he was standing. The boy that was kicked was carried off the grounds.

A girl in a ten-gallon cowboy hat joined Hannah at the rail. Her darkened skin was the color of cocoa. She nodded toward Luke.

"Is he your brother?"

She's an Indian, thought Hannah. Before Cheyenne, she'd never met an Indian in her life, and now she'd brushed with two in the same day, this one dressed like any civilized girl in a gingham blouse and an ankle-length riding skirt. Red ribbons were fastened on the ends of her braids.

"No, that's my husband."

The girl nodded thoughtfully. "You're wearing Indian clothes. Shoshone."

"Yes, Luke bought it for me this morning. I thought it was beautiful."

"It's made for a man. Not a woman. Although you look well in it."

"Are you Shoshone?"

"I am. Most girls don't do beadwork like this anymore. Only the older women do it. Shoshone girls learn to sew with machines at the government school. Crafts like this are not allowed."

"The government school?"

"A government boarding school so the tribes can learn to live same as white people."

"Did you go there?"

"For a few years. If that was how white people lived, I didn't want anything of it. Cold rooms, cold floors, girls coughing and sick all winter. And cold oatmeal. Every fall I would ride into the mountains and hide so they wouldn't take me back. Every time the reservation police...they came searching for me and hauled me back."

"My husband, he's out there now." She pointed to the next cowboy waiting for a bronc.

"Did you meet him at the school?"

"His mother was one of the white teachers. She felt sorry for me when they would bring me back and I would cry that I wanted to go home. She said, come home with me. I will teach you and you can ride horses all the time. Not just in the summers.

"I told her I would pay my way by breaking horses for her. I told her I knew how to do that.

"She got permission to take me home to her ranch. Her horses threw me off ten, twenty times. After that I could break horses." Her eyes twinkled at her punchline.

"Leonard Lefever." That's how the cowboy was announced.

"You're Mrs. Lefever."

"Call me Eleanor."

"I'm Hannah Mangum."

Lefever was mounted on a buckskin named "Hell's Drop." True to his name, Hell's Drop nearly dropped to his knees once Lefever was in the saddle, then shot straight up into the sky. He came down in a twist, but still hadn't dislodged Lefever. After that move, he settled into a bucking pattern until the bell rang. Lefever was the first cowboy to stay on ten seconds.

The crowd roared. Lefever swept off his hat and bowed.

"That was terrific!"

Eleanor glanced at Hannah. A saucy little grin lit up her face. "I can do that, too," she said. Her grin broadened when she saw Hannah's shock. "What? You think broncs are only for the boys?"

Eleanor's jibe rang true. Hannah had never considered joining Luke and the cowhands in riding bucking horses. She'd spent the last two years building her abilities to show that she could be every bit as at home riding with the boys as she could be in a kitchen. But Eleanor's words opened a door. *Why not push even further and tackle the most challenging riding in the world? What would stop a girl?*

Eleanor continued. "It looks impossible to you, doesn't it? It's not. It's all how you see it here inside your own landscape, the only one you can control yourself." She pointed to her temple.

"You mount an untamed horse. He bucks, it shocks you, terrifies you. You fall off because you told yourself you would fall. You have not controlled the inner landscape first. Now, instead picture how you will ride through the motions, pull back on the lead rope, rock with the horse. When he kicks back, you push through your feet, push your backside into the seat. Your power begins only when you admit the violence and ride through it. "

She nodded to the ring. "Next year I will ride in this contest."

Eleanor's confidence was as astounding to Hannah as her words were. Not a hint of misgiving tempered her tone.

"I want to do it with you."

Eleanor smiled. "In your tunic?"

"Yes, in my tunic."

"And what will you be doing today, Hannah Mangum?"

"I'm riding in the relay race."

"Me, too."

Lefever was declared the winner of the saddle bronc riding.

Next on the program was an event called "Wolf Hunt." The announcer pricked the crowd's sensibilities as he spoke of the legendary wolf, the creature that had terrorized the pioneer family— almost as much as the heathen savages—causing them to gather their children close to the fire while the great animal howled its dirge of desolation and death in the enveloping dark. Thankfully, the monstrous beast had been cleared from the plains, but for the education of the assembly, a lone fellow had been captured and would be exhibited.

Murmurs rippled through the spectators.

A group of Indians carried in a large cage and set it in the middle of the ring. They opened it, while the crowd gasped, and a wolf stepped out, thin and mangy. The wolf sniffed the air, took a few tentative steps, then broke into a trot. A few women screamed. Soldiers positioned all around the animal aimed their rifles. At their commander's signal, they fired, and the wolf dropped.

That was the first wolf Hannah had ever seen. She had expected a snarling beast, a demon creature—everyone had—but the animal had looked more pathetic than demonic. Lying in the dirt, the lifeless body brought back Zephira. All the men she knew would kill a wolf on sight, if they saw one, no questions asked. They were solid in their conviction that wild beasts had to be cleared from the Plains. That was what progress exacted.

She heard the murmur of consensus coming from the crowd.

The relay race contestants were summoned to the grandstand as the steer roping started. Eight other women besides Hannah and Eleanor, including Ruth Pickering, had gathered. Ruth was tall, like her daddy, but lacked his outsized personality. She stood apart from the others quietly gripping her riding gloves. Everything about her, from the pearl buttons to the polished boots, indicated she was there to ride, nothing more. She seemed to take no value in the other girls' sharing of where they'd come from or how they'd started riding.

The race judges recorded the women's

names, the names of their horses, the names of their assistants. One of them scrutinized Eleanor.

"You with the tribe?"

"I'm with my husband."

"We got a squaws' race coming up. You don't need to enter this one."

"Yes, I know you have a squaws' race. I want to be in this one."

"I guess we don't have anything about it in the rules, but we set aside events for Indians. We didn't count on them entering the regular events."

"Pardon, sir, but her husband just won the bucking contest," Hannah said.

"Is he an Indian, too?"

"No," said Eleanor.

"Well, if you're his wife and you didn't come here as part of the tribe...hell, I guess we can bend a little for the wife of the saddle-bronc champion," said the judge. "All of you go around back of the grandstand. There's a photographer there who's going to take your picture."

As they walked away, Hannah was worried over how her new friend had taken the man's comments. "Are you all right? I'm sorry he spoke to you like that."

Eleanor stopped. "Hannah. I have ridden horses that have reared and bucked. Horses that have run away with me that I couldn't stop. A horse that sees me for the first time doesn't care whether I am man-woman or white-Indian. If I can get on that horse and ride it, why do I care about words from oafs who fumble about in our country and know nothing about it?"

"You're very brave. I've never met a girl as brave as you."

"I see no bravery in simply being who I am."

They joined the photographer and the other girls. Newspaper reporters from Cheyenne and Denver peppered the girls with questions:

How had they learned to ride? Why didn't they ride sidesaddle? Did they cook and sew with their mothers? Or did they ride horses all day? Had they made their own riding skirts? Did they have time, after domestic chores, horse-breaking, and cattle herding to go out on a Saturday night? What about dancing? Did they do that, too? Did they plan to go to the dance tonight? What did they think of the first ever Cheyenne Rodeo? What was their response to folks back East who would say that their riding was indecorous and that their clothing was scandalous?

Ruth answered first. "I was raised just like my brother. Whatever he did, I did. That's true for all the girls raised out here. We don't know of any other way. We wouldn't want it any other way."

"You're Sam Pickering's daughter. I'm sure you can roll out a pie crust as handily as you can rope a calf, can't you Miss Pickering?"

"I don't care for pie."

Another girl immediately jumped in. "I can! I sell pies at home!"

The men chuckled. "We'll put that down."

"I'm from Ohio originally," Hannah said. "I didn't come from a ranch. This is a brand-new place, for me, anyway. The old ways back East have no place out here. Everyone's making new ways. Girls will, too."

She exchanged glances with Eleanor. None of the reporters had directed a question to her, but she seemed untroubled by it. All this prattle meant nothing, just empty words that she had to endure. She was patient, as if she was accustomed to sitting through talk that didn't include her.

Hannah turned back to the reporter. "Nothing stops us from making ourselves whoever we want to be."

"That's a mighty fancy tunic, young lady," the reporter said. "Are you going to race in that?"

"Sir, I am not only going race in this tunic—I am going to win in it."

The other girls laughed nervously, and Ruth glared at her. "Well, I am going to win if I'm equal to these horsewomen here. I hope I am."

"Good luck to you, Mrs. Mangum. Good luck to all of you!"

The wind had picked up. Towering dark clouds rolled across the sky, and the sun slipped in and out of them, throwing patterns of light and shadow across the green hills west of the rodeo grounds. The air had chilled and smelled of rain and still, Hannah had to sit through the steer roping, the squaws' horse race, and a staged stagecoach attack by the Indians.

Luke bought a half dozen hot dogs and tried to feed her one. He had never had them before and told her she was missing out on the finest food Cheyenne had to offer. But the odor just made her queasy. Everything started to jangle her nerves: the noise of the crowd, the chill raising goosebumps on her arms, the thunder in the distance. She kept glancing to where her horses were tied. They were growing as fidgety as she was.

By the time the women were told to line up, drops of rain pockmarked the dirt. With the starting gun and the first forward lunge of the horses, the sky opened into a downpour. Hannah gasped at the shock of cold rain pouring down her neck even as she struggled to see ahead. Horses thundered around her, and the collective roar of the crowd blended into the roar of the storm. She could barely make out the blur of wagons and buggies at the rail.

The grandstand came up again on her left and there was Luke ahead, holding Helios. Now she saw two horses ahead of her. Both overshot their assistants, and their riders yanked frantically to haul them back. Lightning struck not far off, and one horse threw its rider.

Hannah vaulted off and undid her cinch. She pulled off the saddle and blanket and tried to run but the wind was too strong and the rain—too hard. Luke's hat brim streamed water on his chest and shoulders, and she read the helplessness in his face. He ached to reach out and help her, but the slightest assistance would cost her the race. His gloves tightened around the reins.

She heaved the saddle and blanket on Helios' back and felt for the cinch. There was so much water in her eyes she couldn't see what she was doing. She could only hope her cinch was tight enough. Her boots sloshed with water. She hustled back in the saddle and smacked Helios with her quirt. One rider had taken off already—Eleanor, whose hat flew off behind her.

The rain turned to hail—fat globs beating down like stones. She raised her quirt again, leaned over the horse's neck and shouted, "Go!" but Helios didn't need the quirt anymore. He overtook Eleanor's horse as they came around the final turn.

Just as she felt she would win, Ruth Pickering caught up on her other side. The black horse chuffed as he drew alongside Hannah. He took one stride for every two of Helios'. In another breath, they would pass her.

The anguish she felt was every bit as punishing as her physical misery. There were no more words she could shout. She was out of time and strength for words. She let loose one long wordless howl and brought her quirt down on Helios' hindquarters one more time. and they beat the Pickering horse by a nose.

She let Helios wind down on a track churned to mud. All that followed was noise: thunder and hail and the crowd cheering. She looked to the grandstand where everyone was on their feet and threw her arms straight back into the air and she could have sworn that someone threw flowers although when she looked around, all she saw were melting chunks of hail.

Luke helped her off the saddle and threw a blanket around her. He took a corner of it and began to dry her hair. He and another cowhand lifted her on their shoulders and Hannah laughed and cried at the same time. The clouds split apart, and shards of sunlight appeared in the puddles.

The judge who had pestered Eleanor, met her by the rail. "What's your name, young lady?"

Luke shouted, "Her name's Mrs. Luke Mangum. That's what you ought to write down."

The remark dropped her right out of the clouds sure as a bullet through an eagle's wing. *Shouldn't it be Hannah? Hannah Mangum?*

Oh, she couldn't have done it without Luke. He'd stood there in the same hail she'd endured. He'd paid for their hotel and meals. Did marriage give him the right to wrench away her moment for himself?

He put his arm around her and hugged her tight, just as the camera bulb went off, catching them together.

Eleanor met her at the gate and hugged her. "I'm glad for you, Hannah."

Eleanor's hair was plastered to her head and strands hung in her face. Hannah grasped both her arms.

"What is it? Why are you crying?"

"Because...I don't know when I will see you again," Hannah said.

Eleanor hugged her and spoke in her ear. "You will come next year, and I'll be right here."

Luke pulled Hannah away. "Let's go get our prize money. What are you so caught up with that squaw for?"

Hannah looked over her shoulder and Eleanor waved.

"She's the first true friend I've had since I left Ohio."

"We ought to get you to Alliance more so you can find some better friends."

They picked up her forty-five dollars and went back to the hotel. Hannah wanted to dry off and go out to the dances. Luke wanted to bed her. He stripped her and rubbed her dry. Then he turned her over on her belly and pressed her head into the pillow with one hand. As he started to moan, she closed her eyes and saw the race all over again: the horses, the crowds, the ground churning beneath her, the eye of the Pickering horse and Helios' final lunge.

Mrs. Luke Mangum.

6

February 6th

In all the scrapbooks, there are no photographs of Mollie as an infant. Living on a working ranch in 1899, there was no time for such frivolities. Trips to town were reserved for business, food, supplies. Sitting for photographs was a wasteful luxury.

She has a lock of Mollie's hair. Also, a yellowed pinafore with lace that Francine made. Other than that, she has only fragmented images, insubstantial as floating cottonwood seeds.

If only she had held that infant tighter, squeezed every moment from every hour until they'd hardened like gems so she could have scooped them all up. She'd have had a treasure chest holding her daughter, Mollie.

Now, as she rakes through her mind searching for just one recollection to grasp, she remembers how impatient she was in the nursery when she longed to be outside on a horse. Her drive to master bronc riding had stampeded through the bedroom window, whisked her away from the cradle and out the door.

Eleanor had lit the spark. After the rodeo, Sunny had mulled over her words. Bronc riding presented not only physical challenges. To engage in it, a woman would have to be willing to turn her back on every stricture of femininity. A woman riding broncs would smash all boundaries defining who a woman was and what she could do.

Then, too, there was the lingering effect of her victory. "Mrs. Luke Mangum"—how that still galled after all this time—was the top horsewoman in the world. One hard ride—and the world as they departed from Cheyenne was a far different place. She was not someone's wife. She was a person who had struck her mark. No matter what she was called. No matter that back in Nebraska, she still didn't have the right to vote.

So as the unbroken colts and fillies galloped into the Mangum corral that fall, nostrils flaring, she thought, why not? What was there to lose? The worst that could happen would be a fall, broken bones maybe. What was there to gain? Pride in meeting the challenge.

To climb aboard raw energy, jam your legs down and throw your arm back before that roaring crowd, now that would be horsemanship beyond anything she'd imagined. Winning a contest would almost be beside the point.

And then there was Mollie.

On the wagon ride home from Cheyenne, Hannah tipped her face to the sun, her spirits boundless as the sky. Her elation was so great that she forgave Luke for spoiling her victory with his insistence on recording her married name. And she'd forgiven him for pocketing her earnings, too. Because nothing could change that she—Hannah Mangum—was a champion. A champion at sixteen years old! She batted away Luke's grumbles about the long trip home. Nothing would spoil her joy.

Ollie Mangum rode out to meet them, and she jumped up in the seat, nearly toppling over. She couldn't wait to share her news.

"You must have missed us," said Luke as Ollie pulled up alongside them.

"Luke, Hannah." He nodded to the back of the wagon where Helios and the second horse were tied. "You didn't kill the horses, I see."

"No, sir, but hasn't anyone brought out a newspaper yet?" Hannah asked.

"No, and I wouldn't ride all the way to town for such a rag. What's the news that you think I would want to read?"

Hannah held up her fancy gold and silver belt buckle.

"You won?"

"She sure did, and the rodeo stockman, Pickering, he tried to buy old Helios off of her."

"You should have sold him."

"Why?" cried Hannah.

"Well, he could get struck by a bolt of lightning tomorra. He'll never be worth again what he was when the man made that offer. You shoulda sold him for enough to buy this winter's hay. What with the drought, we need hay more than we need Helios."

"I'll never sell him, never," said Hannah.

"Which brings me around to why I rode out here to meet you in the first place. Tremain's run off. Not sure what day it happened. Your mama rode up here two days ago on Greta. She was sunburnt all to hell and she was in quite a state. She said Tremain left, saying this land was beating him down and he just couldn't make it here and that she'd be better off with you, Hannah."

"Did he say when he's coming back?"

"If he did, she didn't tell me. But he's not the only one. Drought's finished off a lot of 'em. Most of 'em."

"But the land and the cattle and the buildings. Who will take care of it?"

"The bank, I expect."

Instead of a joyful reunion where her mother would share in her triumph, she was met by Francine's howls of shock and grief. During the travel home, she had imagined she would spend weeks talking about the spectacle of all she'd done and seen. Instead, day after day, she listened to her mother grope for some kind of explanation for what had happened.

Not much to it, really—just the collapse of a bridge of dreams too flimsy to bear the weight of Nebraska's seasons.

"Tremain was good enough," Ollie observed, "just not the kind of feller situated for range life."

Hannah replied, "We've never learned what kind of life Tremain was situated for."

All that did was uncork another round of sobs from Francine.

In the end, there was not much more to it than foreclosure and the eventual auction sale of the land to the Mangums, for which she and her mother received nothing.

A week after she arrived home, she met the Mangum cowhands at the corral. She was bored listening to Francine. There was nothing she could do for her mother anyway. She was ready to try bronc riding. She hadn't told anyone yet of her desire. Certainly not Francine. The day was as good as any to try her luck on the young horses the cowhands had wrangled.

Hannah no sooner reached the rail when she doubled over and retched. And she was sick the next day and the next. Francine dabbed her eyes with her hankie and beamed. "You're pregnant, darling."

It rankled that everyone around cooed over "her condition." Family, cowhands, acquaintances in Alliance were more interested in "her condition" than her winning ride. It was a rude awakening to learn that biology trumped all, and that a woman's ambition was expected to yield to the primacy of the womb. Whether you were cowgirl or queen, fecundity, not horsemanship, was the exalted state toward which women were to aspire.

Confinement. Hannah repeated that word to herself by the parlor window with her hand on her bulge while the wind churned snow through the yard. Snow in the morning, snow at noon, snow when the lamps were lit, snow as the horizon faded to black. Confinement, the hours of it slowly flattening her. The days became deserts of yawning time. That girl who had thrown her arms wide to a cheering crowd seemed like a dream someone had told her about. No connection between that girl and the lumbering cow she was becoming.

Snow hushed the grassland, hushed the entire house until even dinnertime became silent. No one had anything to say.

And while her soul diminished every day, the life unknown inside her grew and stretched and kicked.

At the first thaw, Francine turned to Ollie at the noon meal.

"We've got to get a midwife for Hannah."

Ollie stared at her for a moment. "We're still a ways off, aren't we?"

"We have to find someone soon. Maybe a woman who could move out here for the last month."

"We don't need anyone around like that. If we're in a tight spot, we've already got someone here who's well acquainted with birthing. Jax."

With women in the household, Jax had been relieved of his cooking duties and moved to the empty bunkhouse.

"Mr. Mangum, I beg of you. This is my daughter. She's not a heifer."

"I didn't say she was."

Hannah interrupted. "I'm right here. You don't need to talk about me like I'm not in the room." But for the first time since her body had undertaken its own course of action, free of her will, she was frightened. There was an end coming, after all. From what she knew, it would be an end of blinding pain with no certainty that she, or the unknown inside her, would be alive when it was over.

"Jax has delivered babies. He delivered Luke," Ollie said.

"You're not serious. He's a...well, it doesn't matter what he is. He's not an appropriate person for a matter of such importance."

"I don't want a man," said Hannah. "I want a woman."

"Yes," said Francine, "the impropriety."

"Doctors deliver babies and they're men," said Luke.

"Even if a woman could be found," said Ollie, "there's no telling whether she could be found again when the time came or even if she could get here." He pointed his fork at Francine. "I'm telling you Jax is the surest bet you got. I don't think he's lost any yet, has he, Luke?"

"Not that I know of. You'd have to ask him."

"Luke, it's our baby you're talking about!"

"It won't be Jax by himself. Your mama's here. She'll be with you the whole time."

"Luke," said Ollie, "go get Jax from the bunkhouse."

Jax came in wearing his long canvas coat splattered with mud and manure. He took off his hat and nodded to the women.

"Jax," said Ollie, "Mrs. Brandt is concerned for her daughter and believes that she needs a midwife. And Hannah's all rattled, being a young wife and this being her first time. Can you take care of her when the time comes?"

Jax shrugged. "Only God knows the answer to this question."

"There, you see!" said Francine.

Jax continued as if he hadn't heard her. "I've helped mothers many times. I've helped babies into the world in saloons and tipis. No woman has ever died with me. But life and death, these belong to God. All the babies I helped got a good start in life. They came out well, as far as I can know. All alive and none hanged."

Francine jumped up and flung her napkin on her chair. "Outrageous the coarseness you all have! I won't have my daughter treated like an animal in a barn! I'll take her away first."

She strode out to the kitchen and slammed the door behind her.

Hannah stared at the men around her. The pulse of shame she'd felt when Luke first climbed on top of her in the barn pounded in her temple. Her throat clogged and she started to cry. No escaping it. The days, miserable as they had become, were counting down, as they did in the fall when the hogs were penned awaiting slaughter.

The men got up and abandoned her amid the dirty dishes.

A month later when Francine lay the swaddled baby in her arms, her tears at the dinner table seemed like a child's foolishness. It was Francine who delivered the baby and Jax who sat by her head and held out his leathery forearm to be squeezed. He didn't so much as squeak when she dug her nails into his skin. When it was all over and Francine held up the unknown who had now become her baby daughter, she was relieved that Jax, and not Luke, had been there after all.

For the first time in months, she felt alive again with this tiny girl whose eyes struggled to focus on her face.

Jax stood up. "Before I go, what will her name be?"

"Mollie. Mollie Mangum. And she's going to be a cowgirl."

In a month, she weaned Mollie to cow's milk. She was ready to ride with the hands again, she told Luke, and to fend off any objections, she told him she would milk the cow. And that wasn't all. She wanted to go back to the Cheyenne rodeo and ride the broncs. She stood on the porch over a steaming laundry tub of diapers. Rain poured outside, pounding on the porch roof and filling up the potholes in the yard.

Luke crossed his arms over his chest. "I thought you'd want to race again."

"I do, I will."

"You've never ridden a bronc, and we sold the excess horses last fall because we didn't have enough feed. We don't have any broncs here."

"I talked to Jax. He says there's a man at the stockyards who buys up horses people can't ride, and he's renting them out to anyone who wants to try."

"Where are you going to get money for that?"

"You could give me my race money back."

"How are you going to find time to get horses ready to race and learn to ride broncs?"

"The rodeo is not until September. That gives me all summer."

"What about Mollie?"

What about Mollie? "Mama's got her."

Luke sat down heavily on the laundry bin. He took off his cowboy hat and ran his fingers round the brim. With his hair flattened, she noticed a bald spot at the back of his head. How smitten she had been when she'd first seen him riding with the other cowboys that day in Alliance. There were still embers of affection, even after all that had happened. But what would her feelings be when he lost all his hair? And when he grew a plump belly like his daddy's? By that time, the image of him back on that day in Alliance would be dim. What would her feelings be then?

"You are going to go to all that trouble and maybe get hurt, but how do you know, if you get there, that they'll let you ride? Women haven't done that kind of thing before. Never mind winning. There's no way you can win."

"Luke, remember how, when that place filled up, dozens of people, hundreds, were all crammed into the stand and along the rail? They all loved it, every second of it. They loved the wild horses and the cowboys who tried to ride them. They loved it when those boys rode out their ten seconds and when they didn't. And if a woman's riding? They might say it's disgraceful, but they'll want to know—can she do it? Will she ride? They'll be sitting at the edge of their seats. All I have to do is tell those rodeo bosses that Eleanor and I want to ride the broncs, and soon as they blast that in their bullhorns...'Ladies and Gentlemen, the first young ladies ever to attempt to ride a fire-breathing mustang'—they'll sell twenty more tickets, fifty, maybe a hundred!

"The least thing I'm worried about is getting a chance to ride."

"What are you going to tell your mama? She's going to pull her hair out of her head when she hears this."

"If I've said it to her once, I've said it a hundred times. If she wanted to keep me in corsets, we shouldn't have left Ohio. You ride broncs. No reason I shouldn't."

"What about us, Hannah?"

"This is about us. We both wanted to be in that rodeo, remember?"

"No rancher out here has a bronc riding wife. Wives are at home with their babies. They want to be there."

"What does it matter what other people are doing if we both want this? You were as happy as I was when I won that race last summer. You claimed that victory as ours."

"I went ahead with it because I love you, Hannah, that's all. Winning that race, yeah, I'll never forget that we did it. But rodeo is just a one-time thing. Our life is out here. Day in, day out."

She grasped his hands. "Please, Luke. It'll come out all right, you'll see. It means so much that you'd let me do this."

He took her face in his hands. Then he kissed her long and hard, ran his hand underneath her shirt and squeezed her breast. She swiveled her hips against his crotch. Didn't she owe him affection— and passion—no matter the rifts between them? Without Luke, she would never have had a horse, much less won a race. Gratitude. She should be able to manage that. More to the point, her body seemed an easy thing to give—if he'd just let her ride broncs.

Hannah was the only woman to show up to ride the wild broncs at Tawny's riding ring. Tawny was a Negro who ran a blacksmith shop during business hours. He'd said that while all those pasty white fops and their hounds chased his people north, he'd turned west—not a white man or a dog, either one, stout enough to swim the Mississippi.

The ring was behind his shop and a herd of motley, pig-eyed horses were crowded into pens. When a horse's career finished at Tawny's, he made extra dollars by butchering it and selling the meat and hides. There were still enough desperate homesteaders left willing to buy both.

Jax accompanied Hannah for propriety's sake, and she was glad because the men hanging on the rails were as scruffy as the horses and had the same pig-eyes.

The ring opened when the blacksmith shop closed for the day and the boys took turns lassoing the horses, tacking them up and helping the bronc riders into the saddle. The cowboys didn't amount to much, but the horses didn't disappoint. They reared, fishtailed, slammed cowboys into the rails. No one rode for ten seconds.

Jax pulled Tawny aside. "This is Mrs. Hannah Mangum. She wants to ride."

Tawny had a scruffy beard that looked like it had been burned off in patches. He folded his arms across his chest, as if they were wasting his time. "These hosses ain't for the ladies."

"She wants to ride all the same."

"The law's gonna come after me if some gal gets hurt. They already make a beeline over here anytime someone takes out a warrant on these sorry tramps."

"It's not against the law for women to try to ride broncs."

Tawny turned aside and spat his chew. "It don't have to be. You know that. She's a Mangum, why doesn't she go ride her own horses?"

"We don't have any broncs on the place

right now, not like these. Mrs. Mangum—she's not a silly woman out for a thrill. She's a horsewoman. She won a relay race at a big rodeo last year. She wants to go back. Ride the broncs next time."

"Ain't she got a child to look after? That might be a more rewarding pastime."

"Mr. Tawny, Mrs. Mangum has got money just like these other boys."

"And who's gonna stand up for me when her head gets kicked open?"

"I will stay right here until she's through."

"No refunds, now."

"We read your rules posted in the shop."

"You say she's a horsewoman. Why did she wear a white blouse over here to ride broncs?"

Hannah spoke up. "I just wanted to look nice, Mr. Tawny."

"Horses gonna stomp you no matter how you're dressed." Tawny shouted to his crew. "Boys, go get her that half-pony. That should be enough to do her in."

The hands dragged in a tan and white pony. She might have been small, but she fought them like a tornado. Ten of them held her down to get the saddle and halter on.

"Now," said Tawny, as the boys gripped the squealing pony, "you gonna want to make sure there's no slack in your lead rope. Don't pull her head, just keep the rope tight and straight. Put your weight down in the balls of your feet. 'Til you learn the motion, you better hold on to the saddle horn. Once you've sat it out a few times, you can raise your free arm. Ready?"

She thought back to the last time a group of men had watched her—that time out with Helios—and how fearful she'd been of failing. Even more so than on that first occasion, she was muscling in on the fraternity of men, and this time the smug curiosity on the swarthy faces around her was replaced by hostility. They were impatient—eager—for her failure.

Jax whispered, "They can't hold that pony much longer, Mrs. Mangum."

"I'm ready," she said.

They set her in the saddle. She gripped the horn, set her weight in the stirrups, and they let the pony loose. One stride, two, and she struck ground unrelenting as a brick wall.

Jax stood over her. "Are we done?"

"It was all so fast, Jax. I tried to do what he said, but it happens faster than I could think."

Jax heaved her to her feet. "Are you ready to go home?"

"No. I am going to stay here until I make the ten seconds."

"The day's not long enough for that."

"Then I'll have to learn faster."

"You keep doing that you won't be able to get out of bed tomorrow."

And just like he had said, when she woke to Mollie's cries the next morning, she couldn't move. It seemed as if twice as many muscles ached than when she'd collapsed the night before. Luke propped himself up on his elbow.

"Honey, the baby."

If she told him how much she hurt, he wouldn't let her ride again.

"I'm fine. Just slow, is all."

She drew a blanket around herself, picked up her daughter and limped downstairs. Once she'd started a fire, warmed a bottle, sounds soothed away the pain: the rustle and crack of the flames, an owl hooting on the windmill outside, Mollie sucking her bottle.

How would she ever do it? After a dozen tries, she hadn't improved at all, no ride longer than a couple of seconds. She didn't have time to nurse these aches. And Luke had been right. She needed time to get Helios ready to race again and a second horse as well.

Her mother walked in and lit the sconce.

"Are you finished with this madness now?"

"No, Mama."

"You got in so late last night."

Francine continued into the kitchen— Hannah envied how easily she moved—and began grinding coffee. Mollie fell asleep again. Her mouth went slack, and the nipple slipped from her lips. Hannah brushed her finger against the little cheek, wiped away a drop of milk. She closed her eyes and let the room slip away. Weight in the balls of her feet, rope taut, rock back against the cantle. She tried to think of her torso as moving in tandem with the horse, one arm thrown back. Horse plunges down, rider goes back. Jump, whip back, jump, whip back. She had to intend to be part of the motion, not a sack of bones and flesh to be jettisoned into the air.

"You'll be staying home with Mollie today, won't you?" her mother called.

Hannah opened her eyes as the coffee aroma filled the room.

"I'm going back to Tawny's."

Through the doorway, Hannah could see Francine grimace and shake her head.

SUNNY GALE

Come September the whole household packed up for Cheyenne and not just because Luke and Hannah were contestants. By 1899, the rodeo had whipped up a whirlwind of notoriety and had expanded from one day to two. Though Ollie and Jax believed they knew all there was to know about vain buckaroos and feral broncs, even they were tempted by the promised size of the spectacle. Neither one had ever witnessed an exhibition this big. Even Buffalo Bill Cody's Wild West shows hadn't furnished as many cowboys, Indians, soldiers, wild acts, and wild animals. Three trains were scheduled to bring crowds up from Denver a full day before the event.

To Hannah's surprise, Francine said she would go. She felt she had to at least try to watch over her daughter's fate as much as she could in this unbridled frontier where she'd been abandoned and left destitute while her daughter ran wild, unchecked by her husband. Hannah and Francine could still find common ground in the one feminine art crucial to Hannah's enterprise—sewing. Besides baby clothes, Francine had produced more blousy riding skirts and blouses. At Hannah's request, Francine had added a strip of bear hide to the bottom of the Indian tunic so that it swept to Hannah's knees over the riding skirt. And she made Hannah a new silk scarf—scarlet—to wear around her neck.

Ollie even bought her a new ten-gallon cowboy hat.

After flouncing in front of the mirror in her whole outfit while her mother looked on, Hannah threw her arms around Francine's neck.

"It's perfect, Mama."

"If it's what you want, darling."

"Whatever happens now—win or lose—everyone's gonna notice me."

One hurdle remained—whether she, or any other cowgirl, would be allowed to ride broncs at Frontier Days. Through the long wagon journey, worry over the unknown gnawed at Hannah to where she couldn't bear to look after Mollie with her constant fussing. She passed the baby to Francine and turned away as if something on the horizon had distracted her when it was her guilt at her maternal failings that she was struggling to brush aside. Someday she'd be able to explain it to Mollie. She pictured Mollie facing her, tall and solemn, while she explained how everything she had worked for was at stake, and that was why she couldn't attend to an infant. The girl she imagined nodded with understanding. They were of one mind—the ascent of Sunny's livelihood just as one day Mollie, too, would ride.

While horses and buggies lined up for a downtown parade on that crisp morning in September, Hannah shivered in the makeshift office, face to face with the Frontier Days officials. It was more than her nerves. Temperatures had dropped so low the night before that the water troughs had iced over, and she was dressed in her tunic without a coat. She couldn't even draw enough warmth from Luke standing next to her. Eleanor was there, too, along with Sam Pickering, his daughter, Ruth, and three other cowgirls, their faces as pale as hers under their cowboy hats.

The three officials were seated. The one in the middle tapped his pipe tobacco into an ashtray, leaned back in his chair and addressed Pickering, the only one among them who the officials seemed to regard.

"If some girl was to get killed by a bronc, this show will fold, Sam. We'd all be vilified both here and in Denver, too. It would be the end."

Sam Pickering removed his hat and pressed it over his chest. This close to him the magnetism he exuded, along with his cologne, held greater sway over Hannah than in the rodeo parade the year before. His gray hair was waved along his temples, almost as if it had been waxed into place. His height alone seemed to command the room. He was always a showman, she realized, never just a range stockman like Ollie or Luke.

If she was going to get to ride, it would be because he would make it happen.

"Burl, we know each other well enough that you'll recognize that I intend these comments with respect. A man can get busted up out there and killed just as well. It's only been by the will of the Almighty that that hasn't happened yet. But we have to reckon that it will happen one day.

"And I believe the crowd expects that. That's what they've paid to see. All these young women in here—well, they're little sweethearts. The crowd loves to see their skirts flap when they race—hell, it's thrilling—and maybe they will think us a bunch of heartless bastards if we go and perch them on raging beasts."

"Just because they look like prairie flowers doesn't mean they don't have the same skills the men do. I can vouch for every one of them. My own daughter, Ruth, has been riding broncs along with her brother since she was twelve. Before that I had her on goats." He turned and pointed his index finger at the other girls. "Victoria Swanson, Bessie Parks, Rachel Gillespie, ranch-raised, every one of 'em. I know their fathers. They're tougher riders than some of the dandies that showed up here last year. Hannah over here, you saw her ride last year. No cowboy could have outdone her ride in that hailstorm. And the Indian woman, she rides with her husband, and he was champion last year.

"Out on the range, these girls put in their time every bit as hard as their brothers and fathers. And husbands. It's time we acted as if our state motto means what it says and let them be equal in every other way.

"And that's how you can sell this."

Another official leaned forward. "Tell you what," he said. "Why don't we make it an eight second ride for women instead of ten? That gives them less time to get busted up."

"I got another idea," said Pickering. "Let them ride with hobbled stirrups if they choose. Make things a tad easier for them."

"Hobbled stirrups?" said Burl. "What's that?"

"Stirrups are tied together underneath the horse. Gives the ladies a better chance to stay in their seats if the stirrups are tied down and can't move. I let all my bronc riders, men or women, start out that way until they get a feel for broncs."

"They still got to have one of their hands free, don't they?"

"Still have to have a hand free."

Burl gestured with his pipe toward Eleanor. "We're saying the squaw rides, too?"

Hannah squeezed Eleanor's forearm. If Pickering didn't speak up for her, she would.

"Doesn't it show how much these Indians have civilized?" asked Mr. Pickering, "if they've forsaken the ghost dance to compete against us in our own events?"

"Civilizing is one thing. Mingling's another."

Leonard Lefever spoke up. "If my wife doesn't ride, I don't ride."

"There you heard it," said Pickering. "There's your bronc champion from last year. You going to send him away?"

When they stepped out of the office, Hannah's eyes smarted in the blinding sunlight. She paused for a moment to let her eyes adjust and her face soak up the warmth. The September sky above was a wide-open blue prairie beckoning any cowgirl who could throw her leg over a saddle.

"Honey," said Luke, "I like that idea of hobbled stirrups. I think you ought to do it."

"Don't do it," said Eleanor. "Don't even think of doing it."

"Why not?" asked Luke.

"It's tempting to believe that it would make the ride easier. But a foot or leg could get caught and drag the rider underneath the horse. No one would be able save such a rider."

"I've ridden without them all this time," said Hannah. "If Eleanor's not doing it, I won't."

Luke scowled. "You'd listen to an Indian you barely know over me!" He began to walk ahead but turned over his shoulder. "For months you've been all twisted up over what those men in there were going to say. Me and the baby, we've had nothing from you all that time. I'm your husband, Hannah. You know I can say you won't ride at all, right? And that would be the end of it."

Eleanor waited until he was out of earshot. "Is it true, Hannah? He would stop you from riding when you've traveled this far?"

"He doesn't mean it. He won't say no to me because he's scared of what might happen."

"What would happen?"

"Locking the bedroom door is where I'd start. It would gut his day if he couldn't poke me at whatever hour he chooses. No matter. We've got to get going. We've got horses to warm up."

By 1:00 p.m., the time for the Ladies' Relay, the day had grown hot. Unlike the past year, no clouds massed over the mountains and not even a breeze rustled the feathers on the women's hats. Cokes, root beers, and beers floated in tubs where the ice had long since turned to water.

Hannah had brought a chocolate-colored mare, a three-year-old, for the first leg of her race. They'd practiced with a starting gun for weeks, but just before the gun went off, a loose dog ran across the track in front of the horses. Hannah's mare shied and she lost a second or two as the rest of the field lunged away. She was the last of the riders to reach her second horse, and while Helios reliably closed the gap on the leaders, he couldn't catch Ruth Pickering on her thoroughbred. Ruth, Eleanor, Hannah, that was how the horses crossed the finish line.

"I'm sorry," said Luke, "bad luck. I thought the mare would have behaved better than that."

"It's all right. I'm just happy I'm in the bucking contest. That's what I wanted more than anything. If I can just stick out the eight seconds, then I've done as much as I wanted to do.

"Hey, you still mad at me?" She tipped her head and grinned, flirting like in her girlish days.

He blew out a long sigh. "So many times, I say one thing and you say the opposite. I get the feeling you do it just to act contrary without thinking what it might mean. I was only thinking of you back there. If there was anything that could be done to make sure you'd be safe, you know I'd want that. There's your mama to think of. And Mollie. And me.

"But, honey, it's your ride. You sure as hell did work for it. I know there were times you were hurting from your falls and didn't complain. That showed me how much you wanted it. I guess whatever happens, Hannah, I'll be on the other side waiting to take you home."

His words made her feel callous, selfish. She had not been a good wife. Even if he had caused her pain, he was devoted to her. Why shouldn't she bend to meet his expectations? That's what made for bliss in marriage, or so Francine had said. She'd never intended to hurt Luke. Maybe he hadn't intended to hurt her either. Tears blurred her vision. Everything seemed jumbled together in that moment: the days of grueling rides at Tawny's, the long journey here, the worry over whether she would get to ride, the disappointment over her loss in the relay race, the jitters she felt now on her debut saddle bronc performance.

She threw her arms around his neck. He hugged her back tightly and kissed her ear, knocking her hat off her head. They both bent to pick it up, but he grabbed it first, wiped the dirt off the brim and set it on her head.

"I'm proud of you."

The women's bronc riding was to be the last event before the wild horse race. Hannah drew the last rider spot on a horse named "Rounder." By the time men's bronc riding, steer roping, the branding contest, Indian horse races, the wolf hunt and cavalry exhibitions were all completed, the sun had dropped behind the grandstand and its shadow spread long across the arena. The crowd hadn't thinned, even though it was cooler, and the spectators in wagons and buggies reached for their blankets. The odors of popcorn and hot dogs were sharper than ever when the first Ladies' Saddle Bronc event began.

Hannah hung on the rail and bit her thumb while watching her fellow contestants. Half of them chose the hobbled stirrups. Ruth Pickering rode for the full eight seconds. She scored the full fifty points, her bronc scored twenty-five, giving her a total score of seventy-five. Eleanor, who didn't ride with hobbled stirrups, scored seventy. It didn't seem to Hannah that Eleanor's ride was any less skillful than Ruth's. She remembered what she'd heard the officials say that morning and wondered. They hadn't turned Eleanor away, but she suspected that who these women were had shaded the scoring. Still, if Hannah failed her ride, Eleanor would come in second.

The rodeo hands brought out Rounder, a giant paint, seventeen hands tall. He was blindfolded and as he was manhandled out into the arena, he reared, just missing the boys with his front hooves. Every time they tried to fasten the saddle on, he lunged against the ropes, half-dragging some of the boys in the dirt. "Get me a twitch," she heard one of them shout. A twitch was hurriedly passed to the man in the front who twisted it tightly around the horse's upper lip. Rounder panted and heaved but stopped lunging.

"Want your stirrups hobbled, Miss?" the man called.

"No, sir," she shouted.

They helped her into the saddle. She wound her fingers through the lead rope, settled the balls of her feet in the stirrups, lifted her free arm up and nodded to the men.

"Cowgirl up!" she heard, and then Rounder was free.

The horse was so strong that she felt every whiplash kick of his hind legs deep in her spine. With every jump, it seemed as if the ground beneath her was miles away, almost as if they had defied gravity and taken straight off into the air. Rounder didn't twist or turn. He bucked out straight toward the opposite end of the arena, straight toward the crowd gasping at the rail. It looked as if he was going to crash through and Hannah braced for the worst.

He turned off at the last moment. The whistle blew, the pickup men sidled up to her. She kicked her feet loose, grabbed for the nearest rider, and she was lifted free and set down, solid ground beneath her again. The world stopped spinning. Instead of a blur, figures solidified, faces became clear. Some among the crowd were on their feet.

Then she heard her score: fifty for her, forty for Rounder.

Camera bulbs flashed as she threw her hat into the air, caught it, and then spun around. Cowboys—she didn't know who they were—picked her up and carried her on their shoulders. She was hurled into space even farther than Rounder had sent her. The world couldn't contain her joy and the crowd roared it back to her.

At the grandstand, Luke was there, Eleanor, too, and Sam Pickering. Burl, the same official who had opposed a women's bronc riding event, shook her hand, and said, "Mrs. Mangum, right?"

"No, sir," said Hannah, "that's not my name."

Luke stared at her.

"Sunny Gale, my name's Sunny Gale."

Another bulb clicked and a reporter called out. "Sunny Gale! Where would a cowgirl get a name like that?"

"From the sun bursting through a spring snow squall. Have you ever seen it? Wind and snow will be whirling close to the ground, but the sun bursts right through the haze and lightens the space all around you. A sunny gale."

"That's quite an outfit you got on. What's that, bear hide on the bottom of that vest?"

"Yes, sir, I bought the vest here in Cheyenne last year, but my mama added the bear hide. She makes all my blouses and riding skirts. She's out here watching today."

"Will you be cooking supper tonight? Or should we ask Mr. Sunny Gale about that?"

"Ask him. He'll tell you I make the best savory meat pie in Box Butte County. Luke!"

She couldn't see him anywhere. In scanning the crowd, she spotted Eleanor. Listening to the reporters, Eleanor wasn't wearing that disconnected expression. Her brows were furrowed slightly, as if she was looking beyond the grandstand and the throngs. Hannah—no, by God, *Sunny*—understood that her friend wasn't envious. It was that Eleanor had seen a chasm that split Sunny Gale from everything in the former life of Hannah Brandt.

SUNNY GALE

7

February 7th

First fuel. Now water. In the winters, Clem would let the windmill run for only a few hours a day—just enough to keep the tank full. That way he prevented wind damage. Yesterday, she forgot to shut it down and now the wind has ripped off half the blades and blown them yards away. The sun glints off the shards, mocking her for her carelessness.

She won't die from thirst. She melts snow in tubs, a tub in the house for her own use and another tub in the barn to supplement the water in the livestock tank.

Every day, the sun lingers a little longer above the horizon. She may outlast this weather after all.

Thirty-one years since 1900, but it feels more like a hundred. These murderous winters pile up, one on top of the other, until they weigh a mortal soul down. When her life began over again as Sunny Gale, she believed her success was just a straightforward matter of gritting her teeth and enduring whatever trials came her way. She had begun that winter of 1899-1900 in Cheyenne, without Luke, with the hopes of starting her own riding ring and getting her own string of horses. All she needed was to find a partner.

Then Mollie got sick, and all her dreams were scrapped while she spent nights next to the crib hanging on Mollie's every breath. Mothers, she learned, are held hostage by Fate.

Though she was dragged low, too much depended on her. She wouldn't buckle like that scoundrel, Tremain! No, instead, she poured her energy into believing that winter would end, that her child would rise smiling one morning, that she would go back to racing and bronc riding, back to an arena where she would shine.

Francine's whining had been an unneeded hindrance. They were living then in a back alley in a room overlooking the railroad yard. Francine complained that the cold was like nothing she'd ever suffered before. Well, the room was draughty. Ash from the locomotives sifted through the windows and peppered their table, floors, and beds.

Every morning at four a.m. when Sunny left for her kitchen job, she paused at the landing to look across the tracks at the stockyards. The train for the slaughter horses came on Friday. She saw them there in the pens under the yard light: blacks and whites, paints and appaloosas, chestnuts, and palominos. Falling snow blew across the lights. Gusts tossed it back up and then it would fall again, blanketing their backs, frosting the whiskers of the old ones. They milled and stamped. They pressed against the fences, their ears pricked, listening—the young, old, crippled, the ones too rank for anyone's use. She imagined picking her way over the snow-covered tracks, feeling through the snow-covered boards for the gate latch, hearing the metallic snap as it opened and watching them file out one by one to trot through the darkened streets and find their way back to the range where the wind claimed no interest in their fate and their lives were their own.

In those visions, she saw Zephira running with them, galloping in long strides, her hoofprints behind theirs in the snow.

The morning after Sunny's winning bronc ride, everyone was unnaturally quiet. Horses were hitched, luggage was loaded, and no one seemed to find Sunny as remarkable as she now thought she was. Without a word, Francine handed over Mollie. When Sunny saw Luke gently load her trophy saddle in the back of the wagon, her heart jumped at the hope that his pride at her accomplishment outweighed his hurt feelings over the "Sunny Gale" incident. All around, he'd had a rough time. He'd lost out in the men's saddle bronc riding. Which meant that she'd been able to do what he couldn't. And without hobbled stirrups. He hadn't spoken to her since she'd come down off the grandstand. Still, she clung to the belief that once his wounds weren't so fresh, they would pick up where they'd left off. Cordiality, respect, if not love.

But when they'd returned home and she'd told him she was going out with the cowboys to break colts, he clamped his jaw, and he told her no, she wasn't a cute little tag-along anymore. She was a mother and wife. Time she assumed her duties and watched the baby and the house from now on.

Sunny laughed in his face. "You're that jealous? What if I say no?"

"It's time I put my foot down. All the hands are laughing behind my back. I'll lock you in the bedroom if I have to. This rodeoing I let you do, it's confused you, Hannah. You don't know who you are. All those Greek gods and goddesses you rattle on about. That's gone to your head, and you seem to think you're one of them. 'Sunny Gale'. Is that some goddess you read about? You need to keep company with your child for a day or two 'til you can come to your senses. You married ME, remember? You couldn't stand to be without me. Hell, you threw yourself at me so I'd marry you."

"That's a lie. That day in the barn I tried to push you off and told you to stop, or don't you remember that?"

"I said I was sorry if I hurt you, didn't I? But here you are, bringing it up now when it was nowhere in your noggin on the day you said 'I do.'"

"My name's not Hannah."

Luke walked out the door and locked it behind him.

Francine unlocked it after he'd left.

"He's your husband, Hannah. You can't dismiss what he commands. You married your fate to his. You took vows at a Christian altar to place his desires ahead of yours. And as barbaric as this place is, he's a good husband. You'll have a good life here, the life you want. Mollie will grow up riding. She'll own this ranch one day. This horse madness is so little for you to give up when you have so much. Run out to him, Hannah, and tell him you're wrong. Beg his forgiveness."

Sunny stopped sobbing and pushed away from her mother's chest. Francine couldn't see that the woman she was preaching to was done being Hannah.

"This 'horse madness?' I'm not giving it up. Frontier Days is just the beginning. Wild West shows and rodeos are popping up everywhere. I can be a champion any place there's a bronc to ride. I just showed you. Sunny Gale is not going to hurt this ranch or Mollie or you or anyone. It hurts what Luke Mangum wants, that's all. That's not reason enough for me to give it up."

Now that the door was open, she'd be pitched off a thousand broncs before she'd ever let a man lock her in a room again. The next morning, she began packing.

"You'll see," Luke fumed as he watched her. "You won't be gone two weeks."

"I'm taking Helios with me."

"He's not yours. Besides your clothes, there's nothing here that belongs to you."

"I thought he was a gift."

"Damn horse means more to you than any human being, me included."

Mollie had been shocked into silence by all the yelling. Sunny grabbed her with one arm, her suitcase with the other and walked out the door. She heard Luke shout, "You're not going to be able to feed a horse on your own. You'd just end up selling him in the slaughter yard to pay your rent."

She nearly collided with Jax on the porch. Tears welled and spilled down her cheeks because, of all of them, Jax knew how she would feel about leaving Helios behind.

He reached for her suitcase. "I'll drive you and Mrs. Francine into town."

Sunny bit her lip and nodded. Jax paused, watching her.

"It's all right, Miz Hannah. You have to go. But in this world you want to enter, there will be many horses. People will give you horses to ride. Or you will get your own horses. Better than this one here. Cowgirls can't love their horses. You pick them up and discard them as you need. Without feeling. As you have learned to hold on, so you must learn to let go. That's all. No tears."

She would have thrown her arms around his neck and hugged him if she could. But it would only make Luke even angrier and no telling what he'd do then. Jax turned away to put her suitcase in the wagon. Francine joined her on the porch.

"Just how long do you intend to carry on this escapade of yours?"

"As long as I can get on a horse."

But winter overtook her in Cheyenne, and her plans of finding a barn and a corral hadn't fallen in place as quickly as she had believed. Riding and rodeo were over for the year. Francine found work as a seamstress by going door to door along the mansions on Seventeenth Street. The legislature came to town in January. Many had brought their wives who needed suits and gowns— proper city fashion, not ordinary country wear— and off Francine would go.

Sunny guessed her best chance to find someone who knew of her and would help her was at the Cheyenne Club, the haven for rich stockmen and Cheyenne's high society. She jumped at taking a job in the kitchen. But she found herself polishing silver under the eyes of Gustav, the alcoholic Swedish chef, not in the dining room mingling with the members. All the kitchen girls had to watch out for Gustav and his wandering hands. He made no distinction between squeezing a buttock and stuffing a turkey.

Nor did she matter to anyone that she passed in the streets. When she left work every day at three p.m., the wind funneled through the cross streets pelting her with ash and grit. Faces were covered with mufflers. No one spoke. No one knew who she was. Her trophy saddle was stuffed in a corner behind the bed she shared with her mother and covered with old newspapers to keep off the ash.

Eighteen years old and everything around her signaled a dead end. Not to mention the end of her marriage. The girlish passion she'd felt for Luke had vanished a long time ago, but she felt grief all the same. Grief for the love she had wanted to have. She toyed with trying to construct a path back to Luke Mangum. Not because she was desperate. Somehow their failure was her fault, too. Maybe there was a way to where resentments and hurts could be laid to rest. Would Luke be joyful at her return? Vindictive?

No matter because she couldn't bring Hannah Mangum with her. That girl couldn't be retrieved. Not for Luke or Francine. Not for Mollie.

Then one afternoon she came home to find Mollie screaming, a doctor there, and Francine wringing her hands. After that, she forgot Luke entirely.

In April, after Mollie's recovery, Sunny found a riding ring where she could practice for the upcoming Frontier Days. As she meandered among would-be ropers and bronc riders, all of whom shifted to stare at her, she felt relieved to be there, but nearly too exhausted to pull herself on a horse. She hadn't slept a full night in the last month.

And these men dared to regard her with disdain, various shades of *what are you doing here* appearing in their eyes. Who were they? Sunny Gale, the mother, had just escaped Hades with her child alive and warm in her arms. She'd steered her family through the winter in a place where they'd known no one. They hadn't starved or frozen to death.

The tasks shouldered by mothers would crack the spines of these boys.

She found the owner, McCauley, loading steers in a chute for the ropers. His bib overalls and boots were caked with muck. He removed his cap and wiped his bald head with a rag.

"You looking for your husband, Honey?"

"No, I am looking to ride. Saddle broncs is my event."

He stared at her. "Got a couple goats you

can try. After the boys here are done roping."

"Pardon, but I'm Sunny Gale. I won the women's bronc riding last year."

McCauley's little eyes narrowed. "So that was you. About fell out of my seat when I saw that they were going to let y'all ride. A'course, if Pickering got a say, it was bound to happen. 'Specially with his daughter in it. I saw you ride. I got to admit you were better than some of the pokes that hang around here.

"But that was some kind of outfit you were wearing that day." He stepped closer to the rail. "You look like you've lost some weight. You're looking a little pale as well. You haven't been on a horse all winter, have you?"

"I want to compete again this summer. I've got to find a place where I can get ready."

"Didn't you have a husband? Short, skinny guy, right? Not much of a rider himself."

"We're not together anymore."

"I see. Well, I don't know what you expect, Miss Gale, but champion or not, you got to pay to ride here."

"I brought money."

"Seventy-five cent per ride, no matter whether you stay on or not."

"Boys I talked to when I came in said it was fifty cents."

"Prices go up for skirts."

His face was close now, close. She inhaled the sweet-sour odor of his chewing tobacco.

"All right. I'd like two rides today."

"Wait till these steer ropers clear out and we'll set you up."

It was after dark before she got started. McCauley switched the lights on, and the ring was

checker-boarded between light and dark. The
first horse the boys brought in wheeled in and
out of the lights. She knew it was young and
unschooled by the way it shied at the noise and
the men. She didn't last long on it, no more than
a hop or two, and as she lay flat on her back in the
mud, she wondered if she was already too late
for this season. If she couldn't do it, it would
mean another year in the room over the railroad,
another year in the kitchen at the Cheyenne
Club. While other cowgirls out there competing
would get better and better.

"You done?" McCauley called.

"No, sir."

The next horse was also young. A buckskin
colt. Once they released him and Sunny braced
in the saddle for his first jump, he stood there,
quaking. In that abrupt pause, coyotes howled
far out on the prairie. She sensed the stars
above traversing paths distant beyond reckoning,
oblivious to the fate of a young woman on a horse.

Then someone cracked a bullwhip.

She was not caught off guard. She was
planted well enough that when the horse
jumped, she was able to stay in her seat, keep
her bucking rope taut and raise her other arm.
The whirl of light and shadow made her head
swim to where she didn't know where she was.
Stick with him, stick with him! Time stretched as
the two of them moved together. No whistle blew.
The colt suddenly braced, and she knew he'd come
up against the rail. She felt his awareness of the
solid planks alongside them. His head dropped,
he broke into a trot, and they circled around once
until he came back into the light and halted. She
leaned down and stroked his neck.

McCauley was sitting on the top rail. "That's the way, honey. Boys have gone home. Cool him down and put him up in the barn."

Sunny slid off, picked up the lead rope and walked him outside the ring. He was too played out to put up any kind of a fight now. Steam rose from his hide and nostrils. Sweat evaporating from her skin was chilling her. Her jacket wasn't thick enough and she needed to get home.

McCauley was in the barn doorway.

"You can put him in that stall back there."

"Unsaddle him, too?"

"Naw, I'll do it."

"Hay?"

"Yeah, you can give him some. There's a stall full of it back there. Pitchfork is there, too."

She threw some hay over the gate and the horse buried his muzzle in it. It still smelled sweet from the last summer, the summer of her success. It reassured her that that success had been real.

"How you getting' home?"

"I walked here. I can walk home."

"Sure you don't want to spend the night?"

A lump formed in her throat. So this was what it was about. She looked past McCauley to the door.

"No, sir, I just came to ride horses is all."

He moved toward her. "I'm not so bad, honey. I know you need help getting to the top again. I can help you. And you won't have to pay me."

She stepped to the side behind a metal table full of blacksmithing tools. She imagined overturning the table as he got closer. It wasn't heavy enough.

"Give me a try, Sunny." He came closer.

She stepped to the side again behind a wooden stand with an anvil strapped on top.

"How long have you been away from your husband? You got to be lonesome by now."

As menacing as he was, she had to let him come closer. A few more steps.

"Please don't, Mr. McCauley. Please."

He grinned, confident that her failure to move meant the opposite of what she'd said. He took another step forward.

Sunny overturned the anvil on his foot.

McCauley screamed.

She ran out of the barn and didn't look back. Behind her, the screams continued. Doors slammed somewhere and dogs barked. She heard others running to the barn.

But she was gone.

SUNNY GALE

8

Past midnight, February 8th

    She drifts in and out, too much discomfort for slumber and too tired to want to awaken. When she drowses, she hears a voice, patient but insistent. Awakening, she realizes it was Ruth Pickering. Instinctively, she jumps to the old defensiveness. No telling what snide remarks Ruth was murmuring, yet as she blinks and feels the room settle around her, she realizes Ruth's tone was gentle, not scathing. She felt as if Ruth had leaned in close to her to straighten a bit of costume, pull some curls out of her cowboy hat. A Wild West show was about to start. Ruth patted her shoulders. "There you are. Ready?"

The moon has already set, the dark thick as molasses all around. Outside, stars greet her, like angels pulsing with light. Many times during the pinnacles of her career, she has fancied them as her innumerable, if mute, fans. They've drawn in to inspect her close up.

Can they hear her? "Help," she pleads. Then louder. "Help!"

The cattle startle and jostle one another.

She closes the door, lights the lamp. She reaches inside Pandora's Box for the Pickering family show programs. Though there are many photographs of Tad Pickering, her second husband, they don't begin to capture him. Tad roping steers. Tad Roman riding, his feet on two horses, racing them around barrels. Yes, his skill and talent are all there, but not the zeal he brought to every one of his days. She closes her eyes and sees him grinning, washed in sunlight with his cowboy hat pushed to the back of his head, his yellow neck scarf ruffling in the breeze.

When they'd announced their engagement, Francine had pulled her aside. "This marriage promotes your endeavors, but what does he mean to you, really?"

Sunny turns down the lamp and she's plunged into darkness once more.

So simple, really. It meant she would never again have to shiver in a room over the railroad tracks and look down on the miserable slaughter horses.

As Sunny stood in the archway of the main dining room, her heart pounded so hard that she thought all the diners would hear her and look up. A man at table number twelve had called for her, that's all Gustav had growled. At last, someone had found her here! She had never been allowed in the dining room when members were there, only after the dining hours to clean up.

It was a mild May evening and the windows had been opened a crack to let in the evening breeze. Men and women seemed enlivened by the warming season. They talked loudly, laughed loudly. Glasses clinked. She felt the room's collective relief at exiting another winter. Their livestock had come through, most of them anyhow. The hay meadows were flooded with snow runoff. The prairie was greening.

The man at table twelve was waving. Sam Pickering! She threaded through the tables. Eyes lifted and she hoped no one recognized her in her kitchen uniform.

Pickering stood and squeezed her hand. "It's Sunny Gale, right?"

The realization that the great man had remembered her shot her spirits right through the roof. She pumped his hand. "Yes, sir."

"It used to be Anna something or other, right?"

"Yes, sir, it was Hannah, but not anymore."

"I'd like you to meet my son, Tad."

Tad stood. He was tall as his father, but slender as an aspen with a full head of auburn hair. He nodded politely. He didn't reach for her hand. It hadn't been his idea to pull her from the kitchen.

"Sit down with us."

"That's awful kind of you, Mr. Pickering. I'm just so happy you called for me, but I can't stay. I have to get back downstairs. The chef is hot as it is that I came up here. He'll let me go for sure if I don't get back."

Pickering swatted her words away. "Aw, nobody's firing anybody. You got my word on it. Sit down."

She glanced around the room. Some of the diners stared, distracted by a kitchen girl hobnobbing with Pickering. Never mind them. Hadn't the man asked her to sit down? His invitation was all the acknowledgment in the world that she was worthy to be with them.

Tad was so good-looking that she felt jumpy to be next to him. Her gaze dropped to his wrists. *Diamond horseshoe cufflinks.*

"I was over at McCauley's to buy some broncs," Pickering said. "Poor man broke his foot. Said an anvil fell on it. Have you been riding over there?"

Sunny searched their faces to see if they knew more about what had happened. Neither of them gave a sign.

"No, sir. I want to start riding again, but I haven't been over there."

Sam reached for a roll. "Well, what are you doing here, Sunny? A rider with your ability. You should have come out to my place months ago. Start riding? You could have been riding all winter long. Rodeos are starting up all over the West. There's Wild West shows we're planning on doing, too. The costumes you wear, that gorgeous smile. You wouldn't have had to say a word and I would have hired you. Salary and board, too. Why didn't you come to see me when you got to town?"

"I had planned to try and start a riding ring of my own. That's what I wanted. But when we got here—Mama and me—it was full-blown winter. I had to snatch this job just to get by. And then my baby girl got sick."

Silly, her voice was clogging with tears in front of these men. The last thing she wanted was to appear as a helpless woman angling for their pity. She hadn't realized that in dredging up the dark times of the past months, she would feel overwhelmed by how much she had lived through. She pinched herself hard.

"You've got a baby?" Tad asked.

Sunny blinked back her tears, measuring the judgment in his tone. He was disturbed by the idea that she was a single woman with a child. She straightened. "Yes, I do. Mollie—she's wonderful. And she'll be a top rider one day."

Tad turned away. She caught the dismissal in the slight shake of his head.

"Whatever you're thinking, Mr. Pickering, you can say it to my face."

Tad reached for his beer, gulped it halfway down and then wiped the foam from his lips. "I don't guess I know enough to say anything."

Of course, he didn't know enough to say anything. His daddy dictated his every move. That was clear. So easy for this fop to take comfort in his presumptions. *Mr. Diamond Cufflinks.*

"The baby's daddy was in the bronc riding, wasn't he?" Sam batted the quarrel aside. "Sunny, don't get yourself all awry here. You've got nothing to prove with us. Is the baby well now?"

"She is, thank you. Sam—Mr. Pickering—I want to say how grateful I am to you. If it hadn't been for you, I never would have gotten to ride broncs at all."

"Everyone's gonna pay to see a pretty girl on a horse. It helps if the horse looks good, too, but it doesn't matter how the horse behaves. If the pillars of refinement are offended by women on broncs, well, my bet is they're still going to buy tickets to watch women on broncs.

"You'd be welcome to work on bronc riding with Ruth. Horse racing, too, if that's what you want. Tad here is a roper. But he's also started on Roman riding, trick riding. He could use a pretty, young woman as a partner. Once we've got it down, I'll be trying to get the Frontier Days committee to add Roman racing and some trick performances. You interested?"

"What's Roman racing?"

"Riding two horses while standing."

"People race like that?"

"They sure as hell do! I saw them do it in Denver last summer."

"And you believe I can do that?"

"From the day I watched you race that horse—what was his name? Hellfire?—I've been aware that Sunny Gale can do anything she sets her mind to do. Do you think you could work with Tad here?"

The two of them eyed one another. His attitude was offensive, but she couldn't deny her attraction to him.

"I'd be happy to work with him. Give me a horse to ride again and I'll do whatever you say. But I'm not sure he wants to work with me."

"What do you say, son? You heard what the lady asked."

Tad's shrugged. "It's worth a try," he said.

His noncommittal demeanor stung. He

wasn't interested in her. Just another chore to do to please Daddy.

"There you go," said Pickering. "Welcome to Pickering Livestock and Company."

The log bunkhouse on the Pickering ranch didn't look much different than their homestead cabin back in Nebraska. Francine took one look out the small grimy window and sank down on the thin cot.

"You can quit the melodrama, Mama. I know it's not cozy, like how you want it to be, but we don't have to pay anyone to live here. That's an improvement over where we were, isn't it? And you heard Mr. Pickering. He's got a pony already picked out for Mollie. She's going to have sunshine and open country where she won't get sick again." She opened the door. Outside was a beaten patch of bare ground. "Just look. No more railroad ash."

"Melodrama? You're such a fool, Hannah. And I refuse to call you Sunny Gale. All these silly fantasies you chase. Never mind me. Just look where you've dragged your child." She gestured around the cabin. "She has nothing. We have nothing. Had you kept your position at the Club, you could have happened on a man who would marry you. Someone who would have provided for Mollie. Someone who would have bought ponies for Mollie. We're drifting from hovel to hovel no better than beggars and why, Hannah?"

"You're the one being silly. No one's drifting. We've got a good place here. Mr. Pickering believes in me. He knows I can ride. We've been over all this. It gives me the chance to do what I want to do and not have to worry about money. And with him, I'm going to be able to do more than just once-a-year Frontier Days. We'll travel to other rodeos. No matter how you abhor it, Sunny Gale is a name that's going to be heard everywhere."

"This man likes you today. There's no guarantee he'll feel that way tomorrow. You know you refuse to face the worst that could happen. You could break your neck, Hannah. Then where would we be? Will Sam Pickering keep you if you're maimed? If you don't want to live in Cheyenne anymore, at least consider returning to Luke. He has to take his child in."

"I am not going back there, Mama. And we've survived. By ourselves. Without anyone to help us."

"You started down this path because you loved horses, or so you said. I don't see your passion in any of this. All I see is desire for a spectacle. Is that who Sunny Gale is? What does that even have to do with horses?"

"It's not just the spectacle. It's about pushing all your limits to be the best you can be. I'm tired of trying to explain it to you. I'm taking Mollie outside."

It was late afternoon. The evening chill already bit through her light jacket. Shadows lengthened behind the two-story family mansion, the barns, and outbuildings. Spring peepers sang in the wet sloughs. Cows bawled for their calves. West of her bunkhouse the pasture was lush with new grass. A mile out, beneath a small hill, horses lazed around a windmill. Sunlight flashed off the windmill blades.

She picked Mollie up. "Look, horses." The horses were too far off to hold Mollie's attention. She squirmed, and Sunny set her down again. The child toddled off, trying to grab a passing barn cat, and Sunny followed until they wound up at the corral.

Ruth Pickering was there, riding another thoroughbred, a sleek bay. He crow-hopped every time she tried to steer him back to the rail. She halted him, walked him back to the rail and they eased off into a canter. As they came toward Sunny and Mollie, the cat ran into the horse's path. He shied, then bucked, and Ruth yanked hard on the bit. She turned to Sunny.

"See the trouble you're causing! Don't you know any better than to haze a young stallion?"

Sunny snorted at the accusation. "It wasn't us. Look there. It's the barn cat."

"Having you here is my father's idea. If we were going to hire a girl, I don't know why we would have hired you. You don't know anything about what you're doing. And your clothing is tawdry. Hideous, actually. My father's determined to make something of you. That's his business. But understand, Miss Gale, or whatever your name is, you and I will not be companions."

Jealousy, oozy as gangrene, that's what this was. She had bested Ruth Pickering in separate contests before hundreds of spectators. Yet it didn't take a fancy education like Ruth must have had to see that she was being goaded. *Deliberately.* She picked up Mollie and hugged her tightly.

"My apologies. Ruth," she said quietly. "I won't bother you again."

"It's 'Miss Pickering' to you."

Sunny nodded. "Fair enough. And you can call me 'Miss Gale.'"

"Good day, Miss Gale."

How giddy she'd been at that luncheon with Sam at the Cheyenne Club, convinced that she was being ushered into a brighter world, even if Tad's reaction had sullied the day a little. And she hadn't expected to be housed in a palace although it would have been helpful in overcoming Francine's objections if at least they'd been offered curtains. And now she saw that the cost of holding her place there would be eclipsing herself to Ruth.

At mealtimes, Sunny and her family ate with the rest of the ranch hands in a lodge connected to the main house by a breezeway. Some of the men worked on the Pickering ranch as cow herders and fence builders. Others tended the rodeo stock, broke horses, or groomed the family's riding and carriage horses. All the men were loud and ravenous, no matter the meal. At first, in front of Sunny and Francine, they attempted their own rough form of chivalry. They took off their hats and offered to pass dishes, but by the fourth day, the ritual of manners had collapsed like a fence of sticks around a buffalo herd.

As Francine watched them reach over her for platters and guzzle whiskey out of flasks from boots, hats, belts, pouches, or other secreted locations on their persons, she whispered, "Mollie shouldn't be forced to witness such depravity."

But Mollie did watch as she sat on Sunny's lap clutching her spoon. The hands smiled and cooed at her. She grinned back, drool running down her chin.

The cook, Dezzie, was a giantess over six feet tall. Ranch lore was she'd escaped slavery as a young girl and had traveled west by hiding in a U.S. mail sack. Some of the hands looked as if the wind would blow them away. Not Dezzie. She hefted an ax just like a man to chop her own wood, her apron whipping about her in the gusts. Her old border collie never stirred from its bed of flour sacks by the stove, and she kept a crow perched on a line in the breezeway. When she ferried platters through to the lodge, the crow, "Tecumseh Sherman," would hop along the line following her.

With little else to entertain the men, they made sport of Dezzie when they thought she was out of hearing. Their jibes smacked of resentment over the power in her bearing.

"She's never been with a man," one boy said. He glanced at Mollie, and confident that she didn't understand, he continued. "Even if she had been married, goner prob'ly couldn't've survived around her. Whatever happened to him, you can bet she chopped him up and fed him to the crow!" They all laughed until they heard the bolt click on a revolver.

Dezzie stood at the head of the table; her gun pointed at the boy. Francine smothered Mollie against her breast which resulted in Mollie beginning to kick and scream.

"You are all swine, and you know it. That's why you muck around here with nothing better to do than trifle with creatures higher than yourselves. Starting with Tecumseh. I catch any of you hairy boars cuttin' up about him, teasin' him, feedin' him, I'll shoot every damn one of you. I can warrant, if Mr. Pickering hasn't told you himself, he won't miss your lice-bitten hides. You stand up and apologize, boy, or you can hand over your liquor."

The bench legs scraped on the floor as the boy leapt to his feet, and no one uttered a sound. Twenty-some men here, yet Dezzie could rule them all. None even tittered as the boy apologized.

Sunny marveled at the spectacle. Never had she seen men defer to a woman, even if such deference was procured under threat. Francine was always lamenting the uncivilized West. Was this a sign of it?

Dezzie had yanked open a curtain on a world where women didn't need to placate or cajole or comfort to reach their ends. They could just demand respect and receive it. Uncivilized? No, the word "civilization" was itself too stymieing. A new age had begun where women wrenched their own destinies away from those who would deny them.

And I am a part of it, she thought, convinced, again, of the righteousness of her choices.

Dezzie stopped Francine and Sunny after the men had left. "Didn't mean to cause offense to you ladies, but I won't let these boys run over me. You look a little pale, Miz... "

"Francine. You can call me Francine. You are right, Miss Dezzie. These outrages are not suitable for me—or for my granddaughter."

"If it suits, you can bring the child and eat with me in the kitchen. That'll get you away from this rabble."

Francine glanced at Sunny. "Thank you. I

think that will do very well. Hannah will be joining us, of course."

"Hannah?"

"It's my mama's name for me," said Sunny. "It's all right. I'll take my seat with the boys."

Francine glared at her—Francine—ever complacent with the limitations in her life. No, Francine would never fully understand those women, including her daughter, who would no longer concede, but challenge.

Without Francine and Mollie at the table, the men began addressing Sunny directly. Some of them had seen her in Cheyenne, some of them had heard of her. From mingling with Luke's hands, she knew how to talk and joke with them. They asked her for her story, she asked them for theirs. The meal conversations became less constrained, if a touch more bawdy, than when Francine had been there.

A whole week went by before Tad appeared in the doorway at the noon meal. The table fell silent. The Pickering family ate in the main house. No one was used to seeing the boss or his people here. Then, too, the difference between Tad's garments and the rest of the crew's was enough to distract from the gravy and biscuits. Tad wore a fringed buckskin jacket. Someone, no doubt one of the men sitting there, had buffed Tad's boots to a shine. These men Sunny ate with had washed their clothes in a stock tank, if they had washed them at all.

The hands waited, expecting some sort of announcement. Tad, for his part, seemed as if he felt out of place. He wasn't the one who gave the orders around here—the old man was—and his discomfort showed. His gaze flitted over each swarthy face until he found Sunny's.

Sunny thought it was about time he, or Sam, came to look for her. Every morning after breakfast, she'd appeared at the barn and had been met by a foreman who had hustled her out to ride with the cattle crews. When she'd protested that she hadn't been hired to herd cattle, he had insisted that the boss would call her when he was ready for her—and in the meantime, she'd be well advised to expand her skills.

Ruth had orchestrated this, Sunny was sure. Maybe she was trying to restrict the amount of time Sunny had to get ready. Maybe she was trying to hustle her out altogether. Tad's appearance brought some relief, as uncertain as he seemed. Something was getting ready to happen.

Tad cleared his throat. "Didn't mean to cause any stir. You boys go on eating. I came to talk to her."

Sunny started to rise when the foreman called out, "We'd be pleased if you joined us, Tad." Several of the hands scooted aside to make a place at the bench next to Sunny.

As he sat down, her heart jumped like a jackrabbit, which she couldn't explain in light of their troubled introduction. She didn't know what to do with her hands, her mouth, her face, her eyes. Should she turn to him, try to talk to him like one of the men? These boys might think she was currying favor. If she did nothing at all, would she seem too haughty? Her mind flipped through alternate scenes, scrambling to pick one where the men all got up and disappeared while Tad turned his attention to her.

A few boys spoke up and mentioned the dry weather. Warm days for the end of May, but too dry. Was Tad's dad worried there might be too little hay?

Just like that, just like falling off a log, men eased into idle chats with one another. Hit on the drought or cattle prices and off they launched, everyone into their call-and-response patterns. She was the odd man out with no way to insert herself into this gang.

At last, Tad shifted toward her, giving her permission to look in his eyes. "Are you and your mama settling in all right?"

She squeaked. "We're fine, thank you." Her questions were pounding to bust out: when would they let her back on the broncs, what about the Roman riding they'd talked about?

"Saw your mama and baby in the kitchen. That is a beautiful baby. What didj'ya say her name was?"

She tried to warn him with her eyes. He couldn't be so dense as to bumble into this topic again. "I told you. Her name is Mollie."

He grinned. He was taunting her in front of these men. "Yes, I remember now. Mollie. She looks like you."

"I'm pretty sure you didn't trouble yourself to come over here to talk about my child. I don't mean to interrupt you catching up with these boys but the rodeo's coming up. Shouldn't we be getting ready for it?"

"I expect you're getting anxious."

"I am."

"Worried that my dad's only brought you here to punch cows?"

She could feel her face color. They all laughed.

"I did say I'd do anything your daddy wanted as long as I got to ride again. I guess, though, if you push me out in the tumbleweeds, I'm not in front of the crowds beating the Pickerings at any event they choose to enter."

The men whooped. "She got you there, Tad."

She feared it had been the wrong thing to say, but as Tad looked along the row of faces, she could see he hadn't been offended. He laughed along with the rest of them and then turned to her again. Oh, yes, she'd impressed him all right.

"No, Miss Sunny Gale, we won't hide any of your talents in favor of ourselves. The reason I've come over is to ask if we can build on your talents. Care to join me in the corral tomorra morning?"

He was being coy in front of these boys, trying to regain the upper hand. She would play along. At least in the morning she could count on finding out why they were so slow to let her back on the broncs.

"Gladly."

He got up and bowed before setting his cowboy hat back on his head. "Good day, Miss Gale." The gesture made her smile and brought one or two last chuckles from his audience.

He'd meant nothing by it. Still, she wished that it had been more than a joke. She had to kill this attraction for him...a man who thought less of her because of her child.

Next morning the air was frosty, almost as if the calendar had been flipped back several pages. A layer of ice covered the mudholes. The sky radiated with the same baby blues and indigos that colored the wild irises running along the sloughs. Way south, a locomotive chugged eastward. The rumble reverberated farther and farther outward like the waves from a pebble dropped in a pool. Her anxieties about her meeting with Tad dissipated. It felt like a day of new beginnings.

In the corral, Tad rode Roman-style on two bay horses, both at a brisk trot. He seemed to float through the air while the horses beneath him moved in perfect tandem. She studied everything, the way his knees softened to absorb the shock, the way he used the reins for control and balance, the buggy whip in his hand to keep the outer horse close. He urged them into a lope. They circled around once and came down the center toward a small hurdle. Both horses jumped, but one was off stride and Tad bounced off.

She climbed over the rails to get to him. "Are you all right?"

"Hoo-whee that ground is frozen. Come help me up."

She grasped his hand, savoring the return grip that was both light and strong. The tension lasted only a second before he'd jumped to his full height, towering over her.

"What do you think?"

"It's incredible. You were incredible."

"And you?"

"I might be able to do it after a while, but I couldn't be ready by Frontier Days. Not if I'm riding saddle broncs, too."

"The question is do you want to try? That's where we're starting."

The invitation in his eyes—she didn't want to misread it—but it glowed with warmth.

He continued. "What we're thinking is once we get this down, we could work out a routine for the other rodeos and the Wild West shows."

"Yes. I want to do it."

"All right, let's get started."

He boosted her onto the horses and she wavered as she stood up, struggling to find her balance. The horses stirred underneath, and Tad calmed them. She was embarrassed at how clumsy she must appear where he had been graceful. Her perspective felt so skewed that her heart raced as if she'd never been on a horse before. The horses' manes looked as if they were yards away—no way to reach and grab a handful for stability. Instead of her gaze naturally traveling forward over the horse's ears, her eyes bounced around the corral, the house, the outbuildings, the windmill, the range sloping upward and away. She needed to focus on some spot to hold her in space.

"Miss Gale, we all require air to survive. Please go ahead and breathe."

"It's a lot of work just standing here."

"We've got time."

She rocked her feet back and forth until they angled out slightly.

"You all right?"

"I can make it."

"I'm going to hand you their reins. You'll do better if you're holding the reins, but just hold them. Don't try and do anything with them. I got their lead ropes down here, so I have control. They can't get away from you. We're going to walk, okay?"

She nodded because she couldn't speak. Her shirt felt soaked with sweat although she'd been chilled just moments ago. She bent her knees, gathered the reins.

"Let those reins go loose. I got the horses, remember? Just stand up there."

At the first step, she nearly fell off backward. Squeezing the reins brought her back upright. She thought of Eleanor's words about bronc riding. She had to think forward to imagining the movement of horse and rider through space, so she wouldn't surrender to the image of the fall.

"Don't look down. Keep looking outward. You don't have to turn your head if you don't want to, but keep your head up."

"My neck's getting stiff."

"You want to get off and take a break?"

"No. Keep going."

Once around, then twice. After a while, the scenery around her seemed to be settling in place, not shaking up and down.

"Ready to take over for yourself?"

"Yes."

"All right. I'm going to have to stop to release the lead ropes. You need to sit back on your heels as much as you can. Otherwise, you're going to fall forward when they stop. Ready?"

"Ready."

The stop threw her forward and she reached for the horses' necks, but it was no use and she fell off between them. Tad moved them away so she wouldn't get stepped on before he turned to help her up.

"You all right?"

"Yes, I'm fine."

"You're doing fine. Sure you don't want to take a break?"

"No. I am getting back on."

"Thatta girl."

His encouragement boosted her desire to show him she could do it.

He helped her back on and handed her the reins. "Walk alongside me, please, Tad."

"Glad to do it, but you can't look down."

"I'll just listen for your voice. Keep talking."

Tad walked alongside her, and her eyes darted down to glimpse the horses pacing below. The roll underneath her feet had a rhythm, she realized. She was learning it and learning the slight adjustments she had to make as the horses curved around the corners.

"I'm ready to go to a trot now."

"I don't know about that. Your stop needs some refinement and it's that much harder to stop when they're moving faster."

"I want to see what a trot feels like. I'll worry about the stop later."

"They've got to pace together or you'll bounce right off, like you saw me do. Also remember that your outside horse needs to keep a longer stride so don't go pulling on him. Use your inside horse for steering."

"What happens when I want to stop?"

"Sit down on your heels before you even think about stopping. If you think you're gonna fall, just fall down on your heinie on the inside horse. For now, that might be the best way to stop."

She clucked them into a jog and was surprised at how smooth the feeling was. Closer to the feeling of flying than a lope on a regular ride. She started to giggle. So this is how a goddess is ferried through the air! She teetered, realized she was in danger of falling and bottled her exuberance. Falling would surely be ungoddess-like.

She sat back on her heels and the horses slowed to the added pressure on the reins. Then she dropped her legs over the inside horse and they stopped.

"Well, who says you can't be ready for Frontier Days?"

"You're talking about riding routines. And your daddy's talked about racing. I need to practice just this much for weeks. Besides, I have to get on some broncs."

"You can be every bit as good doing this."

"Certainly, I can. But I want to do both."

Tad put his hands on his hips, drew in a deep breath. "You might as well know. Ruth is sore. She says now that we've hired you, she wants saddle broncs as her sole event."

"What does she have to be sore about? You and your daddy didn't bring this up at the Cheyenne Club. I was hired to ride. That's what I came here to do."

"Hey, don't put the blame on me. Problem is Daddy made up his mind about hiring you but didn't tell anyone."

"And you and Ruth don't like it, right?"

"I didn't say that."

"I'm a champion rider and yet both of you act as if I'm not fit to wipe your feet on."

"What are you talking about?"

"The way you acted about me being on my own with a child."

Tad looked away. "I'm sorry you took that so hard. I didn't mean to insult you. Certainly didn't mean to harm a little child. It's just that...

you came up out of nowhere, Sunny. Almost like you just blew up out of the dust. I heard about the family homestead. We saw your husband. He looked like a regular feller. None of that explains how you came out of all that and became this scrappy, curly-headed buckarette. We've never seen anything like it."

"I did come up from nothing. If not for horses, I'd still be nothing. I'd be scrubbing on a washboard and hoeing a potato patch if Mama had her way. All I can say is I've had a hunger since the first time I raced and won. I was racing Luke Mangum and his cowhands, and my mind was in the next stride before the horse was. It was so powerful, that aching to be ahead of where I was.

"Bronc riding? It's about wanting that space beyond the next jump and the next till I've ridden it through. I've owned time. Out-wrestled motion. It's about how much more I can do, how far I can go. That open space in front of me calls for me. Don't you feel the same?"

"Not exactly. Me and Ruth, we grew up riding, racing, roping. We never thought of doing anything different. I do want to win. I guess I'm like you in that way.

"You're a top horsewoman. No one is going to argue with that. But if you want to succeed here, you'll have to dim your light for a little bit."

He pointed to the paired horses now dozing in the sunshine. "You can do this. Give the rest some time. Daddy will bring Ruth around. Just sit out Frontier Days and concentrate on this. By the time you can ride Roman-style, I expect Ruth's pride will be eased to where she'll tolerate you on the broncs. Heck, by that time, she might even start to like you."

"And what if I say no?"

"Well, there's the Cheyenne Club. Call me a miserable heel if you want, but if I learned anything at all about you that day it's that you don't want to be there. You've just about said as much now. I'm not going to speak up and tangle with Ruth. That would be a fool's trail to hell. I'm just asking you to stay and wait for that chance to come around where you can have all you want. Be patient."

"If I'd spent my time waiting for people to give me permission to ride, my name would still be Hannah Mangum."

His laughter put her at ease. He was coming to respect her after all.

"Miss Gale, you are kind of like a gale that kicks things up a bit. I'll tell you what. Ruth's riding broncs this afternoon. You can take her on then if you're up to it."

Sunny waited around the corral two hours or more that afternoon. She knew Tad hadn't lied to her because the boys moved a few broncs into the holding pens. But the sun baked the mudholes until they cracked dry, and no one came. Ruth had had a luncheon in town, one of the hands told her, at the governor's mansion.

"Is Ruth coming?" she asked. "No telling," was the answer. It wasn't unusual for them to have to wait around all day for Ruth. Or Tad. Or even for the boss.

What would it have been like to have been raised here, Sunny wondered. To have men rise before dawn to feed and groom your horses. To have a daddy buy you any horse you could point to. She imagined Zephira again out in the sage, the wind ruffling her mane. Back when she was Hannah Mangum, horses could not be possessed.

She took her scarf off and ran it back and forth between her fingers. What would a woman like Ruth Pickering know of the bar of denial? And if she hadn't ever run smack against it, how would she know of a horse's right to its own being?

The sun hovered just over the hills when Ruth and her father finally arrived. The boys scurried into action. They herded a pinto bronc into the corral, roped him, saddled him, hobbled the stirrups. Sam Pickering rode in on one of his palominos and paced along the rail until he stopped in front of Sunny.

"Sunny. What are you doing here?"

"I've come to ride the broncs."

"Honey, I am sorry I haven't had the time to talk to you. But look here, I've done some figuring. There isn't enough time to get you ready for Frontier Days. We'll get Ruth here ready and then we'll start to work on you for a little shindig in Saratoga."

"There's not time to get me ready? Or are you setting up Ruth to win?"

Ruth was in the saddle. She nodded to the hands to let her go.

"Hold on, will ya?"

Pickering jogged away to watch Ruth. The pinto bucked across the corral in a steady straight line, its white mane and tail flying. The hands were so quiet that Sunny could hear Ruth grunt with every jump. Her arm was back. Her cowboy hat flew off. She lasted the full eight seconds and was still on when her father rode in to pick her up. She vaulted to the back of his horse and then slid off.

"Another one?" one of the hands called.

"Yes," Sunny cried, "for me."

The hands looked to Pickering. "It's all right," he called, "let her have one." Sunny was conscious of Ruth glaring at her as she crossed the corral.

The hands opened the gate for a big bay draft horse that thundered into the corral. He ran twice around before they roped him, all struggling to hold such a big horse.

"No hobbled stirrups," Sunny called out.

The men looked back at Pickering.

"Let 'im go for a moment, boys."

Once released, the horse ran again, slamming straight into a corner, wheeling, then running the other direction. The men coiled their ropes, rolled their cigarettes, leaned back against the fence. They seemed to know Pickering wasn't going to let her ride.

"You had a heck of a ride a year ago without hobbled stirrups. Nobody can take that away from you. But the crowds traveling to see these cowgirls want to see them smiling and waving from their saddles. All of you look a lot better bouncing around on the horses than laying in the dirt. I need you to ride out your full eight seconds and show off those curls and that smile and those costumes of yours. If hobbled stirrups will help that to happen, then I'm all for it."

"You mean you're not going to let me ride if I don't use them?"

"No one's ever going to stop you from riding, Sunny. I don't think anyone could. But you won't be riding here for me." He glanced at Ruth. "For us."

Ruth had crossed her arms over her chest and her thin pale nose stuck straight in the air. She had to be hoping that Sunny Gale would stumble over her own pride.

The last rays of the sun splitting through the corral rails were blinding and Sunny dropped her head. Yes, Ruth wanted her to lose here because if she stayed, she would outshine Ruth every time. Oh, Pickering might have to listen to Ruth complain. But from what she'd seen so far, she didn't think he'd care. It wasn't the personalities or the relationships or ideals that mattered. Just the greenback dollars. He only cared about the ticket receipts pouring in.

To claim the top spot here, all she had to do was to agree to hobbled stirrups.

She walked up to one of the boys leaning against the rail.

"Let me have your rope."

The bay horse rested in a corner. His head jerked as she approached, his eyes wide and wary. Already he was tensing to run again.

She stopped. "Hey, big fella. You're big as Bucephalus. You know that? You know who he was? He was a king's horse. You look like you might be him."

His ears pricked toward her with interest. She took a step forward.

"Will you give me a ride? Just one?" She reached into her pocket for a peppermint and held it out to him. As his soft lips tickled her palm, she slipped the loop over his head.

She turned to Pickering. She could see the admiration in his face at how she'd handled the bronc. Already she was besting Ruth.

"I'll ride with hobbled stirrups."

SUNNY GALE

The 1900 Frontier Days parade was her first. The Pickering family rode directly behind the dignitaries, all on palominos with polished silver on their bridles and black leather tapadero stirrups that had been hand-polished until they gleamed. Mrs. Pickering—Ethel—followed in an open carriage trimmed in white satin.

Predictably, she and Ruth had bickered beforehand over apparel. The family had planned to dress in black suits as they'd always done. Ruth had chosen a white sailor blouse with a lace collar and expected Sunny to wear the same. With Francine's help, Sunny had already sewn her costume: a butter-colored blouse with downy owl feathers covering the cap sleeves and a tan bolero with embroidered roses. She'd borrowed money from Tad for a brand new Stetson "boss of the plains" hat and she'd fixed a white satin ribbon around the crown.

Francine said that it made no sense to defy the Pickerings in public view by not adopting their attire. Ruth's complaint was entirely reasonable, so out of deference to her employers, Sunny should acquiesce. The point, after all, was to showcase the family.

As Sunny stood in front of Dezzie's full-length mirror and set her cowboy hat on her crown, she'd responded, "Someone's got to liven them up. It's not a funeral."

In the end, Pickering responded just like she'd figured. He said Sunny could wear whatever she wanted, so long as she didn't choose to dress like Lady Godiva.

As the parade started down Central Avenue, Ruth stared straight ahead while Sunny waved to the throngs on either side. Here was the proof that she'd been right to shed her name and her marriage, as scandalous as that had seemed. Her heart nearly busted right out of her chest when people in the crowd called out to her. She glanced at Tad to see if he'd noticed. He had, and he tipped his hat to her.

The clop of horse hooves, the breeze rustling the cottonwoods, boys and girls running alongside them—it was blinding glory! How perfect the view was as far as she could see down sun-washed streets lined with people cheering.

Later that day when she met Eleanor at her campsite, she was still under the spell of the amazing parade. The troubles of the winter were too distant to recount while everything that had happened since Sam Pickering had found her at the Cheyenne Club had lifted her to this pinnacle. Unlike Luke Mangum, Sam Pickering wanted her to succeed just much as she did, and now that she had at last felt she'd found her place, nothing seemed unattainable.

Eleanor wasn't relishing her outpouring as she had imagined. Not only was her silence unsettling, but in the light of her campfire, her expression was skeptical, not congratulatory.

"What's the matter? You're so quiet. Aren't you happy for me?"

"I think too much has happened to you in just a year's time. Listening to you, my fear is that you are not looking at where you are with open eyes, so that there will be no surprises, no disappointments."

"What do you mean?"

"You speak of Pickering as if he has accepted you as one of his own. He does not accept you. You are his to use," Eleanor reminded her

"How can you say that about him when he stood up for us so we could ride broncs? I'd think you would appreciate him, like I do."

"Is this how it is, Sunny? My gratitude should be so great as to cancel my opinions?

"Remember what they said about you? You're an ..."

"Indian. So I deserve nothing but what whiteskins will hand out to me so that I may serve them in some fashion."

"That's unfair. You know that's not what I meant."

"It's not what you meant now that it is out in the open between us."

"Please don't say these things. I think of you like a sister. I would feel torn apart if I thought I'd given you offense."

"I think of you like a sister, also. We started down this path together. I would like us to continue down it together for many years. If Leonard agrees, I think you should bring your mother and your daughter and come with us when the rodeo ends. You might not live as well as on the Pickering ranch. But I promise you will have your own horse."

"I don't see Sam the way you do. Sam believes in me and my riding. He believes we girls, no matter our background, should be allowed to ride. Tad's already started me on Roman riding. I understand that you say these things about him because of how you feel toward me, but I think you've misunderstood him. I see him every day. I know him better than you do."

"Let me ask you this: If you win tomorrow, will the prize be yours to keep, or will it belong to Sam Pickering?"

"It'll be mine, of course."

"We'll see."

BOOM! The Fort Russell soldiers fired the cannon, signaling the start of the rodeo finals. Sunny no longer jumped at the cannon blasts, but the usual commotion ensued as spectators fled crazed horses who'd broken loose at the sound. The day was hot, without the usual western gusts, and the calls of hawkers pedaling merchandise reverberated up and down the grounds.

The grandstand was filled. At least three rows of buggies and wagons lined the rail. A drum and fife band played *Yankee Doodle Dandy* as the Fort Russell cavalry loped through their figure eights while everyone sang along.

Sunny couldn't stop grinning. *What a swell crowd!* Another day when, with any luck, she would be their darling.

Men's saddle bronc riding began. First up was a cowboy, George Howell, on a black horse. The instant the rodeo hands released their ropes, the horse shot straight up and flipped over backwards, landing on the cowboy. The crowd gasped. The horse scrambled to its feet and tore around the arena, bucking every few strides. Murmurs ran through the grandstand. They crescendoed as seconds ticked by and the cowboy didn't move. It seemed to take forever for cowboys to reach him. The announcer tried to soothe the crowd. "The wind is just knocked out of him, folks. He'll be up here in another minute. These boys are way tougher than you or I."

Men hustled women and girls from their seats. The announcer turned his attention to the next cowboy. The men remaining with the stricken rider gathered him up and carried him away.

Sunny felt as if she had been slammed down to earth, almost as if she herself had been on that ride. Her forehead burned red hot. She took off her hat and let it fall to the ground. That cowboy was dead. The world ought to stop, take reckoning, but no, motion had resumed in the grandstand: people buying peanuts, children chasing one another, women fluttering their fans as they sat back down. The next bronc launched off with the next cowboy.

A perfect day. A beautiful day.

"You look queasy, Miss."

A rodeo clown stopped in front of her, his face painted blue and white with a red bulb over his nose. He was so close she could see his pores through the paint. "Need some water?"

She nodded and he passed her his canteen. She tilted it back, took a long drink.

"First time seeing someone get killed? You're a youngster. I bet you thought it couldn't happen."

"I knew it could happen. I just never thought about it. Seeing it—that's what's different."

"Well, now you're broke in. Squared your reality a bit. So how do you feel about taking that next ride, Miss?"

His eyes were large and bloodshot. The shock she'd felt—she couldn't wave it aside. He'd seen it.

She wiped her mouth with the back of her hand. "They all walked away. I have to do that, too. I can't give this up. It's too priceless to me. The horses, the crowds, the pretty sky. I've got to believe I'll make it through to the end of my ride. That all of them out there will, too."

The clown's lips stretched wide over huge tobacco-stained teeth. He clapped her on the shoulder. "Mount up, girl."

By the time Leonard Lefever was called, the crowd was restless for a good ride. No rider had stayed in the saddle for the full ten seconds since the first cowboy's tragic ride. The crowd clapped when the announcer bellowed that two-time Cheyenne Frontier Days' champion Leonard Lefever would be aboard a piebald, "Mark Twain." A roar went up as he was mounted.

The horse bucked off in a straight line toward the grandstand and the crowd grew louder the closer it came. Many jumped to their feet. At the ten-second whistle, the pickup man rode in, but as Leonard reached for him, someone set off a firecracker. The pickup horse shied and slammed into the bronc. Leonard was jostled and fell off the other side of the bronc, landing underneath his hooves. Screams erupted as the horse's hind feet hit Leonard's torso.

"Yes, ladies and gentlemen," said the announcer, "the life of the range is unpredictable, full of unforeseen calamities. No one knows it better than these brave boys. Folks, Leonard Lefever didn't become a champion without falling off dozens of devil broncs. There, I see him picking up his head. He's going to be fine. And he's our new leader. Give him a hand."

Leonard, as if taking the hint, tried to sit up on his elbows. The cowboys who'd arrived reached down and helped him up. Now all the crowd was on their feet. The applause was thunderous. Still, Leonard was limping, and the men were half-carrying him.

Sunny pushed through the throng—cowboys, cavalrymen, Indians—around the stock pens to a tent where Leonard had been taken. A mortuary wagon had parked there to pick up the dead rider, *Gallantin Funeral Home* painted in elegant script along the side.

The horses in harness dozed as the mortician quizzed the cowboy's friends about next of kin. Sunny was in a rush to see her friends, but the boy in the wagon was done rushing anywhere, done with desire, done with regret, done with the spark to form a thought. In a sequence as unstoppable as a lightning strike, his story had folded in on itself and collapsed into nothing.

That odd clown. He seemed to possess awareness of the black hole in the arena that only an ill-fated rider would see.

But for Sunny, the all-consuming present was clamoring for her, driving her forward.

Eleanor was standing just inside the tent while the doctor tended to Leonard. His eyes were closed, his face contorted. His shirt lay on the ground in tatters.

Eleanor was pale. Sunny took her hand with both of hers and squeezed it. "He's going to be all right."

"Dislocated shoulder, broken ribs, that's what the doctor says so far."

"What can I do?"

"What you can do is leave us and get ready for your own ride."

"What about your events?"

"I have to scratch. I can't leave Leonard."

"I'm staying with you."

"Your fortune is not with us. It's out there."

Sunny started to choke. "That boy died out there. First him, then Leonard."

"What of it, Sunny? Go, get ready to ride."

"How will you get home?"

A man's shadow filled the entryway—Sam Pickering. "How is everybody in here? Sunny, what are you doing here? I thought you'd be out watching Tad. He's at the top of the steer roping this moment."

Sunny wiped tears off her cheeks. "These are my friends."

"I remember. I came to see how Leonard was doing." He walked over to the cot. "If you're in pain, at least you know you're alive. Glad to see you'll make it. I don't know what these women are all torn up about. 'Fore you know it you'll be back here to ride next year. Sunny, do your friends have money to pay this good doctor?"

"We will take care of it," said Eleanor.

Pickering put his hands on his hips. "Don't doubt you can take care of it. What I asked is if you have it."

"It is very kind of you," said Eleanor. "I am saying we do not need your help."

"You don't want to spend all his winnings on this doctor, do ya?" Pickering reached inside his vest for his billfold, thumbed out a few bills and handed them to the doctor. "Take care of him, will ya, Chance? God willing, he'll be a champion again next year."

"We don't want your money," said Eleanor.

"I heard you the first two times. Don't think of it as my money. It's an advance on the money

Sunny's gonna win today. You'd let me give your friends your money, wouldn't you Sunny?"

"I'd want you to do that, sir."

"Then, go out there and get ready to ride."

Eleanor took the money from the doctor and handed it to Sunny. "What Sunny wins should be hers. What we want from her is only what she came here to do, to ride best as she can."

Pickering gawked. He wasn't used to people opposing him, nor people refusing his money.

"I guess an honest white man's money is too good for these Indians. C'mon, Sunny." He put his arm around her shoulder and hustled her away. Despite her wish to stay behind, she felt gratitude for the warm body beside her towing her away from the day's wreckage. She glanced back over her shoulder at Eleanor who touched her hand to her lips and waved.

Back in the arena, a stagecoach weathered an attack by Indians and Fort Russell cavalryman were flying through the gates for the rescue. Cowgirls were called to get ready for bronc riding. As she went to find her place in line, Tad met her.

"Is Leonard all right?"

She nodded. "I think he's going to be okay."

He stooped slightly to look in her eyes. "You don't sound like yourself. Are you okay?"

"I'm all right. I just wasn't expecting... everything."

His eyes lingered on hers.

"It's just one day. Other shows will come along, good shows, and this one won't punch quite as much."

"I know you're right."

"Did you hear I won the steer roping?"

"Yes, your dad said."

"I wish you'd been there."

"I should have been there. It's just—I've known Leonard and Eleanor for a long time."

He kissed her forehead. "Good luck."

Any other day, she would have thrilled to that kiss. She would have savored it and run the memory through her mind a hundred times. But this day had gone on too long already though the sun was still bright and hot as it dipped toward the grandstand—making it too bright to see the spectators anymore. Her thoughts had been wrenched in too many directions.

The ground wobbled beneath her feet. There was little talk among the women in line. Their faces were anxious but resolute. Ruth was behind her. Her arms were crossed over her chest, her hands adorned with new fringed buckskin gloves, her aquiline nose, as always, in the air. *Nobody's accident would upset her day.*

Sunny watched the riders in front of her, listened to the scores. It seemed as if the pitching broncs and their cowgirls were miles away. At last, she was called. At last, she was boosted into the saddle. With one hand on the lead rope, she nodded and set her other arm back behind her in the air.

As the bronc took off, she couldn't find her center. Shards of her self-awareness seemed to fling out among the bits of dust and manure. It all went around so fast: the crowds, the cowboys, the horses waiting and watching in pens, and the last thing she remembered was the sky above, arcing up and away to indigo, to darkness.

SUNNY GALE

9

February 8th

If Sunny has seen this article before, she doesn't remember it.

Why had Francine preserved it? Surely, she didn't want a reminder of the fear she must have felt. Fear—and bitterness—at the fate that had dragged her to the helpless moment where she'd had to watch her daughter get pitched into the dirt.

She must have intended for Sunny to find this article one day. What had she meant by it? Did she want Sunny to be grateful that she hadn't lost her life? Or did she want Sunny to reflect on Francine's suffering that day? Or had she meant *it as a memento of a crisis happily eclipsed by Sunny's second wedding?*

Bronc Rider Killed! Champions Injured!
September 14, 1900

George Howell, an undaunted buckaroo in the dawn of his manhood, suffered an evil fate when his bronc, Cyclone, flipped over and fell with all his force on the luckless young man. B. Garfield, coroner, states the boy was killed instantly. Howell was from the Howell family ranch in Lovell, Wyoming. His father, Aldon Howell, states the boy was their only son.

Leonard Lefever, two-time Frontier Days bronc riding champion, also suffered grievous, though not mortal, injuries yesterday. After completing his ride in the Finals, he was tossed underneath the bronc's pounding hooves. A full recovery is expected, though he will be confined to bed for an undetermined amount of time. Lefever was the winner in yesterday's contest, making him a three-time Frontier Days champion.

Sunny Gale, a cowgirl of uncommon beauty and also a former champion loved by Frontier Days' fans, is recuperating at the ranch of Sam Pickering and family after falling from her bronc and striking her head. Tad Pickering, this year's steer roping champion, raced to the aid of his fallen cohort and ferried her from the field.

Sam Pickering says the family's own personal physician is attending to Miss Gale, and a complete recovery is expected. He counsels rodeo fans to look out for Miss Gale at any rodeo or wild west show where the Pickering family will next appear.

SUNNY GALE

Well, what Sunny most remembers with this article is that Ruth was the women's saddle bronc champion that year.

She can picture Sam buttonholing the Tribune reporter, his tone resonant with concern, while ensuring that the reporter scribbled down that promotion for the Pickering enterprise. Sunny would give Sam a toast if he were alive today. He had handled her far more deftly than Luke, whose self-interest was as obvious as a skunk in a barn, while Sam Pickering had so dazzled her with the specter of possibility that she had become his to use without the slightest fuss. Just as Eleanor had predicted, Sam collected all her trophy saddles and locked them in an outbuilding. He pocketed her prize money even before she'd left the grandstands.

This article makes her tear up alright, not for its content, but for reminding her of what a giant of a man she believed Sam Pickering was back then. And she'd been so wrong. Was this what Francine had intended?

The rodeo clown she'd seen that day of George Howell's death—the one with bloodshot eyes—she saw from time to time through the years. Always with his makeup on. Once, after she'd lost all her events at a rodeo, he bought her a few drinks. Streaks of sweat ran through his blue and white paint. After they'd had some laughs, he invited her to his room. She declined.

He didn't turn sour, as so many drunk cowboys did. He swept his hat off, bowed low. Those yellowish teeth again. "Some other time, Sunny Gale," he said as he winked. She laughed in response, hoping they'd never meet again.

Ruth told her he'd drunk himself to death, but it wasn't true. She saw him one last time.

The first day Sunny sat up in bed after her fall, Francine brought her a hand mirror and Sunny burst into tears. They'd shaved off her hair to put fifteen stitches at the back of her skull. She ran her hands over her bare head, as if her fingers would tell her something different than her eyes.

Francine pulled the mirror away. "The doctor said your head must have hit a stray rock."

"I can't go out looking like this."

"You're lucky to be alive, unlike that poor boy. Think about your daughter. You haven't even asked about her yet."

"Wait. We're in the ranch house. Why?"

"Sam moved us here after your accident. He said he wanted the best care and attention for you."

"I'll have to stay in this bedroom forever."

"You can wear scarves. You wear a cowboy hat on top of your head, anyway."

"All the rodeos and shows they've talked about doing—I won't get to go. It's all over!"

"Oh, Hannah, as if it wouldn't be a blessed relief for it to be over!"

"Where is Mollie?"

"Go to the window and look."

Sunny rose and lifted the curtain. Out in the corral, Tad was leading Mollie on a paint pony. Her heart jumped. She hadn't told Francine of her discord with Tad over Mollie.

She could tell Francine noted her silence.

"You should know—he bought that animal for her," said Francine.

"I want to go out and be with them."

"Absolutely not. You're not supposed to be

out of bed. And you just said you didn't want to go out."

"Mama, please get me my bandana. I can wrap that around my head. Oh, what if Ruth sees me? It doesn't matter. I am going to have to go out sometime."

Tad saw her crossing the yard, but he kept up a chat with Mollie as the pony ambled along. Francine had fashioned a split riding skirt for her, a miniature of Sunny's own. Her curls spilled out of her cowboy hat.

As Sunny opened the corral gate, she heard Tad shout, "You shouldn't be out of bed, should you?"

"What's the pony's name?"

"'Candy's what Mollie says. She started on her yesterday. She's doing well," he said, smiling.

"Mommy," Mollie said and reached for her. Sunny pulled her off the saddle and held her close.

"You can ride. I am so proud of you."

"How are you feeling?" Tad asked.

"I feel ridiculous. Who's ever seen a cowgirl with her head shorn?"

"It's going to grow back."

With her free hand, she wove her fingers through the pony's coarse mane.

"That was a silly ride I had, sloppy."

"You were upset over Leonard."

"Do you still want me to ride with you?"

"Yes, I do. But that's not all I want."

"What do you mean?"

"I want us to be a team inside and outside the arena." He dropped on one knee and reached for her hand. "Miss Sunny Gale, would you do me the honor of becoming my wife?"

"You'd marry me now though I'm ugly as a baby bird?"

"If you hadn't had the accident, I would have asked you that day, and my mind's not changed now that your head's naked."

"But I thought you thought I was...." *Beneath you.* That's what she meant to say.

"I told you, Sunny. You're like no other woman I've met before."

Sunny held her breath. Hadn't she wanted this? It wasn't so much a matter of how she felt about Tad. Feeling was beside the point. With so little effort, her fortune was becoming more than what she'd dared to dream. A handsome man at her side. They would make a perfect performing team, part of a perfect performing family. A lovely ranch. All the horses she'd ever want to ride. And Francine—she wouldn't ever endure deprivation again.

The world Tad held up to her was bright and glittering. Not one flaw.

"Tad, what will your family say?"

"Let's tell them together and find out."

"You haven't said anything to them yet?"

"What was the point if I hadn't spoken to you first? You still haven't given me an answer!"

She clasped both his hands. "Yes, yes a thousand times!"

Sunny Gale's wedding, held at St. Mark's Episcopal Church, on a blustery November evening was far grander than Hannah Mangum's. The Wyoming State governor—Governor Richards, no less!—and his family held seats of honor in the front pew. As the sunlight faded behind black roiling clouds, the gaslights flared like beacons.

Sam had paid for the Lefevers to travel down from Lander. Eleanor had agreed since Sunny wanted her to come so badly. It was decided that Leonard would walk Sunny down the aisle. At the archway before the sanctuary, she linked her arm in his.

Among the faces turning toward her in the pews, she saw Dezzie—and many of the hands from the ranch. Up at the altar stood Eleanor in a calico dress trimmed with black velvet. Her black hair gleamed in the light and, in her smile, Sunny felt pride and love. Mollie waited next to the Reverend with a basket of spruce twigs and pinecones. Next to Governor Richards, Sam Pickering shifted and beamed at her. Tad stood with his hands crossed in front of him, his eyes burning with adoration.

Francine had made the wedding dress. The second one. The color, ivory, led to howls from Ethel Pickering and Ruth, both of whom had greeted the wedding announcement with tight-lipped grimaces. It was bad enough, Ethel had declaimed, that Tad had rejected the eligible maidens of the Capitol City in favor of a ranch employee, but then to parade her before the community in virginal attire with her own child as a member of the wedding party was a scandal that would besmirch them forever.

Ruth sat at the far end of the front pew next to her mother. Neither one turned their head. Sunny didn't care. The marriage vows sealed her installation into this family, and they would have to accept her. She could feel everyone hold their breath during the long, sweet wedding kiss, and when she was announced as Tad Pickering's wife, she could feel her exhilaration spread to everyone around her, just as in her winning rides. Well, everyone, except for Ruth and her mother.

This was the first winter she'd lived in the West where she did not have to get up in the dark. Tad woke early. She would hear him pulling on layers of clothing to go feed and water livestock. She would pretend to be asleep as he tiptoed over to the bed and looked down at her. She'd hear the door close and fall back to sleep to the sound of the wind knocking about the house. By the time she woke again, the sun would be up mid-sky, shrouded by the squalls that piled more and more snow in the corral and on the road, sealing them in. Farther out, ribbons of blowing snow snaked across the plains.

The winter tunneled inside her like a mole, hollowing her out day by day. In her Nebraska winters, there had been the cookstove to light, water to haul, the search for fuel, the cow to milk. She thought of the cowboys at the Mangum ranch dispersing for points south in December. She could see them so clearly, trotting down the beaten track, loping up the ridge, whooping as they went. While here all around her, the white-out shut her in.

Francine busied herself with sewing. Her needle never stopped, and if drifts mounded against the doors, there were clothes she could make for Mollie using material from her own dresses and skirts. Soon, Mrs. Pickering and Ruth were clustered around her with pictures from *Ladies Home Journal.* Could Francine make this or that.

Their demeanors froze as Sunny walked into the room. Even though Tad had chosen Sunny, even though they were comfortable in persuading her mother to make them clothes, the two ice queens made it clear that Sunny was not to be acknowledged as part of the family. While being "a scrappy buckarette" had endeared her to Tad, it was what the Pickering ladies deplored.

Francine briefly registered the women's glares and then blinked, as if she could smooth over the little schisms by heartily agreeing to make the fashions they desired. The three of them returned to discussions of colors and materials.

Sunny stared at the drifting snow piling over the fences.

On clear Sunday afternoons, Tad took her and Mollie out in a sleigh. Powdery snow flew up from the horses' hooves, the bells on the harnesses jingled. Mollie cried, "Faster, faster!" Tad would pretend to urge the horses on but not too much faster, just enough to please Mollie. Up and down the hills they went, the horizon glazing under the afternoon sun. Tad would stop and pull out a bottle of bourbon from under the seat and there on the hushed range, Sunny felt her numbed senses revive. The steam rolling off the horses' backs, the burn of liquor in her throat, the bite of frost on her cheeks. It was like blood pulsing back into frozen limbs. So much sensation that it hurt.

One Sunday, she said, "Let's not stop. Send the horses on and let's keep going."

"It's too late in the day," said Tad. "We have to turn around."

"I can't stand that house one more minute. Tad, let's go on into Cheyenne. We can spend the night there."

"What about Mollie?"

"We'll have her with us, of course. She'll fall

asleep quickly, and even if she doesn't, I would still love to have a night away."

"No one will know where we are."

"I know. Won't that be delicious?"

"I can't do that, Sunny."

"Let's go back and tell them, then. Tell them we'll go to town for dinner and stay overnight at the Plains Hotel and come home in the morning. That way, we can leave Mollie with my mother."

"Mom and Dad won't like it."

"It has nothing to do with them. We're married, Tad. We can do what we want."

"You've never stayed in one place for long, so you don't understand. Who we are, what we do—it matters. Cheyenne is not as frontier-minded as it pretends to be. You've seen who was at the wedding; businessmen, people in state government, people important for our business. We can't go carrying on like a couple of heathens."

"All these people are going to notice? If a married couple spends one night at a hotel?"

"Once we register, it's the same as if we'd shouted it from the Capitol Building. Expanding Western events in this state and others, too, is what you want, right? You want to perform more than once a year, right? Well, Dad's the one out there working to make it happen for you. We can't undercut him."

"You're right. I don't understand. If I go out for a night in rowdy Cheyenne, I've tarnished the family name. If I stay at home, the family rolls their eyes as if I'm some tramp lounging about the house. Where is my place?"

"With me, you know that. You're churning up a whole lot of mud over nothing. Dad thinks the world of you, and you've known that from the very beginning."

"And you're sticking your head in the mud to avoid seeing how your mother and sister act around me. If my place is with you, you need to say that to them."

"Honey, they were all there when I married you. Before God and everybody."

"They seem to think that was some sort of mistake. Like I bewitched you."

That irresistible grin spread over his face, and he kissed her neck. "You have. Got a little half-way meeting spot for you. Let's go home and we'll pretend we're in a hotel," he said.

"How can we do that with all of them around at the dinner table?"

"We'll skip dinner and head upstairs."

It wasn't the escape she wanted, which he didn't seem to understand anyhow. The sound of muffled voices and clinking plates wafted up to their bedroom, and though they had their pleasures, the ache for a separate life apart from anyone's gaze remained with her deep into the night, after Tad had drifted off into a cowboy's deep slumber.

She didn't doubt her husband's love for her and Mollie. She felt sure that her love for him would grow over time, but how could she persuade him that his identity should be aligned more with her and less with the Pickerings?

The next morning, a chinook cleared a patch of ground in the center of the corral. Over the coming days, she watched as it grew. The corners were still plugged with drifts when she tacked up the two bays and jumped on their backs. She was hardly the rodeo beauty now dressed in layers of Tad's clothing. No mind. Every day of melting brought her closer to that. Standing on top of the horses, she was vulnerable to the wind gusts, and she struggled to stay upright. At least when she fell, the bulky clothing cushioned her.

Day after day, she practiced. Day after day, when she came in and scooped up Mollie from her mother's care, Ruth glanced at her and turned away. Sunny crowed inside. She knew Ruth had been looking out that window, watching her. When the crusts of the remaining drifts blackened from blowing dirt, Sunny set up cross rails in the center of the corral. On the day the drifts were no more than lumps, the horses sailed over and for the first time, Sunny didn't fall. She began to laugh. She laughed so hard that she had to sit down on one of the horses. The sun warmed her shoulders, laughing with her. She laughed the hardest when she looked to the house and saw the curtain fall shut.

Though it was June, and one would have expected the wind to drop by now, it blew grit across the Wellington arena stinging Sunny's eyes. This show was to be the first trial run of the Pickering Family Wild West show.

The arena wasn't far from the railroad tracks and the noise of the locomotives roaring through made it difficult for the sparse crowd to hear Sam Pickering's introductions. As his palomino jogged out of the way, Sunny and Ruth, the opening act, flew in at full gallop: Ruth on one of her thoroughbreds and Sunny on a white horse, both women in Western shirts sewn and embroidered by Francine. Their hats blew off in seconds.

After they'd finished their drill pattern, they spun their horses around and met in the center. They stood side by side, and as practiced, entwined their arms around one another, waving with their free arms. Ruth counted out the seconds under her breath—one, two, three—and then, still smiling, she ripped her arm away and turned her horse aside without ever looking at Sunny.

A little girl climbed to the top of the rail and waved back. As her father pulled her back down, Sunny could feel her longing to join them. She trotted over to the girl and shook her hand.

"You're Sunny Gale, the bronc rider," the girl said.

"Yes, I am, honey."

"I want to be like you when I grow up."

Sunny glanced at the girl's father. "You can. Don't let anyone stop you."

She found the show was more taxing than a rodeo. At a rodeo, all Sunny's concentration went into the contest events. But here, she was either preparing for her events or helping others prepare horses and livestock for theirs. Sam had rounded up a few more cowgirls and they'd performed exhibition bronc riding. Every cowgirl was riding with hobbled stirrups.

Tad had hitched a buffalo to a cart. Some of the women in the crowd shrieked at the size of the beast, but at the end of his performance when the buffalo bowed, the crowd stood to applaud. No sooner had that ended then Sunny and Tad began their Roman riding performance. Tad could now twirl his rope while balanced on two horses and Sunny could go over a jump three feet high. Even though Tad fell, the crowd loved them.

Sunny fell asleep in the carriage and didn't wake up until deep in the night when Tad woke her to say they'd arrived home. She had been dreaming of riding. The stars dipped so close that it seemed as if she had been riding broncs all around them. Instead of roaring cheers, a million lights radiated their admiration.

Before Frontier Days began, Sam invited her to come to town with him. They would have lunch at the Cheyenne Club. Just her. No one else. When Ruth's eyebrows arched, he'd said, "I can take my only daughter-in-law to town, can't I? You and your mother are always at those legislature's wives' teas and luncheons. It won't hurt for folks to see Sunny out and about as one of the family."

Sunny refused to wear a skirt. She strode through the Club doorway in her boots and standard riding knickers, now made of suede. She expected to feel the sense of grandeur that she'd always felt on the main floor, so she was surprised when she spotted the decay: threadbare runs in the rugs, holes in the upholstery, dust lining the display cabinets. The giant bar, which used to have liquor bottles stacked floor to ceiling, was half empty and there was a huge crack in the mirror, caused, it was said, by a down-and-out stockman who'd hurled his bottle at it when he'd been asked to leave.

She didn't recognize any of the waitresses and there were far fewer of them than when she'd worked there. Fewer tables were occupied, too, although there were still enough livestock and government men to greet Sam Pickering and shake his hand. They shook her hand, too, and she felt proud that it wasn't just because she was now a member of the Pickering family. Some of them remembered her relay race win—"You went by another name back then, didn't you?"

Sam chose a table by a west window, and in the pause between them, she watched the carriages pass by. The bustle of people and horses captivated her after such a long stretch on the prairie. She faced Sam and saw that his eyes had been on her the whole time. Even with tendrils of hair combed over his balding head, he was still a good-looking man, his blue eyes ice-crisp and warm at the same time, the way chill on a spring dawn gives way to the warmth of the rising sun.

"We've come full circle," he said.

"Yes, we have."

"I couldn't have predicted that you and Tad would get together, but I'm sure tickled that it happened. He couldn't have found a better girl among these Cheyenne butterflies. A real girl of the range, that's what he needed."

"I'm not entirely a 'real girl of the range.' We only homesteaded a couple of years."

"You get what I mean. You're fresh. You're real. Convention stripped down to yes-please-and-thank-you. No extra frumpery tacked on. It's not only good for my boy. As we expand, the whole world's going to learn about you. It's just around the corner. A'course we'll let you have some time off when you pop out those grandbabies."

Sunny ran her fingers through her hair, flustered by the hint of flirtation in his manner.

"And we love your mama. She's a treasure."

"I want to thank you for how you have looked after Mama. And Mollie, too."

"They would have become family even if
you hadn't married Tad. We'd be tickled if Mollie
thought of us as her family. I'd like her to call Tad
her daddy. I think he'd like that, too. You haven't
talked to her about her real father, have you?"

"No, we haven't heard from him," she lied,
thinking of the packet of letters that she'd hidden
in her wardrobe. "I am grateful for the money you
give Mama, too."

"I don't give her anything. Ethel and Ruth
have her whipping up clothing nonstop. Francine
won't ever say no to them, and she doesn't have to
do it."

"Mama loves to sew."

"Dezzie loves that suit jacket she made her.
She wears it every time she goes to town. Seems
even my hired help parade in style with your
mama around."

"Dezzie's been kind to us."

"I know Ruth's acted like a poked porcupine.
Don't take her to heart. She doesn't mean ill. I've
just spoiled her, I'm afraid. You're not letting her
bother you, are you?"

"No." Another lie. Yet she wanted to live up
to the image Sam had of her. "There is something
that I'd...we'd appreciate having."

"What's that?"

"Tad and I would like to be more free to...."

"Free to what?"

"Well, have our own life."

"What in hell does that mean?"

His bristling made her stammer. "Well, just,
not to have to do everything with the family. To be
able to go off on our own. Every now and then."

He bit into a biscuit and stared at her.

"After today you'll forget all about that. Because in addition to the bronc riding and Roman riding, I found you something that'll keep you so occupied you'll barely have time for Tad, anyway."

"What's that?"

"Let's hurry up and eat, if we can get some service here, and you'll see."

They drove out to the stockyards. Horses filled the pens. Sam ushered her to a pen where a young palomino, with a burnished coat as gold as fall aspens, paced up and down.

"What do you think?"

"He's beautiful. May I go in?"

She walked into the pen and held out her hand. The horse stopped to watch her.

"Where did he come from?"

"Roped out of a wild herd is what they told me. But I don't think he's a mustang. He must have escaped from somewhere. They'd penned him with the horses to be shipped for slaughter when I saw him."

The horse came to her hand. She reached up and began unwinding the knots in his mane.

"Are you going to get him?"

"Yes. For you."

She looked back over her shoulder. "Really?"

"You're the only one in the family who doesn't have a horse of your own. High time we got you one."

"I haven't had a horse since.."

"Since Hell's Bells?"

She smiled. "You're making fun of me. You know it was Helios."

"Beautiful golden girl, beautiful golden horse. Both out of the dust of the plains. You two are made for each other."

She looked into the horse's brown eyes. How long had he been away from his masters, forgetting human voices, human odors, human touch, surrendering only to the cycle of the seasons on ranges that stretched to infinity?

And then another image replaced it. She'd name him Aeolus—god of the winds, of course. They would ride out next to Sam as he led his Western entourage into the ring. She could feel the horse anticipating, as she did, the exuberance of the crowd. A touch of her heels and he would lunge into a ring of cheering fans.

This would be her special partner. Nothing could take him away.

"Well, what do you say? I haven't paid for him yet."

"Yes," she said. Then she shouted it. "Yes!"

She stepped out of the pen. "Sam, I can't thank you enough. If you only knew how much this means."

He clutched her close to him and kissed her on the mouth. While holding her firm, he whispered in her ear. "Anything your heart desires, Sunny, I want you to have it."

10

February 9th

> *At first, she'd felt shamed by the way Sam had manhandled her. Somehow her behavior had encouraged him—that feeling had riled her for months. So many miles and years between then and now, and now she knows better. It had been part of Sam's scheme to plunge her into confusion—a simple manner of control, just as one would twitch a horse.*
>
> *Sam had known that she had no escape. She had become devoted to Tad. Her loyalty alone kept her from confiding in him. In the first place,*

Tad wouldn't have believed her. Nor would he have been able to listen to unfavorable reports of his father, whose bidding he did without question. Tad's entire world was the Pickering enterprise: the rodeo events, the exhibitions, the livestock supply for rodeos, and finally, the ranch itself. The last thing he would have wanted would be to call it into question. If she truly loved him, wasn't it better to preserve that world for him? For all his horsemanship, Tad wasn't a range cowboy, able to persevere through all conditions. He was more like a prairie gentian that a May frost could shrivel.

Then there was her own tainted complicity. She didn't refuse the horse. Sam had counted on that circumstance, as well.

Sunny threw herself into training Aeolus. For over a year, she had missed the sense of fulfillment that she'd gained while working with Helios and, before that, her poor Zephira. She had longed for another horse of her own.

At least, she was able to prevent Sam from mauling her again. She declined further invitations no matter what they were for. Didn't she want to meet a famed Montana cowgirl? Didn't she want to travel with him to buy broncs? She wouldn't so much as go in the barn if he were there by himself. How it burned to have to skulk around her own house and grounds!

And meanwhile, all the shows with Sunny Gale ever the sweetheart of the arena. Wild West shows from Lincoln, Nebraska, all the way to Salt Lake City. Well, Ruth rode, too, but what with her tight-lipped little smile, her nose in the air, and her odd detachment, crowds didn't go half as wild for her as they did for Sunny.

But all those clicking camera lights couldn't capture the shadows of Sunny's complicated life.

No sooner had she broke Aeolus to ride in the fall of 1901 when morning sickness overtook her. For a while, she had concealed her condition, anticipating that Sam would shunt her from rodeo rider to broodmare. Then Tad had caught her retching in one of the stalls, and she'd been forced to tell him. He skipped off to trumpet the news to the family even before she'd picked herself up off her knees.

It was midmorning, but Sam poured whiskeys for anyone near, even Dezzie and the cowboys. Sunny forced a smile despite her nausea, because it was expected, and she couldn't disappoint Tad and her mother, who stood there beaming at her. Once again, her fecundity, soon to be on display as in a freak circus show, was going to overrule her will and dictate who she would be.

Just as she had predicted, Sam proclaimed that her performances were to be set aside while she was in "the maternal condition." And so she stood there stupidly smiling while hating his power over her.

She glanced at Ruth. She had anticipated a smirk—smug satisfaction at Sunny's confinement. Instead, to her surprise, Ruth had stepped forward and squeezed her wrist. "Congratulations, Sunny. I want to help you if I can. Please let me know if there is something I can do."

Had that been a sincere offer or part of the family show?

Nine months out of the arena—and then Scott Matthew Pickering was born.

All of Cheyenne was invited to the baptism and from what she could tell it was as well attended as Frontier Days. It was Easter, and even though a blizzard had closed all the side streets, people were ready, after the long winter, to break out of their houses and join a party. Any party.

Scott's birth had cured Ethel Pickering of all her distress at her son's marriage. The way she paraded that baby around the reception hall, one would have thought it was hers.

And Tad, he'd had so much to drink by then that he could barely stand. Seeing him from a distance she noticed that, like his father, he was now combing his hair to cover the thinning spot on his crown. But the weather lines deepening around his eyes made him look distinguished, seasoned, more desirable to Sunny than ever.

Ruth promenaded arm-in-arm with her fiancé, Arthur Smithey, son of the lawyer, Lewis Smithey, and advisor to the governor. Arthur was attending law school and they expected to be married when he passed the bar. The way Ruth tugged him around, he could have been another thoroughbred, or maybe a prize Hereford bull. Odd, Sunny thought, that no one was speaking of just how Ruth would shift from cowgirl to matron and settle down in a mansion on Seventeenth Street. If Arthur had consented for Ruth to continue her racing and bronc riding, it had not been publicized.

SUNNY GALE

For Sam, the public presentation of his grandson was yet another performance. Booze gurgled and flowed in the church's social hall like spring runoff in the Laramie River. All the guests mobbed him to offer yet more toasts.

Sam spotted Sunny across the room and raised his glass. It seemed like a taunt, a reminder that everything of hers belonged to him.

Over the next three years, Sunny's attention was divided between "the maternal state" and her riding. She did enjoy mothering little Scott more than she had Mollie. Without the worry over making an income, she had the space and freedom to watch her boy grow. And her resentment toward Sam diminished to a simmer. She didn't have so much time anymore to tend to it.

Scott was Sam's darling. When he rode out to introduce his Wild West shows, the baby sat in front of him, to the delight of the crowds. By his third birthday, Scott had his own role in the show, with a cart and goats.

While Sunny was spending less time in the ring, younger women appeared at the rodeos, fresh from their home corrals, hungry for their own chance at a championship buckle. It was easier for them, she observed. From the time she got in line to ride a bronc until her eight seconds were done, she fretted over whether anyone was minding her children. One day Francine became distracted with Mollie, and Scott had been found wandering among the bucking steers.

With Scott out of diapers, he often spent his days with his father or grandfather. Sunny slipped away and took long rides over the range. Aeolus threw out his white-stocking legs in a long, extended stride, and she sat back in the saddle, transported over the countryside as if she were floating. No bleachers in the rolling hills, no cheers. No performance expected. Golden eagles wheeled overhead, gliding ever higher until they were no more than specks. Antelope watched her, then sprinted away. Like all the range creatures, she was just a wayfarer here, and like them, she would leave nothing behind. When the hours and miles with Aeolus as her only companion had eclipsed the preoccupations that had haunted her at the house, she could, at last, notice how the horse's cream-colored mane rippled in an evening breeze, how tendrils of light fingered through it. The gift of open country made you a champion, no matter who you were.

When Aeolus jumped a gully one day, Sunny started thinking about jumping him just for fun. They didn't need it in their exhibitions. The Roman riding act already included jumps. She started with poles, then old gates cut down to half height, then gates at full height, then two gates together.

"Bet he can jump my Model A," Sam called to her one day. She hadn't seen him sneak up to the rail to watch her. She leaned over and patted the horse's neck so she wouldn't have to make eye contact with him.

"He can do it. But I wouldn't want any harm to come to it. Mother Ethel would sure be mad."

"Automobiles are blasting horses off the roads every which way these days. It'd be nice if we could turn the tables and show how a horse can top these contraptions, don't ya think?"

Sam drove the Model A into the center of the

corral and cut the engine. He walked around to the front. "Go ahead!"

"You sure?"

He waved her on. She loped Aeolus twice around the corral, then picked up speed and aimed straight for the car. Up and over they went. Both breathless and relieved, she pulled the horse up at the rail.

Sam's grin spread over his tobacco-stained teeth. "I had no doubt that you'd be able to do that," he said, "no doubt at all." He reached through the rail and squeezed her thigh. "You're an incredible woman. You know that?"

Sunny nudged Aelous aside to pull away from him, but not before Ruth saw them. Though her cowboy hat was low on her forehead, Sunny could feel her measuring the scene. A knot of fear twisted inside of her. She felt the old shame coloring her face from his advance on her four years earlier. She hated this feeling—this sense of responsibility—when she'd done nothing to bring on his attentions.

"What's the Model A doing in here, Daddy?" Ruth said.

"We've just made ourselves a new act. Your sister-in-law jumped that car! I think it'd be a helluva showstopper if the two of you could jump cars side by side. 'Pickering Horsewomen Top Henry Ford.' What do ya say?"

Ruth shrugged. "If it's what you want."

"C'mon in here and watch. Sunny, do it again. We can park two cars end to end and have both of you go over 'em at the same time."

Sunny nudged Aeolus into a trot while Sam put his arm over Ruth's shoulder and hugged her. There was no way to tell what Ruth was thinking as she circled the corral and flew over the car a second time.

She cornered Tad the first moment she could and begged him, again, to get a them place of their own.

"What's got you all out of whack? I don't know why you are bringing this up. Your mama loves it here. And Daddy would be heartbroken without Scott. Scott and Mollie both. You know he treats Mollie like his own. What's this about a new act you and Ruth are working up?"

The only solution was to get as far away from all of them as much as she could. Put them out of her mind and just ride. Racing, bronc riding, Roman riding. If she was busy, then there was no time to dwell on all this. No time to fret over what Ruth might think. Not a moment to spare in Sam's presence. Her children only saw her at bedtime.

1910 Cheyenne Frontier Days. Biggest crowd ever. Two additional grandstands had been erected and they were packed. And a special gazebo draped in red, white, and blue flags had been built outside the racetrack as special seating for the former president—President Teddy Roosevelt—and dignitaries.

As Sunny climbed aboard her two horses for the Roman racing event, she couldn't see the legendary Rough Rider. People in the grandstands and around the gazebo looked like one seething mass. Behind the starting line, she rocked back and forth on her horses testing her balance. Back when they'd begun Roman racing, she thought she'd never learn the take-off. She had tumbled backwards in the dirt so many times that her shirts had been torn to rags and her skin was scraped and bloody. Twenty starts, thirty, more before she finally got the hang of counter-balancing both heels and arms.

One of the horses underneath her, Thaddeus, fidgeted, trying to sidestep a horsefly. If she took her whip and swatted at it, no telling what both horses would do, and any second the starting gun would...*BOOM!*

The sound caught her with her head lowered and she nearly lost her balance. Her gaze snapped forward just in time.

There were four racing teams. Sunny was the only woman. Tad and his team were on her left. Left of Tad was a buckskin team and on her right was a dappled grey team. Her chestnuts pulled ahead. The buckskins passed Tad. She could hear him shouting behind her. Just when the buckskins were nose to nose with her team, she barely flicked her whip near Thaddeus's withers, and at the sound, his ears flattened and his legs stretched out. Samson, his mate, caught the cue and united the three of them in one thundering surge.

They passed the finish line. She couldn't hear the crowds for the pounding of the other teams coming up behind her. She'd won—her first win at Cheyenne Frontier Days since her saddle bronc ride eleven years earlier.

The championship buckle for bronc riding— she won that, too. President Roosevelt himself presented it to her. Face to face with him, she was surprised to see that she was taller. He grasped her hand with both his own.

"By God, it's astounding the way you women ride! The thought that I have lived to see it renders me entirely humble, and grateful to all my hosts. Miss Gale, you and your sisters in this ring demonstrate what can be achieved with the courage and independence so prevalent among the citizens of our Western territories. I see how, beyond my time, women are not only going to have the vote, as they do in this state. They will lead."

She stepped down from the gazebo beaming at her younger competitors. Their eyes met hers smoldering with determination. They would continue to chase her from one event to another. It was all about riding and training as much as she could so that when circumstances flipped over like lucky cards, she would have her best chance. Today it had happened, and as Tad swept her up and kissed her mouth, there wasn't the slightest need to think about tomorrow.

Ruth Pickering's reign at the Seventeenth Street mansion barely outlasted her honeymoon. From what Sunny could overhear on the stair landing, as Ruth sobbed below, surrounded by her trunks, it was as she had suspected. The marriage was foundering on the parties' expectations about Ruth's cowgirl pursuits. Whatever wifely duties Smithey had envisioned Ruth had found to be too restrictive. When she had thought he was out having dinner with his colleagues, she'd sneaked away and had been caught on the rodeo grounds taking turn after turn on the bucking broncs.

Francine quietly unpacked the trunks and ferried the clothes to Ruth's armoire.

In her defense, Ruth protested that she had agreed to give up all rodeos and exhibitions except

Frontier Days, and at Frontier Days, the only events she would participate in were the parades and horse races. In return, Smithey had agreed to see to it that she would be seated on the Frontier Days' Committee, a ceremonial position only, of course. But in the long hours while Smithey toiled at his law office, not all the stimulations the city of Cheyenne had to offer could replace the freedom that came with choosing one's horse to ride every day.

"Don't know why anyone thought that hot filly would pace in traces." That's what Dezzie muttered in her steaming kitchen.

"I understand you now," Ruth said to Sunny, "why you broke from Luke Mangum and became Sunny Gale." Sunny was brushing Aeolus in the barn when Ruth's long shadow telescoped across the floor from the doorway.

Sunny shrugged. She reached for a comb and ran it through the horse's mane. "I don't see what you wanted it for, Ruth. What did you hope to gain that you didn't have already?"

Ruth's tears were running down her face again. "Love. I wanted to be loved. You can be at the top and still want a man's arms around you through the night."

"Sure. Doesn't mean you have to marry him, though."

Ruth snorted. "Only a tramp like you would say that."

"That's what you've always thought of me. But while you're judging everyone else, you need to look in the mirror. It didn't look to me like you wanted love. It looked like you wanted a pretty little picture of what you thought love would look like. A picture someone nailed up in your head. Now the picture doesn't match up with what you have. Do you have someone in mind to blame?"

"I'm to blame...."

"That's a start."

"For not understanding all he needed from me. Maybe I haven't been fair to you, Sunny, but you talk about me like I'm some sort of scheming vixen. You're wrong about me, too. I always loved Arthur. We just misread so much about each other. It's hard for him to understand our life. He's not like Tad."

Sunny stopped and looked at her. For all Ruth's protestations, Sunny didn't place much credence in her confession. Wasn't the public shaming at play here? If Ruth had run away with one of Sam's ranch hands and the romance had fallen apart, it wouldn't get the same scrutiny as a marriage that had been lavishly detailed over three columns in *The Wyoming Tribune.*

Well, they would have smeared her all the same. It was a new age all right, but not a great many had welcomed it. The good people of Cheyenne wanted the West to look exactly like where they'd come from. Which meant they'd countenance a girl riding like a cowboy, but not acting like one.

Sunny set her grooming tools down, walked to the doorway and touched Ruth's arm.

"Forget all this. Go get one of your horses. Let's go ride."

Not long after Francine began sewing Ruth's new rodeo blouse, chambray with a high collar and puffed sleeves, the Smithey family drove out to the ranch to discuss the impasse. All the hands, and

Dezzie, too, were allowed to drop what they were doing, for the Smitheys were the first visitors ever to arrive by motorcar. The vehicle, a royal green, was covered in dust and so was Mama Smithey, whose first words, upon disembarking, were, "That was most awful." She untied her hat and shook it out in the yard. "The jostling and the ruts—it took us hours to get here. And look at the doors—just ruined with dings from grit thrown up by the tires. I told you, Joseph, we would have been much better off in a carriage. After all that money for this extravagance. It's much easier to replace a horse."

Arthur Smithey unfolded from the rear seat. He stretched, took a deep breath, and said, "Lovely air out here. Beautiful country."

Sunny followed his gaze to Ruth on the porch with her hair brushed to one side over her shoulder and tied with a white ribbon. Yearning—that was a feeling she'd never seen on Ruth's face, not in her riding, not even at the wedding. Yet there she was, about to topple over the rail from it.

In the face of Ruth's passion, Arthur turned away and offered his arm to his mother, communicating that his wife's disobedience would not be condoned. The elder Pickerings and all the Smitheys then filed into Sam's office behind closed doors.

An hour or so later when they came out, Arthur appeared placated and Ruth, relieved. She clasped Arthur's hand with both of her own. Sam had given them a thousand acres along the main road to Cheyenne. They could use the land however they liked. The Smitheys would donate the motorcar so Arthur could get back and forth to his office. The property already had an existing well.

Both families would contribute to the expenses for building a home. Sam would build them a barn and corral.

The increase in Arthur's assets had mollified his pride to where he had consented to allow Ruth to rejoin the family's rodeo and Wild West show enterprises and to compete in whatever event suited her.

Sunny complained to Francine. "I'd like to have my own house, too, Mama. I've asked Tad a hundred times if we couldn't get away from here, even for a short while. I'd love to be able to have a conversation with my husband and children without a dozen people listening in."

"That's an exaggeration. No one interferes with you and Tad."

"You don't know."

Francine had been fitting Sunny's latest split riding skirt. She set her pin cushion down. "I don't know what?"

Sunny stared at herself in the full-length mirror. "Sam interferes. With us. With me."

"What are you saying?"

"I'm saying Tad and I need to have our own home where we can be alone."

"He's your employer. The employer of both of you. And a grandfather. What would have happened to Mollie if the Pickerings hadn't adopted her?"

"There's more to it, Mama."

"Don't be silly."

"He kissed me. The day he bought Aeolus for me."

Francine sat up and considered. They both stared at one another in the mirror.

"The horse that you've had for years now? You must have misunderstood, Hannah. You've taken a moment from ancient history and blown it all out of proportion. I don't understand you. You wanted an impossible life, and you succeeded in getting it. And along with everything you wanted came a marvelous husband, beautiful children. Why would you allow obsession to destroy it all?"

"There's no obsession, Mama."

Francine began pinning material on the inner side of her thigh. Of course, she would minimize what Sunny'd told her. Her concentration indicated she'd already forgotten it. Her mother, having endured losing everything, would bolt the door against anything that might threaten her security, even if it meant denying her daughter.

Sunny bit her lip as she watched her. *I had hoped that you'd want to stand up for me, Mama.*

Once the Smithey marriage was patched, rodeos and western shows proliferated just as Sam had always predicted they would. South to Greeley, Denver, Colorado Springs. North to Torrington, Douglas, Casper. Sam purchased draft teams to pull stock wagons loaded with their horses and gear. Whether they won prize money at the rodeos or not, their names became so well known that they had no trouble drawing spectators to their exhibition shows. On the show programs, *Pickering Wild West Show* was arched over a photo of Tad riding a buffalo. *"Each family member a champion! Exhibition riding! Bronc riding! Steer roping! Gun battle with Real Indians!"*

The "Indians" were anything but—they were pulled from the summer's cowhands and given costumes and makeup. As they were plucky

riders—willing to ride bareback with no bridles—
no one noticed. Or cared. It was a welcome
diversion on a summer's evening for lonely
homesteaders and their wind-battered wives,
for the ranch hands and sheepherders and the
daughters they'd managed to coax off the ranches
to accompany them.

Over the winter of 1911, Ruth gave birth
to a daughter, Beatrice, but no sooner had the
snowdrifts puddled in the yard than Ruth broke
from the family enterprise and began competing
on her own. Over the next three years, she took off
to distant rodeos that Sunny hadn't ever thought
of attending. The Snake River Classic. Belle
Fourche. Wolfe Pointe. She raced horses owned by
others since the events were too far away to haul
her own horses. Newspaper clippings trickled
back of her victories at horse races, relay races,
bronc riding.

"Ruth Pickering Smithey!" read the caption
underneath her picture in the Missourian, "Queen
of Northern Plains Rodeo!"

Beatrice joined the grandchildren at the
main house. Mollie was eleven, old enough to take
over much of her care.

Now that they lived in separate houses,
Sunny rarely saw Ruth, though she heard that
Ruth came home between rodeos. After Beatrice's
first Christmas, Sunny didn't see Ruth again until
July 1912. She and Arthur drove into the yard
on a hot summer evening, spraying dust all over
the tables Dezzie had set up for dinner. Ethel
and Francine had given up on the tables anyway,
complaining that they couldn't eat when they were
dinner themselves for the swarms of mosquitoes,
but the children were happy running through the

yard, freed from all table manners, and Dezzie herself ferried Beatrice on her hip while she served the food.

Everyone was dumbstruck at the changes in Ruth, but Dezzie was the first to announce it. "Miz Ruth, you look jus' like you walked off a magazine cover!"

Not that she had been plain before. But with makeup and red lipstick, a red silk bandana and a white bolero decorated in sequins, she no longer looked like just another ranch daughter fresh off the plains. It wasn't a stretch to see why someone would have called her the queen of rodeo. Sunny had always intended her own apparel to be eye-catching, but this was more than eye-catching. It was something Sunny had never been exposed to before: glamour!

Ethel swept down the stairs to greet her daughter. "Ruth, I hardly recognize you."

Ruth pressed her cheek against her mother's, careful not to leave a lipstick stain. "Hello, Mama, I've missed you."

"But—where did all this come from?"

"I've been making a name for myself, Mama."

"At least you're home in time for Frontier Days," boomed Sam.

"I'd never miss being part of the family at Frontier Days," Ruth said. "That will never change."

"To make a name for yourself, must you look gaudier than the rest of us?" pressed Ethel.

"There're more and more cowgirls out there competing all the time," said Tad. "Ruth's right. You got to stand out for the fans and organizers to remember you."

"She was a champion before. Without lipstick and with decorum," said Ethel. "People knew her name then. Arthur, what do you have to say about all this?"

Heads snapped to him. He took Ruth's hand. "Her appearance doesn't disturb me in the slightest. She is a new woman for a new country and a new century. I just hope the day arrives soon when she's had enough acclaim and wants to stay home."

"When is this new woman going to fetch her baby?" said Dezzie.

"Well, of course, Dezzie," said Ruth as she hefted Beatrice. "She's grown so much in just a few weeks."

"Seems like yesterday you couldn't live without this man," said Dezzie. "You howled like you'd been peppered with buckshot when you thought he was leaving you. How many days have you been with him since the first of May?"

Ruth hugged her baby. "Arthur and I came to an arrangement a long time ago."

However settled the "arrangement" was in Ruth's mind, Arthur's concurrence was eroding. Income from their land was cold comfort when people talked of a wife gone six months out of a year, roaming through lawless enclaves astride wild horses. The last straw was when Arthur concluded that his wife's occupation was hurting his own. He had not been made partner in his law firm.

He first announced it to Sam. Ruth would no longer be allowed to compete.

From there, the couple's decline proceeded as slowly and as steadily as the collapse of an abandoned homestead. Doors falling off hinges. Roof caving in. Rumors of the couple's discord were whispered about behind closed doors all over Cheyenne.

SUNNY GALE

Ranch hands who worked on their place reported that there were crates of empty liquor bottles on the porch. At times, when Ruth came to ride, the family noticed bluish bruises here and there covered by makeup, sleeves, scarves. She didn't respond to questions, even from Sam. Her jaw would slam shut and off she'd pivot to the barn to tack up another horse.

Sunny pitied her as she watched her walk away. Ruth's marriage had become just another bronc to ride with no ending bell.

Sam threw up his hands. There was nothing more he could do, he said. Ruth was a married woman and grown. The two of them had to learn to manage on their own. And then months went by when nothing more was said until the night little Beatrice, now five, walked the three miles between houses and pounded on the door to tell them that she was scared that her father was going to kill her mother.

Tad was the first one out the door.

Sunny stayed awake watching the yard for Tad's truck. After an hour, Sam got dressed and went to look for him. Francine sat with Sunny and held her hand. As the night dragged on, Francine's murmured comforts dribbled away. There was no use pretending. Some catastrophe lurked out there and was coming for them.

At daybreak when Sunny saw headlights, she jerked away from her mother and ran outside. It was Sam's car rumbling over the dirt road. Sam was alone.

Arthur had a shotgun, he sobbed. In the struggle among the three of them, Tad had been shot, killed.

It seemed as if the world should return to darkness. Somehow the sun climbed anyway. At Gallantin Funeral Home, she asked for a lock of Tad's hair. It was brought to her, and she fingered the texture, thick and wiry. From that lock of hair, it seemed he should spring to life. There he was waving from the backs of two flying horses, dust billowing around him, his cowboy hat flying off and his reddened face, beaming.

"I heard him outside and begged him not to come in. If only he'd listened to me," said Ruth.

"You brought this on all of us," said Sunny.

"Hush, Hannah!" said Francine. "This is not the time."

"When is the time, Mama? When we first came, she treated us like beggars. Even when we became family, we weren't good enough for her. Now she wants to say it was Tad's fault he was shot while trying to save her hide."

Ruth interrupted. "I didn't say that. I didn't mean that!"

"Her brother. My husband. Instead of blaming herself. I think it's time, Mama, I think it's high time."

"To think how you pretended to befriend me," hissed Ruth. "To think how you inserted yourself into our family like a plague. The only reason you are here is because of Daddy's charity. Dragging your mother and child over the countryside with no husband who would have you. Daddy pitied you. That's how he came to fall in love with you. You've known how he felt all along, and you've used him. I've seen you with him. I've seen how you carry on with him when you think no one's looking. Your marriage was nothing more than a sham to give you a boost in this profession that you never would have had otherwise."

"The two of you, stop!" said Ethel. "Your children are here!"

And there they were—Mollie, Scott, Beatrice—their eyes wide open watching the fabric of their lives ripped apart.

Sam sat rubbing his knees with his palms and then more sobs broke from him, sobs loud enough to rip him apart.

The show was over. Nothing left to see.

Days after the funeral Sam summoned Sunny to his study. His pipe smoked in the ashtray beside him. Smoke snaked upwards flicking along the ceiling.

"Ruth's moving home today. I know how you will feel, but she's my daughter, Sunny. You understand that.

"Ethel won't leave her room. I fear I may lose her, too. And the disgrace. Arthur in jail. Our granddaughter's father in jail. A horrific accident spewed from passions of the moment. Arthur didn't mean to kill Tad. I don't think he meant to harm Ruth either. He loved her. He just lost hope of reaching her. A man's desperations overtake him. You know that.

"I pray we can keep Arthur out of prison. A trial, incarceration, all that won't bring Tad back. Arthur's ruined in town, but we can find him a job here at the ranch.

"Now, what will you do? Do you have plans?"

"You would bring Arthur—the murderer of your son—here?"

"Sunny, I know how you feel. But what good will vengeance do? For Arthur to live with his deed is punishment enough. Every day he will have to see Tad's son grow up an orphan."

"What do you mean 'do I have plans?' Are we having a picnic?"

Sam grimaced. "There's no need for rudeness, Sunny, not now. Ethel has asked that you leave. Those words Ruth said at the funeral home, she can't set them aside—I know you understand. I can't say that everything Ruth said was mistaken. Some of it—not all of it. I have felt all along that you were drawn to me. Though you agree I've never given you cause to hope."

Sunny's cheeks burned. "What a goddamn liar you are!"

"A young woman alone in the wilderness without a father." He shook his head sadly. "She would feel such a great longing."

"I never told Tad about your advances! I did that to protect him!"

Sam almost seemed to be muttering to himself. "The children can remain here, of course. I will always care for them. Mollie, too. Contrary to anything Ruth suggested, she will not be treated like a bastard. You'll have what inheritance Tad's left you, of course. You could leave the rodeo life. Find yourself a little place."

"After all these years, you're not doing right by me."

His blue eyes shone out of his sunken sockets. "You're a shrewd woman, Sunny, more than your years would suggest. I have to clean up this mess, you see. By late summer, I hope to have it out of all the papers to salvage what's left of the season. The family wounds must heal. We must reorder ourselves going forward. Without Tad, I don't see a place for you in our business anymore."

"If you think I am giving up my life and all I've worked for, you're wrong."

"And your mother? You can wander from ring to ring if you want, but what about her?"

"She's always been behind me. Even if she didn't agree with me."

"You're still young. There's much you can endure. But Francine? Back in the cold at her age? Is that what she's earned?"

Sunny fought back her tears. He wouldn't have the satisfaction of them.

"You still have ambition, hunger. I don't begrudge you those desires. I hope they won't wear you out. Let me keep Francine with us. Out of respect for Tad. And you."

He reached for her arm.

"You lecherous piece of filth. Don't you ever touch me again!"

In her final gaze before she slammed the door, he looked deathly pale in contrast to the light streaming in the window. Pale, decrepit, with his mouth gaping. She'd devoted half her life to Sam Pickering, and, here, it had ended. How bright that noon all those years ago when she'd stepped into the dining room of the Cheyenne Club. All that promise awaiting her at Sam's table.

She'd been so eager then to buy tickets for his show.

11

February 10th

    Sunny slams the cabin door behind her. Slams it on the blizzard outside, although the snow and wind are battering against the walls, like an animal trying to get in. She struggles to catch her breath. She's shaking with cold. She loads the stove with coal, she uses the whole bucket. Oh, God, that's too much! But she's so cold she can't stand it.

    She had been hauling melted snow-water to the livestock tank when everything had vanished in the whiteout. House, outbuildings, fences. She had tried to maintain a straight line toward the gate, but she'd found herself walking and walking, arriving at nothing. She had panicked and dropped the bucket. She turned round and round, frozen in place, desperate to find any landmark to orient herself to.

Nothing but white.

Stillness would be a certain death. She had begun walking again. She became colder, more frightened. Hours seemed to pass before she ran into a fencepost. She looked down at the barbed wire. Which way was it going? Was she pointed toward home or away from it? Which fence line was it? North, South, East, West? She had gripped the wire as she walked alongside it. And there, finally, the cabin chimney emerging through the gusts of snow.

Everything inside the cabin is spinning. She looks for any familiar object to focus on. Nothing seems familiar. For a moment she wonders whether she has stumbled into someone else's cabin. As the room settles, she's able to laugh at the thought.

At last, the fire roars. At last, warmth is surrounding her. She sits down in her rocking chair and hugs herself.

She cries. There's no way out. She's not going to make it. It's not just the coal. She's running out of food. She's rationed herself down to one bowl of beans a day. It's just a matter of time before the end.

What would Francine say? She longs to bury her head against Francine's shoulder.

The cattle. She still has the cattle to feed and water. She'll try again when she's warmed herself. Maybe, by then, the storm will have moved on. She wipes her face, reaches for Francine's packet of letters.

1917. The letter and newspaper clippings had been forwarded all the way to her boarding house in Pendleton, Oregon. The envelope was so battered it was a wonder it had survived the journey. Sunny cried out as the clippings unfolded. There was Mollie in a wedding dress only Francine could have made: a square lace collar and a silk drape pinned at the shoulder and at the waist and from there, angled across the hip to the hem. Her little girl beamed under a crown of flowers. So young. Eighteen years old. Still, two years older than the age when she herself had been married.

"Mollie Pickering marries Hiram Lansing" reads the caption and there was the two-column article describing the wedding at St. Matthew's. Scott Pickering had been the ring-bearer.

Sunny closed her eyes and tried to whisk herself a thousand miles away to where Sam was striding down the aisle with Mollie on his arm. Scott at the altar, his curly hair slicked down, so solemn with his responsibility. *How tall would he be now?* Last time she saw him, he was still shorter than she, but he could look her straight in the eye. He was on track to be as tall as Tad, maybe taller. Such a fine-boned face he had, long hands—just like his dad.

And then there would be Francine dabbing at tears with her white gloves. Dezzie would be sitting somewhere in the back of the church in the suit Francine had made her. Maybe wearing a new hat with pheasant feathers. The only ones missing there at the flower-laden altar were Mollie's mommy and daddy.

Tears burned Sunny's eyes as she opened them to her gloomy room. A breeze ruffled the curtains, blowing in the dust stirred by carriages and automobiles as people poured into town for the Pendleton Roundup.

"Did she remember Lansing Hardware?" Francine wrote. Hiram was one of the sons in that family. He and Mollie had met at a cakewalk dance last year at Frontier Days. Hiram was "most proper." He had come to ask Sam for Mollie's hand before saying a word to Mollie. The couple would move to Laramie where they would both begin studies at the university. With the war on, Hiram had begged his parents to volunteer. Wisely, he had deferred to their counsel and had set such escapades aside for now. Ridiculous to think that American boys, needed to man American farms and build American industry, would be sent halfway across the globe for purposes that in Francine's humble opinion were impossible to discern. In any event, the whole matter would be settled by Christmas, anyway. Isn't that what Wilson had said?

Had she heard from Mollie at all, Francine inquired. Well, Mollie wanted to be a teacher. Francine was so thankful that Mollie was striking out on her own. She hadn't felt that way when Hannah had married, but then Hannah had been no more than a child! Conversely, Mollie was so ready to step out into her own space in the world and claim it for her own, wrote Francine, "claim" being underlined.

Sunny smiled. How times had changed! She'd been the captive audience to endless, tedious lectures on fulfilling one's role as "Wife" and "Mother," and, at last, the growing clamor for "Women's Rights" had touched Francine.

"You would be so proud of your daughter," Francine concluded. "I pray the rodeo circuit will draw you here next summer so you can see her and meet Hiram."

Sunny stuffed the envelope under her pillow. Then she put on makeup and lipstick—a practice she'd picked up from Ruth—and went down to the street. She still wore her blousy riding skirt fastened at the knees, and she had bought a new fringed and beaded top from an Indian seamstress. Her bust had expanded a few sizes since the first one. She'd wound eagle feathers around the crown of her cowboy hat.

There would be no looking back. She'd lashed herself to that idea since she'd left Cheyenne. All that grief—it had threatened to pull her under, drown her. Why should that happen when out under the sun-drenched sky there were horses to race, broncs to ride, grandstands with excited crowds waiting for a show. And—win or lose—plenty of revelers for company at the end of the day. The images of Tad dissipated among men ready to buy dinners and share pleasure.

The way forward was into the night and into the bars.

In the first bar she entered, a slim Indian cowboy in angora chaps recognized her. "Sunny Gale," he said, "I've seen pictures of your rides."

"Glad to meet you," she said, extending her hand. "What's your name, cowboy?"

"Joey Cimarron. Is this your first time at Pendleton, Ma'am?"

"Yes, I'm excited to be here."

"I've been coming here seven years now, since it began."

"So long? You can't be more than twenty."

He grinned. "Twenty-three. Buy you a drink?"

Twenty-three—he might as well be a boy! She could be his mother, well, not his mother but maybe his big sister. What did it matter? She had no one to answer to anymore. And Joey's grin was so broad, his teeth so white.

He ordered whiskeys. She tossed hers down.

"You drink as hard as you ride," Joey said.

She giggled and wiped her mouth with the back of her hand. "Never had one at all before my husband died."

"Sorry. Rodeo accident?"

"You could say that."

He squeezed her hand. "Let's drink a toast to him."

"Let's."

More glasses appeared. Two. Three.

"What events are you competing in here?" asked Joey.

"Horse racing, hat race, the saddle broncs."

"Did you know the hat race is not separated? Men and women will compete together in that one."

"I know. I've been practicing all winter."

"You're known for your bronc riding, right?"

"That—and the Roman racing I used to do with my husband."

"And you've learned the hat race? Picking up hats from the ground on a horse at full speed?"

"I'm here to try it."

He lifted his glass. "Good luck to you, Sunny Gale. And good luck to me. I'm your competitor."

"What about you?" she asked. "Have you done this before?"

His Adam's apple bobbed as he downed his whiskey. He set the glass down, leaned over and kissed her neck. "I won it last year."

Later, in his room, she expected an explosion of passion. Instead, she lay on his bed while he neatly folded every item: the angora chaps, pants, socks, the sweat-stained wool shirt, the bandana. The little pile was topped with his hat.

"Did you learn to fold your clothes like that at a laundry?"

"No. Out herding sheep, you learn to keep track of your things. Fold them up small. Keep them close. Or they could get stolen from you."

"Fold mine, too, Cowboy."

He smiled and reached for her bloomers. She never dreamed how arousing it would be to watch a man finger her garments and fold them. He stacked her clothes side-by-side with his, suggesting a familiarity as if they'd known one another for years. The kind of familiarity she used to have with someone else. She felt a pang of sorrow until Joey slipped under the sheet and slid his tongue from her collar bone all the way to her ear.

"I'm sorry to tell you I am going to beat you tomorrow, Sunny Gale," he whispered.

Then she closed her eyes and the images of Tad and Francine and her children receded as swiftly as if they'd been photographs dropped down a well.

Early the next morning the women contestants gathered around the grandstand for photographs. Sunny had been sharing a room with Eleanor but hadn't told her where she'd gone the night before, so to see Eleanor waiting there, proud and trim in her vest and deerskin riding skirt, guilt at how Sunny had treated her added to her queasiness from last night's liquor. She tried to minimize it by telling herself that Eleanor would be the last person on earth who would place demands on her. A lame excuse, really, when it had been Eleanor who had helped her without question, or reproach, when she had arrived in Lander.

With what she had inherited from Tad, Sunny had bought a two-acre lot outside of town with a dirt yard and a small barn. A place for Aeolus. From there it was an easy ride to the Lefever ranch on the Popo Agie River. Leonard no longer rode broncs. Because of his marriage to Eleanor, he had been allowed to purchase grazing allotments on the reservation, and he and their son, Hank, ran a large, thriving ranch.

Eleanor ran a free rodeo and horsemanship school for reservation children. She broke horses, as well, and the money was used for rodeo trips. Sunny had found comfort assisting in her enterprises. And it was Eleanor who had taught hat racing to Sunny—and the riding students, too—after Frontier Days had introduced the event the previous summer.

Eleanor spotted her. "Is something wrong?" she asked. "You didn't come in last night and you look pale this morning."

"Nothing's wrong. I went out last night without telling you. I shouldn't have."

"You don't owe me anything."

"You say that, but I don't feel that way. If nothing else, you paid me to teach your students when you weren't charging them yourself."

"Are we to compare accounts this morning? About who has done what? We entered rodeo together. That's what matters." She squeezed Sunny's arm. "All right?"

Tears welled in Sunny's eyes. "All right."

"Now, tears? What happened last night?"

"Nothing, nothing happened."

Streaks of gray ran through Eleanor's hair, and it was thinning on her forehead. Her skin had contracted across her cheekbones, making them more prominent, and small wrinkles etched her face. To Sunny, she had never looked more beautiful. She could see that Eleanor didn't believe what she'd said and wanted to press further, but the photographer interrupted.

"All right, Ladies, line up! Let's do something different. Each of you turn to the side and look over your shoulder at the camera. Tallest girls at each end."

Sunny and Ruth Pickering were the tallest.

The photographer put his hands on his hips and squinted at the lineup. "Must have gotten you girls up too early. Some of you look half asleep. Especially you on the end, Sunny Gale. Where are those million-dollar smiles? C'mon now. Think of those lucky cowboys out there waiting for you!"

Flash went the bulb.

The group started to break up. Sunny ran to catch up with Ruth.

"Hey, Ruth."

"Sunny."

She was relieved that Ruth acknowledged her without hostility. She didn't care what Ruth thought of her, nor would she ever, but, at least, they should have a truce.

"Is Scott with you?"

"No, he's in school now."

"How is he?"

"He's doing well. He competed in his first Frontier Days this summer. Calf roping. He didn't win, but the day will come."

"And you?"

Ruth paused, as if reflecting. Then she said, "I'm well. You look well."

"I am."

"Scott helped break our thoroughbred colts this spring. He's turning into a fine horseman. Having him there eases the loss for Daddy. We're grateful to you, I guess. For letting us keep him."

"He's better off there."

"I'll give him your love."

Does he mention me, Sunny had wanted to ask. But Ruth had already pivoted, and she didn't look back.

The hat race was a mile long, with ten-gallon hats placed on the ground at quarter mile intervals, three hats in all. The riders drew lots for the horses they would ride. They were assured that all the horses had done this race at least once to minimize the possibility of any rider being thrown. Any rider who was thrown would get a second chance.

"Watch," Eleanor had said to Sunny and the other students back on a thawing day in February. The mud in her corral had been ankle deep. Eleanor had urged her horse up to racing speed, then in an instant almost too quick to see, she scooped all the way to the ground, picked up a hat and straightened.

She circled back around to the group. "This was a tribal exercise so warriors could learn to pick up weapons from the ground during battle. Now we will be one happy family in rodeo."

To Sunny's chagrin, the younger riders caught on much faster than she did. After two sessions of practice, they made it look so easy while Sunny had fallen off so many times that she'd been covered in mud like a pig. The young riders had laughed and laughed at her, and she had to laugh with them because mastering the event had seemed too hopeless.

"We will put you on a pony until you get it," Eleanor said. And after weeks of falling in the mud, she had.

No chance of mud at Pendleton. The track was dry and fast. Sunny drew the first slot. Her horse lunged to a good start, but on her final bend, she missed the last hat and was disqualified.

As she dismounted, Joey sprung up on an appaloosa. "No sadness, Sunny Gale," he said.

The fact that he had turned to speak to her lessened the sting. She grinned back as broadly as she could. Million-dollar smile. "No sadness. There'll be a next time."

The gun went off and the appaloosa tore down the track. One-two-three hats. Joey set the last one on his head and the crowd went wild.

"Joey Cimarron, folks," the announcer said, "last year's hat racing champion and set up to win this year as well!"

Except Eleanor's ride was faster. When her time was announced, Sunny jumped up and down cheering with the rest of the spectators, as Eleanor galloped a victory lap. Beautiful beneficent sunlight, gift of the gods, streamed down on the crowds who had leapt to their feet. It glinted off the grey streaks in Eleanor's shining hair. Eleanor dropped the reins and threw both arms in the air. Her mouth opened and she sang. Not a song of this world, not of the white world anyway. A song of joy and triumph. Eleanor, the Indian girl who'd refused to stay in the white man's school.

Pendleton was a washout for Sunny. She didn't place in any of her events. Ruth won the saddle bronc riding. As the rodeo ended, Sunny looked for Joey to say goodbye. No, she wasn't seeking a farewell, she was seeking consolation. She was hoping he would look at her and smile and then ask her to stay for the night, then maybe for the next day, the next week.

He was downing a beer when she spotted him. Their eyes met and he nodded. There it was— the little smile at the corner of his mouth. But then another woman, a younger woman, came between them. She grabbed his arm and tugged him away. He knew her. He was happy to see her. He put his arm around her waist, and they turned into the crowd. Before they disappeared, he looked over his shoulder and waved his hat.

Back in Lander, the top tiers of the aspen were already bare. Aeolus' winter coat had grown in. In the mornings, frost covered the hillsides. When she got up, her teeth chattered so hard she thought they'd fall out of her head before she could get her stove lit. One morning, she didn't light the fire. Instead, she splashed cold water on her face, dressed, took Tad's diamond horseshoe cufflinks downtown and pawned them. Her engagement ring and wedding band, too. One of her early costumes brought some money.

Wrapped in a quilt, and with a cup of coffee and watching the frost glisten in the first rays of the sun, she heard a whisper in the stillness: *you can't stay.*

Soon snow would plug the streets. There would be no riding then, not riding that paid anyway. Eleanor could afford to wait for the thaw to start riding again, no matter how many weeks that took. But Sunny would soon be juggling money for food and fuel.

That image from her Nebraska girlhood returned: the crisp fall air as the Mangum cowboys rode south, turning to specks in the distance before cresting the bluff.

If she wanted to keep riding, she'd have to follow their example.

The rancher who bought Aeolus came in a wagon to pick him up. The last she saw of her beautiful golden horse he was tied to the back of the wagon, and as he threw out his front legs in the extended trot she knew so well, the breeze riffled through his mane. One more curve in the road and they were gone. She heard Jax's whisper in her ear: "Cowgirls can't love their horses."

"Leave the house and come stay with us," Eleanor said.

"Winters are too long," she answered. "I know what's it's like inside a house day after day with the wind blowing outside. Everyone goes stark crazy, don't they—if they don't get to hating one another first. All I want to do is ride. It's the only way to keep my mind clear. And if I can ride through the winter, I'll be ready come next rodeo season. I can't get anything done staying here."

"You didn't have to sell Aeolus. We would have kept him for you."

"When you have your own cattle and horses to feed? And I don't know if I'll ever be back. Naw, it's not worth it. I'm sure I'll have another horse again someday."

"I wish you would stay. For me."

"Look at you, the tough old girl. You look like you're ready to bawl as if we're never going to see each other again. I'll let you know where I end up. We'll meet at Frontier Days next summer."

Eleanor hugged her, and as Sunny's eyes started to tear up, she pushed Eleanor away.

"No more nonsense now."

"Please take care of yourself, Sunny. Write." said Eleanor.

Instead of riding south on horseback, Sunny caught a ride with a lumber truck driver.

At a crossroad in New Mexico consisting of a bar, an outhouse, and an automobile repair shack, she found a one-legged rancher, Angus Laroche. Laroche had lost his leg when he'd been pinned and stomped by a bull.

"I'm a one-legged rancher with a three-legged dog," said Laroche, grinning and pointing to the brindle dog at his feet. Laroche had only a few tobacco-stained teeth left. He still cut a striking figure: six feet tall with a full head of black hair and black bushy eyebrows. Son of a French Canadian and an Apache, that was what he claimed to be.

He'd heard of rodeo some. There were some local contests. But he'd never heard of a woman bronc rider although his own mother, God rest her soul, could have ridden the Devil if he had had a mane and tail.

Yeah, he'd hire her as a ranch hand over the winter. If she could ride like she said.

She slept in the back room in the bar that night, and the next morning Laroche's cook picked her up. The car was open, and the wind was bitter cold. She was chilled through by the time they drove under the arch that read "The Purple Orchid." Odd name for a ranch that was unlikely to have grown an orchid, much less seen one.

Laroche was resting on his crutches while holding on to the horse he wanted her to ride, a brownish-black Thoroughbred named Jack. Jack used to be his, he explained, but hadn't seen a rider nor saddle and bridle since Laroche's accident. Jack did look bewildered at all the human attention after years of living on the range. He kept looking over their heads as if longing to be released. Still, his eyes were large and kind. He was no killer bronc.

With Sunny on board, he crow-hopped several times in protest as Laroche, his cook, and three weathered cowboys watched. There'd been snickers when she'd mounted, and while she listened with satisfaction as they trickled off, she could see Laroche's boys had not been won over, no matter how well she'd ridden. Their squinty pig eyes told her she was just a foreigner on their turf. When they heard her mention prizes she'd won at rodeos, one of them leered and said, "She didn't get those prizes for riding. They were for her cooking."

"Yeah, it must have been her Rocky Mountain oyster recipe."

"Yum, yum."

They looked at her and laughed.

She looked to Laroche, expecting him

to intervene, but he only stared back at her, measuring her response. The test wasn't whether she could handle the horse. It was whether she could work among these men.

His eyes reflected the disappointment on her face.

"You think you'll be all right here?" Laroche asked.

"Yes, sir."

"Cook can take you back to the bar...."

"I'll be fine."

"Suit yourself."

That was her start as The Purple Orchid's new hired hand, in a place where her past as a rodeo champion meant nothing. She could have moved on, but there was no guarantee she'd find anything different. She was unknown here, but after all, hadn't she wanted a little anonymity to put as much distance as possible between her and Sam Pickering?

Laroche did go so far as to acknowledge that the bunkhouse would be no place for her. One of the stalls in the barn was converted to her bedroom. She was given a cot and a half dozen bearskin blankets.

"You'll need this as well," said Laroche as he handed her a shotgun. "Ever used one before?"

"My step-father showed me how to use a rifle, not a shotgun. What would I need it for?"

"The immediate use would be to deter any of those boys who might trouble you should they come along. I believe if they see you're serious, they'll leave you alone."

Maybe it was because Laroche told the men of her shotgun, but though she lay awake night after night fearing the worst, no one came. Mice skittered in the stalls. An owl hooted on the roof. When the owl flew off, the coyotes would begin howling.

As had been true everywhere she'd lived, the horse became her refuge. Jack's lunge from a stand to a full gallop contained so much power that it took her breath away. She raced him over the juniper-covered hills, through the sandy washes, while her heart released its aches and opened to the sound of pounding hooves and wind.

One late afternoon as they slowed, she spotted an owl perched in a dead cottonwood. He eyed her as they passed underneath him.

"You're the same fella that keeps me awake at the barn."

He answered her. *Who, who?* The slopes around them framed a sky awash in violets, saffrons, blushes, fluid colors rippling on into twilight and an emptiness without end. *Who, who are you?*

One night, after she'd been with Laroche for a month, she wrapped herself in a bearskin blanket and opened the barn door. Cold air struck her cheeks and whooshed down her neck. A bloated moon hung over Laroche's house. Fresh snow had fallen, and shadows pooled in the tracks of the mountain lion that had crossed the yard. On the roof, she could make out the owl's silhouette. He was watching.

She put on her boots and crossed to the front door of Laroche's house. It creaked as she opened it. She left the boots on the rug next to Laroche's and padded through to the bedroom.

When she pushed open the bedroom door, there was Laroche sitting straight up with his shotgun pointed at her.

"I'm cold," she said.

Laroche threw his legs over the side of the bed. One foot came down and then there was the stump. The way it jiggled repulsed her. She hadn't considered how it would look.

He set the shotgun down.

"It won't do."

"I don't know why'd you say that. My husband's gone. You don't have anyone."

"You don't know that."

"Whoever she is, she's not here right now."

Laroche nodded to a photograph of a woman on his bureau. "You're wrong about that, too."

"Just for tonight we can put her picture face down."

"There's no 'just tonight.' You'd be back tomorrow. You'd decide that you belong here. When we know you don't belong. All those places you've been to. The shows, the crowds, the costumes, and the bronc riding you've told me about. That's what has made you who you are, and you'll be headed back before long. I'm an old, useless son-of-a-bitch and I don't have any business being anywhere else."

"I don't expect you to marry me, Laroche."

"Good thing because I can't see why I'd hitch myself to a woman bent on chasing glory. Next spring, you'll ask me for money so you can be on your way. Maybe you'll pay me back with the money you win. Maybe you'll pay me back by punching cattle or breaking horses. Maybe you'll just disappear, and you won't be the first hand who has taken more from me than he's given. But we'll just waller in a muddy bog if we mix business. ..." he nodded to the pillows, "and this."

"I don't believe that you don't want me."

Laroche snorted. "Because every man you meet wants you? I'd have thought that by the ripe old age of—what, thirty-five?—you would have acquired some perspective. Whatever comfort a man's loving on you brings doesn't last past dawn, does it? Ain't it just you that's left in the end? Sunny Gale has got to learn to live with herself outside of the limelight."

He pulled his leg back over the bed, turned his back to her and lay down. "There's a three-mile race in Santa Fe next Saturday. You can take Jack."

She hadn't expected rejection, so it was a long cold walk back to the barn. It smarted that she was being turned out of a man's bed, a cripple's, no less. Still, when spring came and she was preparing to depart, she had to admit that his refusal to make love to her made things tidier. No balances to be adjusted.

"Will you let someone else ride Jack?" she asked as they settled up at the kitchen table.

"No. He's yours from now on."

"Then I'll try to come back."

"We'll be watching out for you when you've worn yourself out, or the fall comes, whichevern happens first."

He laid an extra hundred-dollar bill on top of her wages.

"I don't need this."

"Your wages plus your winnings on the racetrack ain't going to last a month."

She put the bills in her shirt pocket. "It looks to me like you're trying to get me to stay here with you."

"Nope. But there'll always be a place here for you."

She smiled at him. "In the barn."

He nodded. "That's right. In the barn."

"You think on this, old man, while I'm gone." She came around to his side of the table and kissed him.

He didn't return the gesture, didn't even look at her. "Be on your way," he said.

Utah, Idaho, Montana. End of July found her back in Cheyenne. She caught a lift over the Medicine Bow Range with a steer roper who remembered Tad Pickering and was happy to help his widow. As they sped out of the evergreens and aspen, the plain rolled before them just as she remembered it, cattle and horses grazing in the gullies or dozing at the windmills. Hardly changed since she'd first seen it some two decades ago. If it was still here, then the story of Hannah Mangum turned to Sunny Gale was here, too. She was coming home to herself.

"You all right?" said the steer roper. "You can take my handkerchief if you need it. I guess it's got to be hard. Never mind. You're gonna show 'em all up this year, ain't you?"

She was booked in the same hotel, same room that she'd shared with Luke on her first Frontier Days in 1898. Looking at it now, patches

231

of the wallpaper were torn off, the rugs frayed and stained. She'd been so lit with excitement back then. Maybe the room had looked the same, and she hadn't noticed. She had been swept along that day by everything that had happened and then, when they'd shut that door, it had been just the two of them, her and Luke. She imagined him in the air in front of her, still young, boyish. *"Give old Atlas a nudge with your feet and take off."* For all she knew, he'd been in the crowd at any number of rodeos she'd performed in, just another shape in the stands, another blur.

Down below, the horses and carriages were gone. No more horses bolting when a motorcar blew a tire. All automobiles now, sedately parked.

But the desires of Hannah Mangum were still as palpable as they were back then.

Where had that steer roper said he was staying? What bar did he say she could find him in?

Next morning, he gave her a ride to the Pickering ranch.

"You want me to come in with you? Wait out here?" he asked.

"Don't waste your time. Go on back. They'll give me a ride when it's time for me to leave."

The truck pulled away and she watched a young man in the corral on horseback. He was swinging his rope, getting ready to pick out a calf. God, he looked like his father must have looked in his teens.

"Scott," she called.

He looked up. "Mom?" He dismounted and

ambled to the rail. "Where did you come from?"

"'Where did you come from?' Is that all you can say? Get over this rail so I can squeeze my boy!"

Scott grimaced a little. Probably too big for squeezes, she thought. He submitted to the embrace but didn't return it.

"You're here for Frontier Days."

"Yeah, I am. How about you?"

"Entered calf roping again. Hope I do better this year."

"Sunny Gale and her boy entered in the same rodeo. Bet they'll talk about that!"

"Yeah." He looked away.

"You're not excited about it?"

"No. I wish my name wasn't Pickering so it wouldn't mean nothing if I won or lost."

She studied his face for a moment. "I know it's hard work to try to make it in that arena. Hours of practice and then on rodeo day you get out there, something throws you off and your chance flies away from you. Only thing I can say, honey, is that if you want to be on top, it's gonna come. Maybe not when you would like it to. But one day, when you least expect it, everything will fall into place, and it'll happen just as you've dreamed. I know you think you have a lot to live up to but you're lucky to have this ranch to grow up on, this family behind you. When I was your age. . .."

The expression on his face made it seem as if he'd stopped listening after her first sentence.

Dezzie had come out of the door. She shouted back into the house, "Sunny's home!" It had only been two years, but Dezzie was walking with a cane—the very same woman who used to stride across the yard, nearly four feet for every step, her skirts whooshing over the dirt. Sunny rushed to her and threw her arms around her.

Dezzie held her head to her chest as they both cried. "Thank God!" Dezzie said. "Thank God I have been here to see you again!"

Her statement drew a fresh round of sobs from Sunny. In all those years they had dwelt in the same household, why hadn't she ever stopped to tell this woman how much she meant to her? She'd been so immersed in her own struggles and rivalries that she hadn't ever thought of it. How shallow she had been after all.

Francine had also aged beyond what Sunny had imagined. She now wore glasses thick as bottle glass.

"Don't worry about me. I'm just fine," she said. "But this is likely my last outfit for you. I don't think I can sew much longer. I didn't put as much fullness in your skirt this time. It's immodest but women's riding skirts are looking more and more like trousers. Have you noticed? As much as I abhor it, I thought it's what you would prefer. And I've got a surprise for you."

She unfolded a new suede bolero and handed it to her daughter. "Sunny Gale" was embroidered in gold stitching across the back.

"After all these years, you've used my name!"

"Your courage. The way you've fashioned your life as you imagined it to be, even in the face of your defeats. You really are—Sunny Gale."

Acceptance, after all this time. Sunny's voice started to break. "Oh, Mama!"

"So good to have you standing right in front of us. Not just letters. The real you."

"I should have come back sooner."

"Ssssh, no regrets. We're here now."

Sunny collected herself, and folded her handkerchief. "I stopped in Laramie to see Mollie and Hiram. They weren't at the address that you gave me."

"My letter must not have caught up to you. Hiram couldn't be dissuaded any longer. He joined the army. They moved all the way across the country to Fort Devens in Massachusetts. Hiram's in the barracks. Mollie is in Avery nearby. She's teaching illiterate soldiers how to read. How wonderful she is, Hannah."

"Massachusetts! How on earth will we ever see her again?"

Francine put her arm through Sunny's. "She'll come home when Hiram ships out. By then rodeo season will be ending. You can see her then."

The front door opened.

"Sunny Gale!"Sam leaned against the doorway, panting for breath. The man who had once thrilled crowds.

"Stand up here close and let me look at you."

Slowly, Sunny mounted the porch steps. What pity he might have had from her was swallowed by the old resentments. He raised his hand to touch her cheek, but it fell to his side before she'd had time to step back.

"Same glorious spirit. Time's been good to you, young lady. Is Tad with you, too?"

Sunny looked past him and saw Ruth.

"Daddy, you don't mean Tad. You mean Scott. Scott's roping out in the corral."

Ruth stepped out on the porch. While everyone had declined, she had grown more beautiful. She'd cut her hair in a bob and the new style showed off her cheekbones and jaw.

The same old pride was there but tempered.

"It's good of you to visit, Sunny. I know Scott and Francine are happy to see you."

Sunny glanced over her shoulder toward the corral. "I'm not so sure about Scott. He barely seems to know me."

"He doesn't know how to show his feelings," Ruth said.

They watched while Scott mounted his horse, coiled his rope. The calves, pocketed into a corner, shifted as they eyed him. If Scott knew the women were watching him, he didn't show it. He fingered his loop and began to twirl it, committed to the motions that would unfold.

She shouldn't have expected him to look at her, but the way his absorption shut her out made her feel insignificant all the same. Sure was peculiar how she'd felt more like herself in an old hotel room where she hadn't spent more than two nights than here on this ranch where she'd spent more than ten years, given birth to that boy and suckled him. She'd been part of a renowned enterprise, but there was no trace of that history to be found here today. She'd become no more than a faded image on a poster.

No wonder that boy didn't know her.

Just as she'd predicted, *The Tribune* picked up the story: "Sunny Gale to Appear at Frontier Days with Son" and a photograph was taken of the two of them with their arms around one another's waists. Sunny was smiling. Scott's mouth was a rigid little line.

After the flash, she'd held on to him for one moment longer though he tried to pull away.

"Good luck, son."

Neither one of them won anything.

The end of August swept her to a dusty rodeo in Rapid City. The air of excitement she'd become accustomed to at rodeo time was missing, despite half-hearted attempts by the local newspaper to fan it into life. People in the bar told her there had been a hailstorm the week before. Hailstones the size of gourds. All the hay and wheat that hadn't already been harvested was pelted down, ruined, they'd said. With the country tilting towards winter, no one wanted to spend money on frivolity.

She found boarding at the fairground stables. She had run out of money for hotels.

On rodeo day, the spectators were sparse. Not even the front rows had been filled, and despite Indian dances and savage broncs, the crowd's response was subdued. The children lining the rail looked grimy and half-starved. Sunny leased racehorses from a stockman to run in the women's relay and won that event. But two strides into her bronc ride, the roan mustang buckled to his knees, and the last thing she remembered was her sensation that they were falling over together.

The room she woke in was darkened. She couldn't tell if evening had come already or if the gloom was because drapes had been drawn. She sat up quickly only to feel jagged flashes of pain.

Dry. Her mouth was so dry. She licked her lips and tasted dirt.

"What's happened to me?" she said, although she didn't know if anyone at all was with her.

"Mustang's knee blew out," a masculine voice said. "He came down and landed on you. Broken ribs, collarbone broke both sides. Fear you broke your neck as well. Does your husband know where you are?"

"Husband?"

"You lost your baby, too."

Husband, husband? Laroche's image came to mind instead of the boys she'd slept with over the last few months. Was it the steer roper in Cheyenne? "Laroche knows I'm traveling."

"Did he know you were pregnant?"

"Why are you asking?"

"I can't believe he would have let you roam wild like this when you ought to have been home preparing for this child. You didn't tell him, did you?"

"Tell me something, Doc. You are a doctor, aren't you?"

"Yes."

"Do you doctor on cowboys?"

"Several a month. Shot, punched, busted by horses, trampled by cattle, snake-bit. Last week we had one crushed by an automobile."

"Tell me, do you think they were meeting their paternal obligations?"

"I don't understand what you're asking me. A woman with child has a sacred duty to bring life into the world."

"One sex has a sacred duty while the other has freedom, no duty, no morality?"

"Didn't you want this child, Miss....?"

"Gale."

"Miss Gale."

"I might have wanted it if I'd known it was there. It didn't speak up."

"You are a most blasphemous woman."

"One more thing, Mister Doctor. What happened to my horse?"

"The horse? They shot the poor devil."

Yes, she'd heard it, report. And there was Tremain again, lifting the gun to his shoulder.

"Shall I send for your husband?"

"Yes. Angus Laroche."

Laroche didn't come. Instead, she lay in that same room for six weeks watching the daylight blanche the sky and from there spread across the ceiling and then drain out through the same dirty windowpanes. Her head was strapped in place. She was not to move, the doctor said, if she wanted to ensure that she'd walk again, much less ride.

Laroche was always on her mind. She could never think of him without remembering the night she'd seen the stump. She had plenty of time now to mull over the shame she felt at her disgust. If she was to be a cripple, would others look at her with revulsion? She'd rather be dead. Had Laroche ever wanted to die? On the day when someone told him he'd never ride again? If you couldn't ride, there was no life.

He sent a letter with money. "Heal up and come on back." When she wrote back that the doctor had cautioned that she might not walk again, his reply was: "Quack doesn't know a damn thing about you."

She sent word to Francine not to come. As comforting as it would have been to have her there,

Francine was too old to sit alone through the long train ride, too old to find lodging and meals in a place where she knew no one, too old to see her daughter strapped to a bed like a broken doll.

"Mama," she telegrammed, "don't come. Doc says I will be up in no time. Love to Scott."

In the first week of November, she walked. Five tiny steps that exhausted her, but she walked. Her first steps back toward The Purple Orchid.

Laroche moved a couch onto his porch so she could rest in the sun during the day. She asked him why he would keep her at all if she wouldn't be able to do any work. She wasn't the first cowpuncher given time to recuperate, he said. But to date, she had been a damn poor investment.

"You'll have to sell Jack, won't you?"

"I don't give it more than a couple of days before you'll be itching to get back in the saddle, ready or not," he said.

"Laroche, I...." *I don't deserve you. I don't deserve what you've done for me. You've lost so much more, and I didn't appreciate how you endured it.*

"What?"

"I hope you won't be angry. Up in Rapid City, I told them you were my husband."

"I saw that and pondered on it. Those folks probably think that I'm a miserable cuss for not traveling up there to be with you."

"No. Not at all. They thought I was just a wicked woman for deserting you while I traipsed around the countryside."

"We make a rotten couple."

"We do. Good thing we don't have children."

"Good thing we'll never have to worry about that," he said pointedly.

That was the closest she could come to the truth before he hobbled away to bark orders at the hands.

From her seat on the porch, mornings were chilly. The leaves on the cottonwood yellowed. At first, they fell in handfuls. Then in a whoosh, they dropped to the ground and the tree's arms were empty. Midmorning the days warmed, she tipped her face to the sun, and the crickets sang through the noon hour and on until late afternoon when only a handful remained to trill a welcome to the pale moon.

About that time of day, she would see a band of wild horses trailing down the hills toward their waterholes.

Laroche went to Galisteo once a week for the mail. One morning he came back and didn't get out of the car. He seemed to be staring at something in his lap.

"What are you doing?" she called out. "Is something wrong?"

He didn't answer. He reached for his crutches and opened the door. The three-legged dog went to greet him. He stopped to pat its head.

"You're moving as slow as molasses. Do you need some help?"

He waited until he was standing right in front of her.

"You got a telegram."

"Well, give it to me."

"In another minute, I will."

The dread in his eyes. Such a calm morning

and yet everything in his face portended calamity.

"You read it."

He nodded but stood motionless.

"Tell me."

"Let me sit down next to you."

She scooted over. He put his hand over hers.

"There was a plague at Fort Devens. Spanish flu they call it."

"Mollie."

"I'd rather lose my other leg than hand this to you."

SUNNY GALE

12

February 11th

    Her first sensation is silence. The storm has blown over. Grey light seeps into the cabin, retrieving her belongings from the darkness one by one. Here is your life, the light shows her. You have survived another day.
    She used to feel a sense of triumph enduring these blizzards. Not anymore. This morning, the weariness of it smothers every inclination toward moving forward, even rising to light the stove.
    Why bother when she can only be warm for a few short hours?

She pulls the elk hide over her head and closes her eyes. Go back in the darkness to find the sunlight.

One fall, after the rodeo season had ended, Sunny and Tad had taken a camping trip with the children at Laramie Peak. On their last day, Tad had sat next to her on a buffalo rug, shoulders and knees touching. With the warmth between them in this casual contact, it had been easy to forget that the day would end, that in a matter of hours they'd have to load up, harness the horses and ride down the mountain.

The day had seemed poised to last forever.

She had taken off Mollie's skirt so the child could play in the creek. At first, Mollie had squealed when her toes touched the water, but then she'd squatted down to cup it through her fingers. How long and pale her legs had been. Her hair had come loose and fallen down her back. The sun was behind her—a halo of gold from the gods.

Why hadn't it enveloped and protected her forever?

Sunny and Tad had looked at one another. For once, his cowboy hat was off, and his hair was tousled.

"What are you smiling about?" she'd asked.

"I'm thinking of the ruckus Miz Francine would raise if she saw that child's bare legs naked for all the world to see."

"They're perfectly lovely."

"As lovely as her mother. With you and the children, this is the closest this scruffy buckaroo will ever get to paradise."

She had jabbed him with her elbow. "'Scruffy buckaroo?' As if!" And he had laughed.

Paradise. She sits up and looks at the sunlight blazing through the dirty windowpanes. Maybe she shouldn't be so scared of death. It could be just a door through which she will live that day on Laramie Peak forever with Tad's light touch against her shoulder, and glittering water dropping off Mollie's forearms.

She paws through Pandora's Box searching for letters from Scott. There aren't many. He didn't write much after he married and moved to California in 1922. His wife wrote notes on the Christmas cards. Sunny finds the last one from 1929. There's the photograph: Three young handsome children. She sees Tad in every one of them. She remembers writing back, "Do they have red hair?" She never got an answer.

She had attended Scott's wedding, of course, but the last frank conversation they had had was much earlier in the summer of 1919. They had gone to visit Mollie's grave. Beatrice, Ruth's daughter, had joined them, and Sunny remembers how the three of them had stood that evening side by side. Scott had hugged Beatrice to him. She remembers being touched by how close those children were. More like siblings than cousins. She smiles to herself. Her manner of motherhood—leaving children behind to be raised by others—hadn't been so abominable after all.

Once Laroche has handed over the telegram, Sunny is hurtled into an underworld captive to a vision repeats and there is no escape. She is back on the Mangum ranch riding Helios. She's been sent on some task—to round up cattle or find a stray cow. She is riding up and over the hills, down into the washes. A fall storm is blowing in. The black clouds rear up and overcome her. Hail bounces in the dirt.

She hears Mollie. She has left the baby behind in her crib wet and hungry. Mollie's cries reverberate all around her, even louder than the storm's fury.

What kind of mother are you?

She turns for home, but the wind pushes her back. She's lost her hat, and water streams down her face. She can't see through the hail.

She never reaches the house.

She is stuck inside the vision even while pallbearers shoulder the casket down the aisle at St. Matthew's, even while the distraught groom, Hiram, holds his head in his hands, and Scott sits pale in his black suit, even while a parade of people in black closes in on the canopy in the cemetery, the canopy...the canopy, the hole in the ground.

She can't hear a word over that baby's screams in her mind.

After a month, Laroche's voice finally broke through to her. "Wallowing in this grief won't bring her back."

"I was an awful mother. I was never there for her."

It seemed as if he'd stepped into the vision with her, as if he was looking up at the hail and hearing the baby cry from the house that couldn't be seen.

"From what you've told me, she never suffered a day in her life. How many daughters out there, do ya think, have a bronc riding champion for a mother? But for that, how else would she have known to get away from those Pickering folks and follow her dreams? She had a mother who showed her how it could be done."

He put his hand on her knee. "I guess there's no end to the punishment you can put yourself through, but it's useless, isn't it, if no amount of punishment will let you go back."

"I would have done everything differently."

"Even if that were true, she was going to marry that boy. They were going to get on a train and seek their fortunes as young'uns are bound to do. The end is the same."

Laroche walked away. The vision parted like a curtain to let him through. And then he was outside in the bright winter sun. It was near Christmas. The cook had lined up luminaries on the porch.

"You're well enough to ride again," he called back over his shoulder.

One night she woke and the vision was gone. No wind or hail. She sat up in her cot and listened. There were the small rodent scratches, the sighs and creaks of barn wood contracting in the dry cold. She wrapped herself in her blanket and slid open the door to millions of stars. Not the glittering throng of fans as she sometimes imagined, just beautiful shards of ice. Once Mollie had been under those stars with her, maybe not near her, maybe hundreds of miles away, but there and alive. Sunny's loss was an enormity to her alone, not to these bright travelers riding the eons. What was one human being or another? In the unfolding of time humankind itself would cease to matter.

A horrible place, this world. She wanted to scream, as if screaming would clear the sky.

Screaming would only wake everyone up.

Once again, she entered the house. The light was on behind the bedroom door. When she pushed it open, Laroche was waiting for her, sitting up in bed. The gun was there. He didn't reach for it. White chest hair curled out of his open undershirt.

She pulled the blanket tighter around her.

"Let me in."

Laroche shook his head. "No."

"You waited up for me."

"I knew you were coming."

"I've seen the women the cook brings out for you. Why not me?"

"You'll run to anyone in your frenzy to get your baby back." He threw back the covers. "She's not here."

"Please."

"In the morning, you'll still be out chasing her, still miles away from the only place you need to be, the place where you decide to live."

"I never saw a man play so hard to get."

"And you'll never be the kind of woman I can have."

In the end, her pain remained. Over the weeks, the cycle of small things wore it down until it was as familiar as Laroche's stump. Small things—the sun cracking the horizon, ice shards twirling in the water tanks, steam rising from the horses' nostrils. The Purple Orchid's first calf of the year was born, followed by another and another. The pastures were soon teeming with a new wave of creatures all ignorant of anything that had ever come before.

Sunny stayed on even after the wildflowers withered and turned to husks. Laroche never remarked on it though she felt he was glad. When she returned from cattle drives, she could see him from a mile off, shading his eyes against the sun. She felt he was searching for her. When she swung off the saddle, she'd tease him about it. "You were standing there so long I thought you were a cactus."

"Prickly as I am I won't ever flower, so I guess they're more useful."

He'd hand her a jug of water fresh from the underground spring, water that tasted of cooled stone. The hotter it was outside the sweeter it tasted.

One evening at twilight, she knocked on his door. He was sitting at his kitchen table with a glass of whiskey and a rolled cigarette smoking in the ashtray.

"Glad you've come around to knocking before you enter."

"I'm sorry about the times before. I've come to tell you I'll be going."

"I figured the heat would move you up and out of here."

"It's not the heat. I'd like to see my son. It's about Frontier Days' time now."

He picked up the cigarette and inhaled. "Are you going to compete?"

"No. My neck still throbs and I still feel... hollowed out, I guess, is how I'd describe it. The old

Sunny Gale's in a past long gone. I never admitted it, but she was gone when I lost Tad. And the new Sunny Gale...can't find her seat in this old rocking world now."

He flicked ash off the butt. "You're not done."

"You'll let me come back, won't you?"

"Try to come back in one piece this time."

Sunny couldn't find her seat in the grandstand. She chafed at being a spectator— such a chasm between her and the contestants! Up close, she knew how they sweated, grunted, joked, cursed, prayed, gloated. These cowboys and cowgirls were so far away she felt she was watching them through a telescope.

Dang it! She ought to be out there cresting the thrill of countless eyes on her. She missed the explosion in her pulse when the hands let her bronc loose. How she craved winning. The chase for it and the grasp of it as one's own. It was lust pure and simple. How it had made her feel like one of the gods.

No, not a god, just one of those fortunates uplifted by them to the heights of heaven.

She had expected to feel content in this seat, reminiscing about her own glories, and enjoying those of the contestants below. Instead, she felt the arena tugging at her. Laroche was right: *You're not done!*

Beyond the dissatisfaction of being a spectator, she was surprised to see chutes in the arena. Chutes! No more need for dozens of men to rope and hold horses while they were saddled. Now the animals were saddled in tight pens and a gate flew open when the rider was ready. Less like cowboys on the range. More like the assembly line Mr. Ford was so famous for. The activities that took place on the open range were turning into show business.

The crowd was captivated by a new young woman. Hazel O'Malley. Hazel O'Malley won the women's relay race. Hazel O'Malley beat Ruth Pickering for the championship saddle bronc ride. *Without hobbled stirrups!* She was slighter than a cattail, twenty years old, they said, and she wore a ruby-red smile that said, *There isn't anything I can't do.*

The crowd gasped when she was announced as a contestant in Tad's old event, steer roping. Women had never competed in that event before, much less against men. There was a buzz in the stands as Hazel rode a white spotted mare into the roper's box. Once the steer burst loose, Hazel dropped her reins, and from there the white mare worked entirely on her own. Two lunges and she was at the steer's heels. Hazel's rope sailed up and around the horns while the mare had already veered aside to set up the trip. The rope snapped taut, the steer was tripped, and before it hit the ground, Hazel vaulted off the saddle. Three more strides and the mare stopped cold with the steer at the toe of Hazel's boots. She bent to make her tie. The pickup men held up their flags waiting the six seconds to see if the tie would hold. The flags came down. Everyone jumped to their feet. Sunny, too.

Eighteen seconds! Faster than Tad's best time. Faster than anyone's time. Ever.

After the rodeo ended, Sunny searched for her but couldn't push through the newsmen and photographers and fans. Between heads, she watched Hazel pose for every shot. Her face was dust-caked, but she had taken the time to reapply her lipstick.

How had such a little woman pulled off a feat like that?

"I train sunup to sundown," she said. They all chuckled, and she added, "And when the sun's gone down, I set lamps up on the posts, splash some water on my face and tack up again."

She was from Texas, Sunny heard her say. No, she wouldn't be dancing with the other cowboys tonight. She had a husband, Gabriel. She yanked him from the crowd and linked her arm in his.

What did he think about his pretty little wife setting a record at Frontier Days? He took a breath as if he was going to answer, but Hazel jumped in and said Gabriel O'Malley was the finest horseman around and was out riding as many hours as she was. "I wouldn't be here without him."

Was her cooking as smoking as her rodeo performances?

Everyone laughed. The flash went off as Gabriel dipped his head.

"Heck!" he said, "who's got time to eat?"

Sunny felt someone bump her shoulder. It was Ruth. She nodded to the O'Malleys. "You get to thinking that you own it," Ruth said, "especially this place, this rodeo where we started. Cowgirls have been coming up for years, some good, some just trying their luck. Some stick with it, some disappear, but I guess it was only a matter of time before someone like this would pop up and upend all of us."

"Oh, honey," Sunny answered, "it's just one day. One glorious day. We've had them and we have years left."

"We? I've been wondering if you would ever ride again."

Sunny cast a glance back toward the grandstand. "It will never be enough just to watch. The cramped little life Mama wanted for me, I couldn't live it. And I'll never be able to settle in it now, even with everything that's happened to me. I'll see you in Kalispell. If not before."

"Not much time for you to get ready."

"What made you think I wasn't ready today?"

The corner of Ruth's mouth twisted in a half-smile. They were still rivals. They'd be rivals until one of them couldn't throw her leg over a saddle anymore.

Scott joined them and after the hug which he returned, just a little, she wondered where had her boy gone? She'd missed it at Mollie's funeral—how the soft, boyish face had turned into a man's broad forehead and square jaw. Planted in front of her was a muscled cowboy no different from the hundreds of them who had come and gone in Frontier Park over twenty-some years.

"Here, Mama, you need a handkerchief?"

"No, put it away. Just dust in my eyes is all."

Scott glanced at the knot of people around the O'Malleys. "Do you have plans right now? I thought you'd want to visit the grave."

She followed his gaze. "No, I don't have plans."

Eight-year-old Beatrice was at his side. She gazed up at her mother. "Can I go with them?"

"No, we're going home. Scott would like some time alone with his mother."

"Can't they spend time at our house?"

"They're going out to Mollie's grave."

"I want to go."

Ruth looked more exasperated than she had ever seemed with a horse. "It's not a playground. You'll be very bored."

"Scotty, I can go, can't I?"

"Beatrice," said Sunny, "how lovely you are. Braids and ribbons and such a lovely shirt. Did Mama make it?"

Beatrice looked confused.

"She means her mama, Grandma Francine," said Scott. "Mama, you know she stopped sewing years ago. C'mon, Bea, if you're coming."

On the drive out to the cemetery, Beatrice did more talking than Scott did. She had a horse, a spotted paint, that she was already riding. She wanted to do just what her mama did. Racing and bronc riding. She'd already raced with Scott and beaten him once.

"You know my mama's a champion, too, right?" said Scott.

Surprised, Beatrice looked closely at Sunny. "I didn't see her ride."

"I didn't ride today. But I will soon."

"Have you beat my mama?"

"A few times."

"I didn't know anyone could beat my mama, except that girl that rode today."

"That girl won all-around champion because she was the winner in every one of her events," said Scott.

"I could be all-around champion."

Scott snorted. "You have to be able to pick yourself up out of the dirt when you fall off, not sit there and bawl like you do."

"Daddy says I ride like a beautiful princess."

"Daddy?" said Sunny.

"Arthur was released just this spring," Scott said tersely.

"And he's there at the ranch?"

Scott clamped his jaw and stared straight ahead. There was no response.

"Tell me, Beatrice, does anyone ever speak about your uncle Tad?"

"Mama," said Scott, "let it go."

"I've seen a lot of pictures of him. There's pictures of you and him together. How come you're not with us anymore?"

Scott jumped in. "Ruth runs the ranch now. Grandpa's out of it. No more exhibition shows. Other than Ruth's events, we just raise cattle. Yes, Uncle Arthur is home. He's become foreman. And he works hard. He doesn't trouble anyone."

"Well, the reason you don't have a father...."

"I don't need a history lesson. Beatrice doesn't need it, either."

"Just when you were of an age to really get to know him...."

Scott shouted over her. "I've heard all I want to hear from Grandpa. Everyone looks at me like I'm supposed to spend my life worshiping his memory. That's what Grandpa does. I wish everyone would see that his life has nothing to do with me.

"Look, we're here," he added.

Once the pickup cut off, the sound of wind tossing the cottonwood leaves filled the cab. After the clamor of the rodeo grounds, the sound seemed disconsolate and lonesome. The rustling crescendoed almost to a roar, then dropped to a murmur, only to rise again in another group of trees. Above the trees, the clouds billowed. Their undersides flamed as if someone had torched them, and the colors bled across the sky.

Sunny expected the vision to return and fold around her like fog. She listened for the thunder and hail, for the baby's screams. There was only that breeze romping back and forth in the trees. Nothing but that. Tomorrow, planning would begin for the next rodeo and then the next and the vision would never return.

How queer that she missed it.

A lone meadowlark sang on a tombstone. Rows of stones marched into the distance, intoning the inscriptions of the lost ones who lay beneath. If only the chorus were louder, loud as the wind, thought Sunny, then maybe she could hear Mollie's voice.

"Dezzie is here, too," said Beatrice.

"She is?" Sunny glanced at Scott.

Scott shrugged. "She died last winter, after Mollie."

"Why didn't someone tell me?"

"Grandma Francine can't see to write anymore. And even if she could have, she was too heartbroke. She loved Dezzie as much as she did Mollie."

"Someone could have telegraphed me. Why am I saying 'someone'? You could have done that. I loved her, too."

"We're telling you now. Isn't that enough?"

"Why the bitterness, Scott? Have they turned you against me?"

"Here it is," said Beatrice.

Sunny hadn't yet seen the stone, so she was surprised by the white marble with her daughter's name and dates. Time locked in brackets which even the stoutest heart couldn't break.

The inscription read, *Unable are the loved to die, for love is immortality.*

"Aunt Sunny, don't cry. She's gone to live with Our Father, that's what Grandma Francine says, where she won't ever be sick again."

"Is that what Grandma Francine says?"

"She cries, too, but she says it's only because she misses Mollie so much. I miss her, too."

This is not my daughter. Sunny wiped her eyes. "It's a beautiful stone. Did Grandpa Sam pay for it?"

"Yes, he did," said Scott. "And after that, Aunt Ruth told me Mollie wasn't even a Pickering. You never told me that. Why? Who was Mollie's daddy? Were you even married to him?"

Sunny stared at him, realizing that with her absence, the Pickerings could recite her history as they saw fit.

"Of course, I was. Mollie's daddy and I were young. Too young at the time. Your daddy, the one you seem to want to get away from, said he would always treat Mollie as his own. What's the difference? She was your sister all the same."

"Why did you leave us, Mama?"

"Because...." What to say to her eighteen-year-old son? The truth? About Sam's advances and Ruth's spitefulness? How would it help him now? There he stood—blondish whiskers on his chin—on the brink of scouting out his own path, as she had done at his age. No. Competing with the Pickerings for her son's heart and mind wouldn't do him any good at all.

"Your father and I—we were performers. With Tad gone, I still had my life ahead of me. I still wanted to go on. It was no life for you traveling from rodeo to rodeo. Begging food from bars and restaurants. Stuck in a hotel room while I looked for horses to break to put a little extra money in my pocket. Or for riding rings where I could practice. And what if I'd been injured while you were with me? Or killed? You know that can happen. It does happen. What would have become of you alone and in a strange town?

"Whatever had happened here, I knew they were going to take care of you. You were Tad Pickering's son, and his daddy was going to see to it that you had the best. A ranch all your own. Warm and well-fed every day. All the horses in the world to ride. Pick one out any day of the week."

Scott wiped his own eyes. "It was no kind of life here without you and Daddy."

"I thought you loved to ride and rope just like him."

"I loved him, but I'm not him. I'm not anything like him. I couldn't win anything. Didn't you see I wasn't on the roster this year? I'm never going back to it. Never. Uncle Arthur—he understands. He says he knows how I feel."

"Because he's trying to fill your daddy's shoes, the daddy that he..."

"He's apologized for that, Mama."

"So you know. Somebody's told you."

"Aunt Ruth. A long time ago. And she said she was sorry, too. She said she'd never be able to forgive herself."

The shadows spilled out from under the cottonwoods swallowing row after row of graves. Beatrice broke a sprig of larkspur and placed it on Mollie's tombstone.

"Well, I'm sorry, too, if you missed me and I wasn't here. I thought I was doing what was best."

"Is that true? Other mamas stay at home and tend to their children."

"That's not true," said Beatrice. "My mama doesn't stay home, but I'm never lonesome because I've got you."

Scott turned to her. "You always have something to say, don't you?" He kissed the top of her head and slipped an arm over her shoulder.

And there they all stood as the shadows overtook them.

Eventually, she met Hazel O'Malley. The two of them did an exhibition show the next year at Frontier Days 1920. When she had proposed it to Hazel, the girl had seemed agreeable, but by that time Hazel had eclipsed all other cowgirls. If Hazel appeared at any rodeo, she was almost guaranteed to win at least one event, if not all. Sunny thought Hazel must have taken pity on her as an older performer, barely scraping by. They worked up a routine that ended with each of them jumping Model T roadsters at the same time. With passengers in the vehicles.

Despite the success of the performance, they didn't repeat it. That day, Sunny had worn a costume she had made. She had taken her split riding skirt, slit open the legs and inserted strips of deer hide as panels. She wore a fringed leather tunic over that with eagle feathers sewn in at the chest. Hazel hadn't seen the costume prior to the performance, and she looked startled at Sunny's appearance. Hazel wore long pants—men's trousers!—that showed off her slender legs and buttocks—as shocking as that was—and a sailor blouse.

"That's what you're wearing?" asked Hazel.

"Well, yes. You must have seen me in pictures dressed like this."

"I know you're from Nebraska. Were you raised on the reservation?"

"No, I was raised on a homestead, and back then we wore long skirts every day. I've always believed in being...different...so people will remember me. These outfits—they're who Sunny Gale is."

"Have you ever picked up a magazine? *Ladies' Home Journal? McCall's?*"

"No."

"Fashion—that's not something you're familiar with?"

"I'm not sure what you mean. I thought fashion was something that's important in places like New York City where people don't have farms and livestock to attend to. Horses don't care how I look."

"Cows and horses don't buy tickets. People buy tickets. And the people you are performing for all read fashion magazines and they want to look like those women, and they want other women to look like those women. They don't want to see women dressed in skins. And what's on your face?"

"Makeup, like yours."

"And you have no lipstick?"

"Yours is pretty cherry-colored."

"That is the way it is worn. At least, let's redo your makeup."

After all Hazel's fuss, it hadn't made a difference. The crowd had gone wild as Hazel O'Malley and Sunny Gale jumped automobiles side-by-side.

Damn Hazel's "fashion." As if those magazines she'd spoken of ever made it out to Wyoming farms and ranches, anyhow.

Sunny wore her same costume to the Carbon County Stampede in Rawlins two weeks later. In the bronc riding, she drew a small appaloosa bronc named Squall, not much bigger than a pony, but she scored high and won the event. The pickup cowboy congratulated her and said, "Meet me afterwards?"

Too bad Hazel wasn't around to see this young buckaroo's interest, even if Sunny was wearing her "skins" as Hazel had called them. Although, in truth, she had adopted all of Hazel's makeup tips, including eyeliner and mascara.

"Sure."

His face was lean with sharp cheekbones, brown eyes, stubble on his cheeks. Roughened ranch boy come to town for a Saturday night. And Rawlins was more spirited than it used to be, in more ways than one, thanks to Prohibition. Instead of the usual talk of water and cattle prices, the town was abuzz with plans of where the parties and booze would be. Concealing drinking from the authorities, if only superficially, had boosted its thrill.

"Almeida's Auto Repair?" the cowboy asked.

She read his face. It was clear that's where he'd found liquor.

"Sure."

She found the place at twilight after she'd picked up her trophy belt buckle and cash. The windows in the garage doors had been blackened. A boy, who must have been Almeida's son, acted as the lookout, scanning the streets and motioning people inside through a side door. Almeida, still with grease on his face, served the drinks behind an oak counter. Tires had been stacked for seating, and although the place reeked of gasoline and rubber, a drink or two cured the ambience. Cowboys and cowgirls mingled around the welding equipment and tool shelves. One couple was kissing in the back seat of an automobile.

As far as Sunny could tell, the party would last until dawn. Almeida said he had barrels stored in a root cellar that he'd camouflaged with junked cars.

The ranch boy stood by himself leaning against an oil barrel, a country bumpkin if ever there was one. That wouldn't matter, as long as he had money.

"You're not drinking," she said.

He shrugged. "Don't care to. I just came here to wait for you. I wasn't sure you'd really come."

"I would never leave my pickup man high and dry."

She'd expected more enthusiasm at her flirtation, but if this one anticipated a romantic finale to their evening, he didn't show it. His eyes were more soulful. That was okay. She'd known those outwardly bashful cowboys, too.

"Would you like to go for a walk?" he asked.

"A walk?"

"It's awful loud in here, unless you want another one." He gestured to the tumbler in her hand. "Outside it's a beautiful evening. There won't be many more like it before winter comes."

"All right. Let's take a walk."

"Are you sure? " He studied her. "You look like I've disappointed you."

"No. It's all right. We'll take a walk."

Back on the street, he put his hands lightly on her shoulders to step to the outside, but he left space between them. He didn't offer her his arm. He walked with his head bowed, hands shoved in his pockets. The reddened skin at the back of his neck was peeling. When was the last time this boy had sought out female society?

"Are you from around here? I've never seen you at any rodeos before."

"I live 'bout a day and a half ride from here. I've got a ranch north of Medicine Bow. I heard they needed pickup men for this rodeo, and I could use the money, so I rode over." A shy little smile played over his face. "Never imagined I'd get to meet the great Sunny Gale."

"That's kind of you. With so many performers nowadays, I don't expect to stand out anymore."

"My dad saw your first bronc ride in Cheyenne. He said you rode better than any of the men that day. And I bet you were just a girl back then."

She bridled at the mention of her age and then sluffed it aside. Bumpkin hadn't meant it as an insult. "Your dad? How old are you?"

"Twenty-five."

"Well, I guess that makes me old enough to be your mother."

"Does that mean you'd rather be with someone else right now?"

"No, no," she lied. She looked ahead. They were just yards away from the train depot where the town ended. Maybe when this "walk" wrapped up, the boy would head for his ranch, and she could circle back to Almeida's and find other company.

"Rawlins doesn't have as much to offer as Cheyenne," he said.

"Don't worry that I'm missing anything. I've been to more small towns than big ones. It's only what happens in the arena that matters. Outside of that, it doesn't make a difference where I am."

"Beg pardon, Miz Gale, but why do you keep doing it?"

"I just won forty dollars. Are you thinking I should be put out to pasture?"

"I didn't mean it that way. I'm just asking if there are times when you'd like to be more settled."

"'Settled?' When people talk about 'settled,' they mean the washing and cleaning they wish you would do. I never found anything in the 'settled' life to my taste."

"I guess I understand. You want your freedom. But I've always felt freedom living on the plains. It might be a hard life, but no one's over me. Seems like you're locked into traveling place to place, working like hell to stay on top and whether you win or lose comes down to luck, no matter how good you are. Eight seconds and you lose, no money. That looks meaner than my life. Lonelier, too. What I gain or lose, it's all my own doing. My only limit is myself."

How many more men would she have to listen to before she could go home to Laroche who would never ask her to explain herself.

"I've got someone. I'm not lonely."

"A husband?"

"No, it's my boss in New Mexico. I work for him during the winters."

"Do you...are the two of you together?"

Sunny laughed. "What a nosey boy you are! No, we're not together like that. On Laroche's place, The Purple Orchid, I sleep in the barn. We're just good friends accustomed to one another."

"Sleeping in a barn. That's the freedom you've got to have?"

"I don't have any complaints with my life."

They'd reached the depot. Their conversation had blunted the alcohol, leaving her somber. With or without him, she realized she didn't feel like going back to Almeida's.

"I know this wasn't much of a walk, but we can sit out here on the benches for a little while if you'd like," he said.

On the other side of the tracks lay miles of empty prairie. Her next rodeo was in Logan. She would take the train from here, meet the rodeo organizers, find stockmen looking for cowboys or cowgirls to race their horses, find a hotel, another watering hole, another cowboy.

She hoped the next cowboy would be more fun than this one was.

"I never did ask you your name."

"Oh, I'm Clem Albright."

She held out her hand. "Pleased to meet you, Clem Albright."

He hesitated, trying to gauge whether she was being sincere. At last, he took her hand, and she was surprised at his touch. Not a grip but the gentlest squeeze. Tenderness.

"I know this might sound too sudden, but I'd like it if you came hunting with me in the fall."

"Hunting?"

"Elk hunting."

"By then, I'll have gone back to New Mexico."

"You'll finish up the rodeo season in Pendleton, at the Roundup, right?"

"Right. I always go there."

"It can't be too much out of your way to come back through here. You can take the train through Medicine Bow, stay at the Virginian Hotel and I'll pick you up from there."

"This is pretty sudden."

"Please don't take offense, Miz Gale. And maybe you're not interested. I just thought I might be able take you on a different kind of trip—one where you don't have to perform for a crowd. A trip you could just enjoy."

"All right. It's an engagement, cowboy."

Had she spent the night with him, she might not have returned. She might have dismissed his invitation as time-wasting foolery and, aching for Laroche and Jack after her disappointing rout at Pendleton, she might have bypassed Medicine Bow with no word to him at all, leaving him standing at the Virginian all by himself. It had been two years since her accident, two years since Mollie's death. Had she lain in his arms that night in Rawlins, she might have thought that she'd had her fill of the Bumpkin and that she'd rather reflect on her losses, all of them, back in the crisp air of a New Mexico winter.

But after they'd made their arrangements that evening, Clem had left. He'd needed to start out for home, he had said. If he started out that evening, he could make it home by next nightfall. He shrugged off the suggestion of a warm bed. He didn't need to spend the money and he was fine with camping.

He might have been simple, but with the notion stuck in her mind that she'd left a stone unturned, she had to go back. *Hadn't he invited her after all?*

The morning of their meeting, she wondered if she was the one who'd been abandoned. She hadn't slept the whole night and had risen several hours before dawn. Still, after the kitchen opened and she'd downed a cup of coffee, she didn't see him anywhere. Other travelers prepared to leave. The bellhop helped them haul their bags to the train station. While she stood on the hotel porch shivering in the chill, the train to Cheyenne came and went.

I should have gotten on it, she thought. She watched as it chugged into the blinding sunrise. At least waiting there, the sun would soon warm her.

And then he rounded the corner of the hotel with an extra horse for her and three pack horses. His chin was tucked into the collar of his wool coat and pipe smoke hung in the air around him.

He pulled up at the hitching post.

"You look like you thought I wasn't coming."

"That is what I thought."

"I was cursing myself for bringing the extra horse because I figured you wouldn't show up."

"It seems we have misjudged one another."

"I'm sorry if I made you worry," he said with a smile. "We don't have time to dally. We need to be on the mountain by dark."

They set off on the wagon trail south of town. After an hour, the day was as warm as a day in August, and they stopped to pack up their bulky coats. When she set her foot back in the stirrup, she felt a surge of enthusiasm for this adventure. The sky was too wide and shimmering to want anything else other than to ride through country that opened before them mile by mile. Minutes and hours ceased to matter. Only sensations were important: the sun on her forearms, the last grasshoppers buzzing in the shade of the sagebrush.

"How'd you do in Pendleton?" Clem asked.

"It was a bust. I guess you saw my last win for the season."

"That doesn't change my opinion of you one whit."

"And what is that opinion?"

"You're a champion. Through and through. Everything about you."

"You don't know that. You don't know anything about me."

"I know what I've seen and heard. You hung on to your dreams. You never gave up on them through all the down times. Most people wouldn't have the stamina to do what you do year after year. Don't know any other word for that but 'champion.'"

"You talk about it like I'd been given a choice. I never felt like I had one. Doing something you feel bound to do—that's not so extraordinary, is it?"

"It is when there's a rabble out there who believes what you do is scandalous. A lot of 'em say it's a sin the way you cowgirls ride and dress. No 'decorum' to it. No guidance from your fathers and husbands." He grinned at her.

Sunny smiled back. "Aw, I don't worry about that bunch. They write letters to the editor and then they buy tickets to the show."

"Well, I'm a lucky man, lucky that you decided to give me a chance."

"Give you a chance? How?"

"By going with me when you wanted to be somewhere else."

Well, yes, hours ago she'd been anxious to be on her way to The Purple Orchid, but now, as the range fell silent under the glaring sun, she wanted to linger and let her thoughts decouple from her life. People, places, horses—they fled the enclosure of her mind and stampeded away. She couldn't hold on to them. Snatches of voices heard over her thirty-nine years hung in the air before dissipating.

Once, riding the rapture of those early victories in Cheyenne, she had believed that she was special, unique. Greater glory and fame were just around the corner. With the whole panorama of her life at a distance, all she saw was just an ordinary pioneer daughter in a scramble to fill her heart. Oh, young Hannah had been right to reject Francine's plans for her. How miserable she would have been in the Mangum house chained between stove and washboard, but what had been the worth of this calling after all? With its discomforts and pain. Yes—she had to admit—loneliness, too. Had Hannah's early passion justified this existence?

The least she could say was that here and there her heart had been filled—filled to the very brim. Not often, but enough.

"Are you still back there?" Clem called.

"Yes."

"You're so quiet I thought you dozed off in the saddle."

I am as far away as I can be, she thought, in places you can't go.

By the time they started up the mountain, the day's heat had faded. A tart breeze rattled the sagebrush. The horses heaved up the rocky trail. Sunny looked up and saw groves of aspen along the ridgeline, flaring gold, their leaves sounding like chimes. Even with her coat back on, she was getting cold. Her musings drained away, leaving her numb.

They dismounted among the lodgepole pines at the summit. Behind them in the east, the plains sank into an ocean of dusk. Tiny homestead lights flickered against the gloom. In the west, the last sun rays splintered over the land, setting the ridges aflame while shadows flooded the gullies. One last crescent of white fire burned on the horizon, sputtered, then vanished, and overhead, stars by the dozens popped out of the dark.

"This is magnificent," said Sunny.

"I'm glad I could show it to you."

"I'm glad I came."

Even with the dusk, she could still make out the line of his cheekbones. She could still feel the warmth of his eyes on her.

"You're cold," he said.

"A little."

"I'll get a fire started."

While he set up their camp, she secured and fed the horses. Once again, he disrupted her expectations. To her surprise, he put up two tents, not one. How had she misread his intentions? His eyes had been on her so intensely just now, she hadn't imagined it. Still, he'd said nothing the entire day to lead her to believe that this outing was a prelude to love-making. She felt shamed by her assumptions, especially in the company of a boy who could choose from unblemished girls his own age. In her vanity, she'd minimized the difference in their ages. He'd been clear on how much he admired her—she was certain of those feelings—but that was all. She was a matron to him, not a lover.

Had he brought her along to show off his skill? Why would her praise matter? They'd done nothing more than share superficial details of their lives. Nothing profound or inspiring. If anything, they were guarded with one another. Why had she been his chosen companion?

Clem fixed their supper of canned stew. Sunny was ravenous. The first few spoonfuls tasted better than any food she'd ever eaten. Her mood lifted even as she felt herself falling asleep next to the fire, warmed inside and out. Even if he wasn't going to guide her to his bed, the trip had been a pleasant interlude, a welcome pause after the rodeo season. He had been right about that.

A high-pitched whistle, close to a squeal, pierced the night air. She jumped.

"Is that a wolf?"

Clem smiled. "Wolves have been run out of here for a long time. That's a bull elk."

Another elk bugled farther away. After a few moments, she grew accustomed to their voices. These clarions were the right sounds for fall, the right sounds to mark the end of green pastures, the coming of snowdrifts, the slow freezing of water, earth, and sky. They were a tribute to the year that had been, a call to take heed of what was to come.

Clem stood to pick up the tin plates. "Still bothered by the sound?'

"No. I'm beginning to enjoy it."

"You're worn out. You've had long travels and I've given you a long day. Go on into your tent and get some sleep."

"Let me help clean up."

He shook his head. "No, it's all right."

She had thought that sleep would overtake her the moment she lay down, but instead, her eyes snapped open. With every exhalation, the tent filled with grief and longing until it pressed against her, suffocating her.

In the light that remained from the embers, she found his tent, found the hides around him, found his warm body inside.

"Is everything all right?" he asked.

"I was too cold."

"I thought I brought you enough hides."

"Sorry, I'm still cold."

He didn't move to pull her in. He seemed to drift off. She circled his chest with her forefinger and as his breath deepened, she circled his ribs, his belly. Then she moved her hand down and found him hard. He uttered a little groan.

"You want me. I knew it."

He grabbed her wrist and pulled it away.

"Listen. I have tried hard to get you to understand that that's not why I brought you here. Taking advantage of you—that's not what this is about. I don't want to sway you. I don't want something from you that I haven't earned. I thought you were worn ragged from a life where you never let yourself just *be*. You're always pushing to be 'Sunny Gale.'

"I wanted to show you that outside of the arena, it's not all drudgery. There's beauty beyond what you've ever imagined."

"You thought I didn't know that already?"

"Maybe, but the woman I picked off that bronc in Rawlins was all played out." He released her hand.

"I'm sorry if I've offended you."

"How can I be offended? I've been pursued by a legendary bronc rider. And a beautiful one, at that.

"Now settle down. We've got to be up before dawn." He crossed his arms over his chest and went back to sleep.

She thought she understood him now. The pinch of rejection lingered until she herself fell asleep into dreams of elk bugling, elk moving through the woods. She was following them on horseback. Though there were hundreds, their steps were soft as falling snow. The woods ended and she pulled her horse up, but the herd kept running through the sky, bounding up and over the stars. She watched them disappear, the sound of them fading until the only sound was wind among the trees.

And then there was nothing until she felt the scratch of Clem's beard on her neck and kisses along her temple and then his calloused hands on her skin. He was taking all of her, all the physical pain, the losses, the grieving into himself. And as he lifted her up on wave after wave of pleasure, her one thought was: *This is where I belong.*

She woke to his voice outside the tent. It seemed as if less than an hour had passed.

"Sunny, you gotta get up."

"It's the middle of the night."

"No, it's time to go."

When she stepped outside, the stars were still thick above them. Only the barest pink light radiated along the horizon. Clem had a small fire going and handed her a cup of coffee.

They blew steam off their cups, each waiting for the other to speak.

"Did you sleep all right?"

She laughed. "Did you?"

He poured the rest of his coffee out in the fire. "Best rest in a long time."

They mounted in the dark, and as the light spread around them, Sunny saw that they were on a ridge overlooking a bowl-shaped meadow below. On the east side the meadow was ringed by pines, and among the shadows cast by the trees, the elk started to emerge, one at a time, cows, and calves.

Clem halted and pulled her off her horse. "We need to be below this ridge where they can't see us."

They moved the horses off the crest and Clem reached into one of the saddlebags and pulled out a hunting bow.

"You're going to hunt with a bow?"

"It's been done for thousands of years," he said with a grin.

"I've never seen anyone hunt without a gun."

"And you might never see a successful bow hunt if you don't shush up and stay down. If you want to watch, that's fine, but you have to hold the horses and keep them from being seen."

He crouched and made his way around the boulders. Occasionally, he would angle up to the crest to check his distance. He stopped when he'd reached the point closest to the meadow. She saw him aim at the nearest cow when a bull stepped out of the woods and sniffed the cow's rump. She took a step forward and he followed. His lips curled at her scent. Vapor rose from his nostrils.

Clem had shifted his aim to the bull. The air was still as a layer of ice over a pond. Sunny rubbed her numb hands against her chaps. The possibility that Clem would shoot and kill the bull was only one of a thousand possibilities in that moment. Any one of them could come to pass. Any of them could mean that the bull would endure into the next moment and the next. Her own beating heart wouldn't alter the outcome one whit. She held her breath.

Thousands of possibilities. Pick one.

The cows farthest out in the meadow stiffened and pricked their ears and Sunny followed their gaze. A pack of coyotes was crossing in front of them. The cows started to flinch and turn to the woods. The bull, curious, moved alongside the cow.

Sunny looked toward Clem. He had already shot. Sunny let her breath go and the arrow pierced the bull's hide. At first, she didn't believe it had wounded him because he took one step and then another. And then toppled.

The herd disappeared. The coyotes raced toward the opposite ridge.

Clem ran back, stumbling over the rocks.

"Now I need a gun to shoot at those coyotes."

"What for?"

"I don't want them scavenging my kill."

"They're gone."

He grabbed his rifle, aimed, and fired at the

last coyote. He missed. The coyotes flew up over the ridge. No live creature remained in the meadow.

Clem gestured to the dead bull below. "What did you think?"

She struggled over how to answer. She was awed by the raw power in his shot and grieved that such a magnificent life had been severed faster than the barest thought, the barest breath.

The sun was overhead now and all around her another fall day radiated golden light. Soon, she would remove her coat and feel the warmth on her forearms once more. Before dawn, she had had no connection to this animal, didn't even know of its existence. Yet the world, full as it was, now lacked the essence of this creature and the only mark to its passing would be her recollection of it.

"It was amazing. You were amazing," was all she could say. Sensations flooded her again of their shared darkness, of his beard, his hands. She laughed out loud. "So much has just happened."

He pulled her close and kissed her. The skin of his neck felt cold, but she could smell the sweat in his clothes. When they broke apart, he touched her face. "I wish I could lay you down right here. But we can't. We've got to get moving."

The next hours, even as the day warmed, were spent in butchering the carcass and packing the meat. By midmorning, when they were ready to leave, the wind turned blustery, and thick clouds scuttled across the sky. The warmth of the past day and a half blew away along with the summer that had been. No escaping the onset of winter now.

Still, they had to take their time descending

the mountain. By the time they had reached the plain, the wind roared, blowing grit in their faces. They pressed on, anxious to reach Medicine Bow by nightfall.

It was after dark when they saw the lights ahead. Sunny felt cramped, cold, hungry. Her back and neck ached. She'd never thought she'd come across a time when she longed to be out of the saddle.

They pulled up in front of the hotel and Clem helped her down. She stumbled a little and he grabbed her arm.

"Are you all right?"

"I'm fine. Just stiffness, that's all."

He followed her up the porch steps. The intensity of the two days they had spent together had drained away in these last grueling hours. They were too numbed to speak. She thought she knew a way to break the renewed awkwardness between them.

"Do you want to spend the night here?"

"Naw, I gotta be on my way with this meat. I can't stay."

His words made the cold all the more unbearable. "Listen, Clem. You read me right. I'm grateful that you thought of me for this trip. I hope I wasn't a burden."

"No, Miz Gale. It was my pleasure to have you with me. I'm the fortunate one."

"The world outside an arena. You were right. Seeing it through you has brought me some peace. A couple months ago, I thought you were such a rough kid. Now, I want to know you better."

"We each have a long winter ahead of us."

Through the lights coming from the lobby,

she saw the glint in his eyes. They mirrored her own longing.

He turned and went back down the steps. "Hope you'll come back through here."

"I will."

He mounted and turned, all the horses behind him. They soon vanished in the dark. She listened for their hoofbeats while she imagined him turning the corner out of town, back out into the wind for God knew how many more miles. She hoped he would reach his ranch before the blizzards began.

Two days later, she met Laroche at the crossroads. She took comfort that nothing had changed in her absence, not the bar, the repair shop, or the outhouse. The only change was that Laroche and the cook were waiting in a rusted pickup. The automobile was gone.

Laroche gestured to the repair shop. "Guillermo found this wreck on the side of the road. He fixed it up and I bought it off him for twenty dollars. Helluva thing, isn't it? You sit so much higher off the road."

She threw her bags in the back and slid in next to the cook. Laroche climbed in after her. He leaned his elbow on the open passenger window, not minding the chilly breeze. He turned to look at her.

"How was it?"

She thought she'd become accustomed to his piercing stare after all these years. It made her squirm now. He was so close, too close to evade. Could he bore through her skull and read what had happened? The nights that she'd spent with other men—that wouldn't have bothered or surprised him. But would he discover that she'd found one who was different?

"All right. The season kind of went bust on me. I didn't come home with much money."

"What took you so long to get here?"

She broke from his gaze and stared straight ahead. "We might sit higher off the road, Laroche, but the ride's a lot rougher. Might as well ride home on a bronc."

"You found a gentleman."

"'Gentleman'? What a kidder you are! You know well as I do that after drinks and dinner, those cowboys aren't too spellbinding. I stopped to see Eleanor in Lander. That's all."

13

February 12th

That lie she told Laroche was ten years ago, but now it's stuck to her memories of him. She jabs her pitchfork in the hay and tosses a load over the wagon to the bawling cattle. It was his own fault—the old codger. Hadn't he shooed her out of his bedroom? Not once, but twice! What did he have a right to expect? He had no right—damn him!— to believe she'd keep on coming back every fall to roost in his barn. If that had been his expectation, well then, he had deserved to be lied to.

At the time, that lie had gnawed through her every night as she lay awake staring up at the barn rafters. How aggravating that it still plagues her now.

SUNNY GALE

Even if she deserved reproach for lying—after all he'd done for her—it wasn't as if she would have ever placed him above her career. She hadn't done that for anyone. And never would. He knew that. Would he have joined her every summer on the rodeo circuit? Picture him leaning against the rail at one of her exhibitions or rodeos. A damn ridiculous sight and not just because he was a cripple. He would have hated it. He would have rolled cigarette after cigarette, his resentment at the noise and the crowds on low boil. It wouldn't have mattered how dazzling her performances were. He'd have been hankering after his porch chair across from the big cottonwood at The Purple Orchid. And she would have come to hate him knowing that was all he wanted.

Sunny didn't admit her involvement with Clem until the telegram she sent to Laroche the following September from Medicine Bow. She burst into tears while dictating the news of her marriage. She had wanted to end the message saying, "I love you and I'll miss you forever." The words sounded so cheap, so unworthy of what he really deserved from her. At last, she had settled on, "Best to The Purple Orchid. Sunny Gale Albright."

He never answered her telegram.

Laroche would have raised an eyebrow that she had taken Clem's last name. Before balling up the telegram and throwing it away, he would have said, "Old girl, I hope he deserves you."

What would he say if he knew what had become of her? Would he pity her? Would he try to help her? Or was he bitter about her desertion?

Was Laroche even still alive? She wanted him and Jack to be there on The Purple Orchid, just as she'd left them.

She sweeps the last wisps of hay off the wagon, shades her eyes against the glare, and looks over the range for some sign of life. There, on the other side of the gully, a black spot in the snow. A horse. It wallows down through the snow in the gully and lunges up the other side, no more than half a mile away from her now.

Cocoa-colored. A white blaze down its nose.

Just like...

Zephira?

The day after Christmas at The Purple Orchid there was a rodeo in Lamy. The plaza had filled with people of all colors, groups of them together, white and dark-skinned, drinking, laughing, sharing news. There was a feeling of relief at having survived another year. The air smelled of fried sopapillas and tamales.

All The Purple Orchid Ranch buckaroos had entered one event or another. Sunny had entered the women's relay race. There was no formal track. Contestants would race one mile south along the railroad tracks, pick up their second horse and race the mile back.

Laroche said to her, "Is Jack going to be your first or second horse?"

"Second."

"Have you noticed he's slowing down?"

"If he gets off ahead of the pack, we should be okay."

"These Navajo ladies who've traveled a day or so to get here aren't going to give it away to you. And the ground's not flat and smooth, like you're used to. You don't have time to dodge the greasewood. You'll have to plow through it. They are used to that. Their ponies are used to it."

"What are you saying, Laroche? Are you saying I don't stand a chance?"

He ground out his cigarette butt in the dirt. "Just want you to be ready."

"It's like you think I've never done this before."

"I want to hold Jack for you at the mile mark."

"It's not a good plan. You don't know what might happen out there. A horse could get loose. It's not like you can get out of the way."

"It's my horse."

"Suit yourself."

The field was large—twenty-two—white, Spanish, Indian. Sunny couldn't remember when she'd seen so many different riding costumes and hats on a group of women. The gun went off and her first mount hesitated too long before lunging forward. A Navajo girl on an Appaloosa pushed in front of her.

With so many horses, Sunny was blinded by dust and pelted by rocks. Between the horses and the greasewood, she couldn't find an opening. Ahead, she could see the line of men holding the second horses. Laroche was taller than any of the others.

She was off her horse before he'd stopped. She released the latigo, ripped off the saddle. Just as she'd predicted, a horse had gotten loose. It ran through the line and bumped into Jack, knocking

Laroche down. She grabbed Jack's reins herself and threw her saddle on. By the time she was in the saddle, ten or more horses were already ahead of her.

She raised her quirt, but Jack didn't need it. He plunged through the greasewood, closing the distance between her and the remaining horses. She passed them, one after another, and now she was neck and neck with the leader, the same Navajo girl who had cut her off at the beginning.

The girl was young, no more than fifteen. She wore deerskin breeches and a maroon vest. Her pigtails flew out behind her. As they raced stride for stride, Sunny thought of being fifteen again, of horses, open country, open sky all new and beckoning. Had this girl even kissed a boy yet? The girl glanced at her and raised her quirt. Sunny started to pick hers up, then let it drop, and the girl beat her by a stride.

"You let her win," said Laroche later as they sat drinking outside the El Ortiz hotel. Dark had fallen early. Torches burned and a band played. People lingered, reluctant to separate from the warmth and light and venture off into the coming of winter.

"How would you know? You were in the dirt. It's a wonder you didn't get trampled and killed."

"I saw you take off. I was sure you could catch them."

"You said he was getting slow."

"If I didn't try to motivate you, you weren't going to work for it."

"We just got bested, that's all. Just like you said would happen."

"You weren't bested."

"If you think you got it all figured out while

you were face down in the dirt, I'm not going to argue with you."

He took another drink and seemed to forget the banter. He shifted to listen to the men outside the bar whose jokes and laughter grew louder. Then he faced her, his eyes hidden in the shadows.

"I've put the gun away."

"What are you talking about?"

"The shotgun I kept in the bedroom."

Sounds bounced all around them while they regarded each other in silence.

"That's not all. The photograph of the woman that you saw. She's not there anymore."

Oh, Laroche, you're too late.

Back at The Purple Orchid, they separated. She lay down on her cot and the image of Clem Albright hovered above her. She could reach out and feel his beard against her palm. He took her palm and kissed it.

She wrote him letters at least once a week. It was impossible to hide them from Laroche since he was the one who went to the post office every week. He would put on his reading glasses and hold up the envelope—"Clem Albright, General Delivery, Medicine Bow, Wyoming." He'd look at her over the top of his glasses but didn't say a word. As time passed and no return letters came, she was grateful that he withheld his remarks.

When the thaw began, she became impatient to leave The Purple Orchid. If only she could get away, she was bound to find Clem at some rodeo somewhere. There had to be an explanation for why he hadn't written. Maybe he couldn't write. Maybe he couldn't read. Anything but that his feelings for her had subsided or been forgotten. Surely the time they'd shared was too overpowering for either of them to set it aside. She thought of him out feeding cattle in the wind and snow. Didn't he say that they had a long winter to get through? By the time he stumbled in the door at dark, he'd been too tired to write. That was all.

She left on a warm, rainy evening after she'd gotten her pay. She didn't even say goodbye. She bribed the cook to drive her to Lamy to catch the train and she was off racing north, every mile whisking her closer to that point where she would meet Clem again.

In each town, she searched for him among the cowboys moving stock in the corrals, among the contestants behind the chutes, in the bleachers, at the dances, at the bars, of course. Other men offered her drinks and she refused. She skipped the hotels and camped at the rodeo grounds. As she lay awake watching the sky overhead, she wondered if something had happened to him. No telling what the winter might have brought. He could have lost his way in a blizzard.

Her heart sank when she didn't find him in Rawlins. No one had seen him. A few told her he was still out on his ranch, far as they knew. His demise hadn't been reported anywhere, though news of a death on the range could take years to learn. A lot of cowboys raised their eyebrows at the mention of his name. "Why do you ask?" they'd say.

She shrugged. "Nothing special. He was here last year, that's all."

Though she hated herself for doing it, she stopped back in Medicine Bow after the fall rodeo in Pendleton. It was a waste of money, a waste of time. She should beat a retreat back to The Purple Orchid, settle down, reckon with her disappointment. What would Laroche say? Nothing. Since the festival in Lamy, he'd been waiting for her to speak.

Would she tell him that she'd been a fool?

The fall weather was not as pleasant as it had been in Medicine Bow a year ago. The wind roared down the town's one street, banging every loose piece of wood or metal. She listened to the clatter as she stood on the train platform. Her images of their time together were blowing away, along with the tumbleweeds and old newspapers in the street.

How worn those images had become.

A flame persisted, nevertheless. She couldn't gut it. She found a hotel clerk willing to drive her out to the Albright ranch. He wouldn't be able to stay, he said. He had to come right back.

She had to believe that if Clem was out there, he would get her back to town. Or whoever was on the place. If worse came to worse, she would walk back. It wouldn't be the toughest thing she'd ever done.

As they drove, the road unspooled over miles of empty range. Here and there, an antelope shifted to watch them pass. Sandstone bluffs towered around them; their dour grimaces sculpted by the wind—and in moments, they were gone again, receding to shapeless lumps behind them. Land and sky stretched so far around them that direction itself lost all meaning. The boundaries of self could shatter here. The passage of day and a night and a day again were of no consequence.

The Albright ranch was set miles off the main road across country that grew more rocks than grass. The vehicle tracks dipped down a sandy gully, and as they drove up the other side, she saw the log cabin, barn, corrals, and outbuildings ahead. A picket fence, long since stripped of whitewash, fronted the little cabin.

She thanked the driver and told him she would get out, though there was no sign there was anyone around.

"You sure?" he asked.

"Yes, I'm sure."

He wheeled the car around and drove away, dust billowing behind him.

Men were working somewhere nearby. She followed the sounds to a low shed on the other side of the barn. There was Clem among half a dozen other cowboys branding cattle.

Her heart stopped as she watched him. For such a long time, he had lived only in her dreams. And now here he was, real again. His stride was so long and confident, his torso so lean. His shirttails had slipped out of his pants. His jacket was ripped at the armholes. She imagined sitting by his hearth, repairing it for him. But as he continued, absorbed in his work, she began to see how empty her fantasies had been. This land, this work, was his passion. The answer she'd sought was that he had no room for her. She was an interruption.

I shouldn't have come.

She turned to leave when he saw her and called out. He dropped the branding iron in the fire and hustled over to the rail.

"God, Sunny, what are you doing here?"

He'd never lost the feelings for her after all. She could feel his impatience at the barrier between them.

"I came to find you."

He glanced to the other men who had stopped to watch. "You fellas keep on without me."

He vaulted over the rail, and they stood face to face. His face was blackened from the branding fire and his clothes smelled of sweat and smoke, same as the last time she'd seen him.

They clasped hands.

"Is there a rodeo here in town?"

"No, it's like I said. I stopped here for you."

Uncertainty clouded his features, blotting out his pleasure at seeing her. "You shouldn't have done that. You should have forgotten about me."

"Didn't you get my letters?"

He looked down at her hands and stroked her fingers.

"I did."

"Then . . .."

There was something he didn't want to say. Surely, he wasn't so distraught at not having answered her letters.

"I was married, Sunny."

She pulled her hands away.

"You were married? When?"

He glanced back at the men and lowered his voice.

"I was married when you and I..."

"You mean you lied to me?"

"Sunny, I didn't..." He started again; his voice more strained. "I told you when we were together. I never meant to take advantage of you or lie to you. That's not why I had asked you to come.

I told you that. I wanted to share all this with you. I never meant for things to be like this and for you to get hurt."

"There was no one at the house."

"She left me."

"When?"

"Mid-March. She couldn't take another day of being alone out here is what she said. She wanted me to sell this place, sell the cattle. She wanted to me to go work at the coal mines in Hanna."

"Did you tell her about me, about us?"

"Sunny..."

"Don't 'Sunny' me."

"This is why I didn't answer your letters. Better to do my work here and let you move on."

"Well, you're right. I was the one who chose to come out here. This wasn't anything more than a losing bronc ride."

He grimaced. "It's not what I wanted."

"We'll leave it as you wanted. I'll go."

"How are you going to get back?"

"I'll walk."

"You can't do that. Take my horse in the corral. The black one. I'll pick him up at the hotel when I'm done."

"I thought people branded their calves in the spring."

"Me and these boys—we had calves born out on the range during the summer. We got together to help brand and then we'll drive all our calves to sale."

"Well, good luck."

"I'm sorry. I really mean that. You'll always be the cowgirl I'll root for over all the others."

"At least spare me the fakery, cowboy. It seems like you should owe me that."

She took the horse and rode away. When she hit the main road, the sun was already low. Miles of emptiness before her and the land all around swallowed by the twilight. She'd never reach Medicine Bow before dark. She pulled her jacket around her. She'd been so daft that she hadn't thought to wear a jacket that would be warm enough in case she had to return alone. Served her right. Now she had to hope that by dark, she'd be able to see the town lights. Otherwise, she would get lost and then she'd really be in trouble. She listened for trains. That would help her with direction, too. Forget the misguided hopes and fantasies. Focus on her direction: taking the next train out of here.

She swore then that she'd never tell any of this to Laroche.

A few pale stars arced overhead when she spotted headlights behind. The road was too bumpy for the vehicle to travel fast. She stayed ahead of it for the next mile. As it neared, she saw it was a large truck that had been modified to haul animals with wooden slats on the side and a back gate.

It was Clem.

"Sunny, stop."

"What for?"

"I'll give you a ride to town. You can load the horse in here. I built this stock truck myself."

"Not interested."

He downshifted and drove alongside her.

"You're cold, aren't you?"

"No, I'm not."

"Here, take my gloves at least."

She reached out and took the gloves. There were lights ahead at last.

"You're going to go back to New Mexico, work for that rancher down there, right?"

"Right."

"I have a better offer."

"Don't think so. You don't even have a bunkhouse."

"Accommodations are shabby, I admit. But I got this nice stock truck. And a cowgirl such as yourself could use it to haul her horses wherever she wanted to go. No more worrying about trains or catching rides. Plus, she wouldn't have to worry about riding somebody else's horses at races. She could ride her very own.

"And that's not all. The cowgirl I'm thinking of could have the use of a nice big corral to do whatever she could think to do with as many horses as she wanted."

"What would I have to do for all of this? You couldn't keep the one woman you had."

"I wouldn't try to keep you, either. You'd be free to go where you want when you want. I'll never tell you what to do. I promise that."

"You still haven't told me what my job is going to be."

"When you're home in the fall and done being the champ, your job would be to ride with me every day the sun is out and the aspen is turning. That's all."

She stopped.

"There's nothing that would make me prouder than to have Sunny Gale by my side for whatever time she'll give me."

Clem hadn't asked her to take his name. She had insisted on it.

14

February 13th

At dawn, she sees the horse is there, right at the gate in front of the house. Sunny pulls on her boots, stumbles through her boot tracks. She stops at the gate, careful not to frighten it. The knots in her mane, the ribs showing through her hide. Zephira, come back after all these years!

She slowly pushes through the gate, then sinks her fingers in the filly's winter hide. She feels the scar, the scar from Tremain's bullet. The filly nudges her, looking for food.

Zephira follows Sunny to the barn. Sunny pours out a pound of oats, untangles the mane, brushes the icicles out of her coat. She throws her arms around the filly's neck, so grateful that the horse has found her at last.

Outdoors, the wind drives plumes of snow fifty feet in the air.

Sunny retreats back indoors, wraps herself in hides. She is hungry. The cattle are bawling. She is too weary to feed them, too weary even to listen to them. A little rest here in her rocking chair and she will try to go out in a few hours.

She closes her eyes and rocks. Clem. Now that her situation has become dire, she returns to the many signs she ignored. It's a loop her mind has run so many times in the past year. Even if, during their marriage, she'd acknowledged that something was amiss, what would she have done? Would she have left him?

When they were together in Medicine Bow, he never offered more than a curt nod to other ranchers they met. "Why?" she had asked him. The answer was these men all ran larger operations than his and they resented the smaller outfits. She'd taken him at his word.

Over ten years of marriage, they never had drinks with anyone at The Virginian. Never made friends with anyone. She hadn't remarked on it.

The fall brandings of calves—Clem claimed the calves had been born over the summer. Had the same number of cows been pregnant when they had turned them out on the range that spring? She had never bothered to count them herself.

Then there were the times when she came home in between rodeos and Clem wasn't there. Sometimes he hadn't returned before she left again. Other times, he rode in covered in dust, reeking of the last night's campfire.

"Where were you?"

"Somebody's got to keep their eyes on the Albright cattle while Mrs. Albright chases her fame and fortune. It's a big range. You know that. How were your travels?"

Her thrill at seeing him drowned all her doubts. Any apprehensions she'd had were silly when here he stood: vibrant, rugged, devoted to her. "The best of them is the homecoming," she said.

"I believe you're right, Mrs. Albright." And he would unbutton her shirt right there in the yard.

There were arguments. There were days when they didn't speak to one another. But, no, if she'd known what was coming, she wouldn't have left him. It hadn't been that way with Luke. She'd left him behind without a second glance. Things were different now. She was an old, played-out nag desperate for a man's love. A boy's love.

Guilty, guilty, guilty. She was guilty of her own downfall.

Christmas Day, 1921. Clem announced that her Christmas present was in the barn. He sat by the fire grinning at her. "I've already done my chores for the morning. I'm not going out again."

"For all I know, you've roped a bear and put it in there."

"Could be. But I'm sure it's nothing you can't handle."

When the doors swung open, two chocolate-colored Clydesdales raised their heads to look at her.

"Well, hello, boys."

She led them out to the corral to get a good

look at them. They were fine youngsters ready to play. They ran up and down the corral, snorting and bucking and looking out over the fence.

Clem joined her at the rail.

"I thought you weren't getting up."

"I had to see your face. What do you think?"

"They're young."

"They were broke to drive last summer. I thought you could have a Roman riding act again." He searched her face for a moment. He knew she was thinking of Tad. "If it's what you want."

"They're perfect."

"What will you name them?"

"Castor and Pollux."

"Sounds like a snake oil company."

"Castor and Pollux were brothers who looked after one another—and they were cattle rustlers."

"Cattle rustlers!" He shook his head and laughed. "Fine characters to introduce in this country! Neighbors get wind of that, we're liable to get shot.

"Question is, will these brothers look after you?" he said.

Sunny put her arm around him. "We'll all look after one another."

Between bouts of bad weather, Clem helped her with her new horses. On days when there was too much snow in the corral, they rode Castor and Pollux out on the range. Crusted snowdrifts up to their bellies were no hindrance to the Clydesdales. They plowed right through them at a lope. Sunny braced in the saddle as the horse smacked the drift and laughed when snow sprayed in her face. If Clem was ahead, he would shift and look back, and once he was assured she hadn't fallen off, he would smile. Bits of ice snagged in his beard.

She'd never adored a man so much. Who'd have thought that this range boy would be smitten with an aging rodeo star? She was forty years old that winter. Looking at him in the lead smiling back at her, she felt as if her passion would burst her ribcage. It wasn't that her feelings for Luke or Tad had been shallow. It was that those relationships had come so easily, maybe too easily. This love had been hard-won after many miles, hundreds of hard falls and losses, heartbreaks that had brought her to her knees. Every trophy saddle, every trophy belt buckle, every newspaper photograph of a radiant Sunny Gale waving to a crowd couldn't equal that image of Clem Albright, his cowboy hat dusted in snow spray.

When they crested one of the buttes, they would stop, let the horses rest, and look across the white plains. Mist rolled off the horizon. Warmth on her face and cold air at the same time, a delicious mix of sensations. The winter hush closed around them, snuffed out any words they could have thought to say. Words would have been blasphemous in those ice-silent sparkling days.

Once the wind had thawed out the corral, they practiced driving the horses together. They trained them to take off towards Sunny at a flying gallop and stop and bow in front of her. By March, Sunny was ready to try Roman riding again. As she balanced on top of her Clydesdales, she swayed and then remembered that first time with Tad. The fear and unsteadiness were the same. She'd performed Roman riding—Roman racing!—with Tad for years. She was angry with herself at having forgotten so much. And in Clem's corral, with the constant wind, it was harder to keep her balance. She felt the old gut-wrench at the vulnerability of her body exposed high above the ground and in motion through space.

She was stiffer than she had been back when she'd started with Tad.

For the first two weeks she fell every day. Her old neck injury ached. Her back hurt. Her ribs hurt. One day she remained on the ground, staring at the sky overhead. She heard Clem's boots and looked up into his face as he knelt next to her.

"You don't have to keep on doing this." He helped her sit up.

"No, I don't." She looked to where Castor and Pollux waited, both watching her.

"Look. They're worried about me. They want to know when I'm going to pull myself together."

"There's time. It doesn't have to be today."

"It used to be so grand on top of two charging horses. I won the Roman racing at Frontier Days when Teddy Roosevelt was there. Come to think of it, you were barely out of swaddling back then."

"I was older than that."

"Do you believe I did it?"

"Of course, I do, Sunny. You've showed me the pictures a hundred times. Look here, I'm going to feel the same about you if you never do it again."

"Yes, but I want to do it again. I want you to see it!"

"I don't need to."

"All right. I'm ready. Help me up."

SUNNY GALE

By April, the time had come to outfit Castor and Pollux. She went to see Eleanor and came home with a carton of hawk and eagle feathers and beaded breast collars. Then she worked on her own costume. There wasn't a cowgirl left who hadn't switched to men's trousers now, but she'd never give up her blowsy split riding skirt. She bought herself another fringed tunic to wear over it. Extra feathers that she hadn't used in the horses' manes were sewn into her new ten-gallon hat. And one last luxury—a tangerine silk blouse with wide lapels from the brand-new Sears catalog. The Virginian Hotel was the only place where the catalog could be found, and a clerk was posted to watch the women perusing it so as to prevent its disappearance.

By the time the blouse came, wrapped in tissue paper, she was jumping Castor and Pollux. She had revived all her Roman riding performances of the Pickering years and in that bittersweet return, she found some consolation. Every day she marked her improvement and recognized that the core of who she was would still go on to light up arenas even if her heart always ached for Tad and Mollie.

And so, the rodeo season of 1922 began. Sunny entered the bronc riding events but gave up racing in favor of exhibitions with her Clydesdales. With Clem's box truck she could haul them anywhere and sleep in the cab at nights. Whether she won or lost bronc riding, she could count on a stream of income from her Roman riding performances.

After the shows, there were photographers and autographs. Children asked to be held up so they could touch Castor and Pollux, awed by how huge they were.

Men would come around, asking her for a drink and a dance.

She refused.

For a couple of years, their marriage rode comfortably on the rhythms of the seasons. In the spring the rodeo schedule beckoned, and they would spend most of their summers apart. In the fall, there were hunts, cattle roundups, trips to Hanna for coal before snow closed the roads. In the winter, long evenings next to the hearth.

More and more, it began to pinch that he wouldn't accompany her to her events. She knew he'd never be a performer like Tad. He'd never have Tad's level of investment in what she did. But she longed for him to be there among the spectators, where she could feel his pride and love for her. She longed to introduce him to the whole rodeo crew: performers, rodeo hands and livestock men she knew. Yes, she wanted to show him off.

So the arguments began. Clem wouldn't so much as go to Cheyenne Frontier Days, less than a day's travel away. He always had a list of excuses ready. No one else could care for his livestock. He had horses and cattle spread over twenty-five miles of country. If he didn't keep an eye out, no telling what would happen. There were as many predators out there on two legs as four. Didn't everyone know he was married to Sunny Gale? Didn't everyone expect him to leave with her?

The more intense the arguing became, the longer the bad feelings lasted to where they bled the fervor out of her homecomings. If Clem was home at all, just a few paltry murmurs were exchanged, a kiss on the cheek maybe, and he would pick up the work he'd left off doing. She would unload and unpack by herself. Then she would sit on the front porch and listen to the windmill creak as it turned. The quiet seemed deafening to her.

No apologies were uttered, no resolutions were negotiated when the love-making resumed. Whatever bitterness she felt, both of them seemed to have arrived at a silent pact not to withhold intimacy. She thought they feared how it would end up between them if that ever happened.

The last day she saw Clem at the ranch was a bright morning in January 1930 when she was loading the horses on her way to her first National Western Stock Show in Denver.

They had argued, again. He had led her to believe that he was going with her but at the last minute, when she'd asked him where his travel bags were, his face had soured, and he said he'd be staying home. His deception infuriated her. He hadn't offered any of the usual excuses when they had first discussed Denver because he had known they wouldn't wash. This was a winter, rather than a summer, event. After opening water holes and tossing out a little hay, Clem spent the rest of his winter days by the fire. When they'd first planned it, he'd told her he could find someone to mind the horses and cattle for a week.

The truck was already running.

"You never think of anything but your damn performances!" he said. "What if a blizzard blows in while we're away? We'd be shut out of here and no one could get to the livestock then."

She heard Castor and Pollux stamp in their places on the truck, eager to be in motion. Expert timing by Clem knowing that she'd be stuck and would have no time left to argue.

To think she'd been so blinded by his ruggedness in the beginning. Of course, a cowgirl who sewed strips of bear hide on her riding breeches would marry a range cowboy like him and live her life untethered from civilization. Isn't that what the crowds came to see? People in cowboy hats living as they themselves never would have dared.

With his full beard and stained coat, what she now saw was a filthy recluse, pure and simple. Even if she could stitch him up in a wool suit and trim his hair and beard, he wouldn't belong among the boot-polished cattlemen in Denver. The cattlemen she needed to impress to help secure her future in these events. Clem would be aloof, awkward. Awkward to the point of embarrassing them both.

He pressed fifty dollars into her hand. "Here. Don't leave sore at me. Take this."

"Where'd you get this kind of money?"

"I want you to stay at a real nice place, the Brown Palace Hotel."

"And where shall I say my husband is?"

"I'll be waiting to hear all about it when you come home. That's enough, isn't it?"

She climbed in the cab. "It's not enough. When I'm always in your world, but you're never in mine, it's not enough."

There he was in her rear-view mirror, waving, until she crossed the gully and couldn't see him any longer.

She left Denver a week later, her head spinning with all that had happened. Roman riding performances to packed arenas. Dozens lingering outside the arena to marvel at her and her horses. Newspaper interviews lauding her as the cowgirl who had trailblazed women's place in rodeo. There'd been a banquet with dignitaries. A duke from Germany who had bowed and kissed her hand. And best of all, drinks with a gentleman from the Sears catalog store who had offered her a sponsorship for the coming rodeo season. A sponsorship—that was as big a boost to a cowgirl as the invention of the rodeo chute. It would mean a chance to travel the nation, maybe the world. No more scrounging for money every season.

But her exhilaration burned out as the hours passed in the unheated truck cab. Farm and ranch houses grew sparser, the tilled land gave way to snow-covered prairie. She pulled blankets around her.

She chugged up over the mountains and there it was again—the range, as brutal and unrelenting as she had left it. The past days, cushioned in the gazes of so many warm faces, were no more than a dream while this wasteland bided. *You're nothing here. Nothing.*

She was exhausted by the time she pulled into the ranch yard. No sign of Clem. He must have taken a horse to wherever he had gone because his pickup was in the shed. The coal stove was cold. It hadn't been lit that day. The cows bawled around the gate, looking for their hay.

She lit the lamp, lit the stove. The winter daylight had already sputtered out, leaving behind a pallid crescent of moon. Snow crunched underfoot. No lights on the horizon.

She waited by the window all night and was still there when the skyline blanched. Now someone was coming. Headlights bounced over the gulch, shooting straight toward her. She knew it wasn't Clem. The closer the lights came the more they blinded. She already knew it was bad news illuming the fence rails, reflecting in the eyes of the horses who looked up to see what was coming.

It was the sheriff come to tell her that he'd arrested Clem Albright for cattle theft, and that her husband was in the county jail.

Had he done it—stolen—and branded other people's cattle? As much as she craved the truth, it was not to be found in the flurry of criminal proceedings: the retention of a lawyer, hearings, the denial of bail. Twice a month, she had hushed, tense meetings with Clem where they tried to make plans for the ranch. She wanted to reach across the table and shake him. *Did you do it?* She couldn't. The jailers were always standing there.

She would walk away admitting that even if she could have asked him, she wouldn't have believed his denial.

One morning in April when the colors on the range had turned runny, no longer winter-bleached, but not quite green, a dozen or more men appeared on horseback, claiming to be the owners of cattle Clem had stolen. They'd come to ride through, they said, to pick out their cattle and take them home.

She'd never seen faces like these before, all hard as stones. The crowds she was used to connected with whatever was in front of them, whether the spectacle was exciting, exhilarating, or gut-wrenching. There was no such connection here, only malice.

She would not let them see her fear, no, she would not, even if she couldn't stop them from taking everything.

One of them gestured to Castor and Pollux. "Those draft horses there, they look like colts I used to have. That one," he pointed at Castor, "has a scar on his knee from where he got tangled in some barbed wire. I know he's mine. I had just broken these two to drive and turned 'em out to pasture. That's when they disappeared."

"Pictures of these horses have been in the papers for years. Not to mention the hundreds of people who have seen them throughout this state. Half the world has seen that scar. Anyone could come along and make up that claim."

The man's eyes bugged out of his head, the eyes of a vulture.

"Nothing's been proven against Clem. It's all a pack of trumped-up lies. But you. You are all trespassers right now."

Another man spoke up. "These cows are heavy. They're about to calve. We'd rather move them now before that happens."

The others nodded.

"If you take even one animal, I'll press charges against all of you. You think it's easy for me here right now? What will your own wives and children do when the sheriff comes out for you?"

There was nothing to stop them from killing her on the spot.

The one who had wanted Castor and Pollux looked down at his saddle horn, licked his lips, then looked up at her again.

"We don't want to hurt you, Mrs. Albright. No one's said you had anything to do with it. Let's just leave it with a warning: don't sell any of these animals before this thing's wrapped up. If we hear of you selling any, we'll come back and take the lot. For safekeeping. Until Clem's business is decided."

The little gang turned around and Sunny watched them until they were gone over the horizon. *What if he did it?*

"I know what you're thinking," Clem said afterward, even with the jailer there. "You're thinking that I might have done this. Don't believe it! It's these big players with hundreds of cattle who want to drive me off so they can grab up my land and water rights! Just wait a little bit. I'll be home in time to go to your first rodeo with you. I promise."

Sunny glanced at the jailer who gazed ahead impassively. *What about her two beloved Clydesdales? Where had they come from?*

The jury convicted him in less than ten minutes. There was testimony from men who'd claimed to see him riding at night when any working cowboy would have been home, testimony about him branding grown steers late in the fall, not just calves born during the summer, testimony of his pushing more branded cattle into the livestock yard in November than he'd had in September.

SUNNY GALE

By the time the judge announced his sentence—ten years—it no longer mattered whether he had done it or not. Their life together was over.

15

February 16th

The contents of Pandora's Box are stacked on the table and the floor. Francine's scraps of material remain in the box: material for the blouses, vests, and riding skirts.

Sunny had retrieved the box from the Pickerings in 1923 when Francine died. To Sunny's amazement, Ruth had staged a lavish funeral. The casket was polished white with gold handles and mounded with roses. And Francine was laid to rest in the family plot next to Mollie.

The gratitude Sunny felt wiped the slate clean between them. As she stood next to Ruth during the service, she thought how peculiar it was that, in the end, the rivalries and resentments dribbled to nothing. Arm in arm, Sunny and Ruth were the sisters they could have been—should have been—at the beginning.

At the grave, that son-of-a-bitch Arthur Smithey, by then turned into portly respectability—and who, one day, would call for the end of her livelihood—squeezed her hand and said the whole family joined in her loss.

Reconciliation with Ruth was one thing. Embracing Arthur, quite another. He might have ingratiated himself with her family members and how he and Ruth had resumed their marriage, heaven knew. That would have had something to do with each family's determination to salvage their perches among Cheyenne's "elite." Nothing would change her view of him as a scoundrel and murderer. Wasn't the proof that, in all his prattle, he could find nothing to say about Tad?

Without a word, she'd withdrawn her hand.

Clem hadn't gone with her, of course. No one had commented on it or asked where he was. Had they all heard he was a cattle thief? Had everyone in the world known it but her?

Scott and his wife had telegraphed their regrets. They had just had a baby.

There's one scrapbook left in the box, the one she herself compiled. Here is the last newspaper article: "Albright beats O'Malley to win saddle bronc riding at 32nd Cheyenne Frontier Days!"

What an upset against the invincible O'Malley that day! A victory nearly as sweet as her first bronc ride in Cheyenne back when she was eighteen!

Hazel had already ridden and had the high score, but that lovely Goddess Fate planted a wet kiss on Sunny that afternoon. She drew a buckskin that leapt so high out of the chute that the crowd went wild. Sunny was amazed herself that she was still aboard when the bronc's feet hit the dirt. Spur once-twice-three times and there was the pickup man, the ride was over.

Everyone in the stands was on their feet. Hazel joined her in the crowd and gave her a big hug. Sunny couldn't hear what she was saying over the roar. Maybe it didn't matter. When they separated, Hazel's fingers interlocked with hers. The warmth of that grip—she feels it even today.

Ruth's daughter, Beatrice, won both the Ladies' horse race and the Ladies' relay that day. In the photograph of the cowgirl contestants, she has a wide, toothy smile beneath her Stetson. Sunny remembers her with freckles, too. Same braids she'd had when she was eight, although waist-length now. First Frontier Day's cowgirl in denim jeans. Outrageous. When Sunny herself was still wearing her split riding skirt, although not as full. Francine would have gasped from the Elysian Fields!

The win at Frontier Days made up for the loss of her sponsorship money from Sears. A check came in the spring, but by the time the season was underway, the news of Clem's conviction had reached Denver.

"Your liaison with a convicted felon who has been imprisoned for cattle thievery has tarnished your standing in the eyes of the public..." the letter read. As if, somehow, she was a thief, as well.

Other cowgirls were picking up sponsorship

money right and left. Hazel had received money
from Maybelline, Beatrice from Snowgirl Flour.
    Sunny wasn't going to see sponsorship
money again.
    Still, her performances with Castor and
Pollux continued to draw fans. The families who
came flocking to see her weren't as concerned
about Clem Albright as the men far away in boxy
office buildings. There were still lines to get her
autograph. Still more rodeos. Still Pendleton ahead.
In 1930.

Pendleton had become as big an event as
Frontier Days, drawing fans from several states
and Canada and performers from all over. Sunny
couldn't have found a hotel room even if she'd
wanted one. Despite talk of a Depression, the
bars and restaurants were crammed. Eleanor
had come up from Lander. She wasn't riding
anymore, but she'd brought her protégées—
young men and women—and they were entered
in all the events.

    For the first time ever, Arthur Smithey had
accompanied his wife and daughter. Guess he
didn't resent cowgirls and their travel schedules
so much anymore. To all eyes he'd come around
to endorsing them. There he was behind the
chutes, in a hundred-dollar cowboy hat with his
belly straining over his silver belt buckle, jawing
with rodeo officials and rodeo hands.

    While watching him, the pain of Tad's loss
stabbed her all over again. She thought it had
gone, smothered by so many other heartbreaks.

But there it was, as vivid as if Tad himself was in the space before her. What made it all the more searing was that it affected her alone. No one else seemed to see Tad, as she did, reveling in another fine rodeo day.

She wiped away a stray tear before it ruined her eye makeup.

Ruth and Beatrice were scheduled to compete in the Women's Saddle Bronc Riding. Ruth had continued in bronc riding all these years though her main income derived from supplying livestock to rodeos, the business she'd taken over when Sam died. She seemed much thinner than she used to be, almost gaunt, her face lined and drawn.

Two generations of cowgirls lined up for the official contestant photograph. Looking at the younger girls, Sunny marveled that they had no experience of what her generation had lived through: sewing one's own riding skirt, mounting broncs before there were chutes, traveling to events by wagon. Still, the freshness in their eyes reminded her of how she'd been when she'd started out: eager, exhilarated, open to whatever possibilities awaited.

The photographer set Ruth in the middle because she was the tallest. She put her arm around Beatrice standing next to her. A breeze ruffled the silk scarf on her sailor blouse. Her chin was uplifted.

Sunny saw that chin uplift one more time as Ruth sat aboard her bronc. Not the slightest worry in her face. With her gloved hand curled around the halter rope, she nodded to the gate man.

A shiver ran down Sunny's spine when she saw that the gate man was the old clown. There was his blue and white paint, his red bulb nose, his handkerchief hanging from the pocket of his baggy pants. She felt an urge to shout for him to stop, but he'd already heaved the gate open.

Thousands of possibilities. Pick one.

The horse popped from the chute, and his first jump was a c-shaped twist in midair. He came down and Ruth was jarred from her seat. She started to fall, but she wasn't free of the animal. Her foot caught in the rope underneath the horse, the hobbled stirrups she had used for every ride as her daddy had wanted. Over she went, still attached to the horse, and the next blow of his hooves struck her head.

Everyone within earshot was screaming. Pickup men raced in, but the horse was thoroughly panicked from the burden dragging underneath his belly. The grass arena was large—too large—and off he stampeded, dragging Ruth and kicking at her every few strides. The pickup men collected themselves, reached for their lariats, charged again. First one rope flew, then the other, and they stopped the bronc at the far end of the arena.

Men ran from all directions. In seconds, there were so many people packed around the bronc and Ruth that no one could see them. The announcer tried to soothe those spectators who had remained in their seats. Many had fled. The medical team was on hand, he said. Everything possible would be done for this legendary cowgirl, he said.

There was a stretcher, there was a blanket.

Behind the chutes, Beatrice hadn't stopped screaming. She tried to push through all the men to get to her mother. Arthur wrenched her away.

Ruth was covered head to toe, all the blankets blood-soaked.

In less than a second, the world was no longer one that Sunny recognized.

Rodeo hands and performers milled about or slumped against the rails, their eyes glazed and aimless. Hazel O'Malley had been the next scheduled rider. She pivoted and walked away from the chute. Her husband, Gabriel, joined her at the rail. With a side-long glance at her, he reached into his back pocket for his snuff can. Hazel crossed her arms over her chest and frowned into the bedlam in front of her.

It had only taken one set of hobbled stirrups to blast the world apart.

Someone was speaking to her. Someone was saying her name. For a few moments, the voice sounded muffled as if she were under water. Then she turned and there was Eleanor.

"Sunny, are you all right?" She couldn't answer. Her thoughts seemed to have been catapulted some distance away, just as they had been at times when she herself had fallen from a horse. One hits the ground and there are the physical sensations—wind knocked from your lungs, nerves exploding with pain—before thoughts coalesce, organize, restart.

Her thoughts rolled out of her reach into another time, another rodeo when her name had been Hannah and breathless with glory, she'd picked a new name, Sunny Gale.

Eleanor was the last person alive who had been there on that day.

Sunny sobbed into her shoulder. "It isn't fair that it should end like this for her!"

314

Eleanor stroked her hair and murmured, "How many women in this life get all they want, as she did?"

The horses remaining in the chutes gazed over the rails. They understood that the rhythm of their lives had somehow disrupted. Chuted, tacked up, bucked—that was what they knew. This new wind of idleness confused them. Some pawed and reared. Some kicked against the rails, lashing out to urge their handlers into action. Slowly, the gates swung open, and they filed back into the alley, snuffling the dirt underneath them, and then breaking into a trot toward the holding corral.

The Women's Saddle Bronc Riding was over.

16

February 17th

Once again, Sunny dreams of Ruth. They are in the saddle together on the bronc, only Sunny jerks awake to find herself alive in a room so cold she can see her breath, while Ruth falls away.

Is there any end to loss?

She rises and goes to the window. Is there any end to this snow? A new blizzard barrels in from the east, swallowing the sun. Pellets of snow are whirling.

For the past three days, she had brought Zephira to the barn and fed her oats. Only for Zephira. There wasn't enough left to give to the other horses. When she had turned her out, Zephira wouldn't join the others. They charged her. She *evaded their bared teeth and loped away, breaking the crusted drifts until she reached the fence line. She wouldn't return when Sunny forked out hay to the others. She didn't paw the snow searching for grass. All day she paced the fence line until, at nightfall, Sunny couldn't make her out any longer.*

Now in the horizontal torrents of snow, Sunny can't see her at all.

She has to find her before the storm worsens. She pulls on coat and boots and runs out on the porch. Some noise behind her—a scratch? A rap? The sound makes her turn and there's Francine and Tremain, their noses pressed against the windowpanes. How young Francine looks! Barely older than Sunny when she'd given birth to Mollie. Francine lifts her hand, presses her palm against the window. Tremain—his brows knitted in the dreaded scowl—beloved uncle of her childhood mutated into an embittered pioneer.

She calls to them. They don't answer. She pivots and pushes the door open. The wind sprays snow inside, covering the floor, the table, the rodeo scrapbooks.

The handprint on the window matches her own.

Zephira is all that's left. Sunny runs out of the cabin again.

Within days after Ruth's funeral, Arthur Smithey began campaigning to end women's saddle bronc riding. Sunny learned of it in the newspapers at the Virginian Hotel. Arthur was eager to spew his story to every reporter he could buttonhole—and the more he told it, the more reporters flocked to Cheyenne. Newspapers with stories of Ruth Pickering piled up in the lobby and every one of them carried the photo of her bronc in mid-air before the accident.

"These barbaric displays borne from the bygone rigors of the frontier era must be stopped," Arthur was quoted as saying. "Our mothers, our wives, our daughters should be shielded from rampaging animals, not mangled by them for leering throngs." Soon followed a chorus of open letters calling for the termination of women's competition in rodeo from ministers, priests, the Anti-Saloon League, the Mothers' Union.

Sunny longed to cry out a response; This isn't what Ruth would want! Ruth Pickering, who had fought with her husband to pursue her dreams was now, in death, being used to end those dreams for all women, for all time. And to think how that buffoon Sam Pickering had sought to shield his son-in-law.

It had always been known and understood among the promoters, the performers, the spectators: no matter man or woman, death was the imp on every rider's shoulder. How could Sunny's livelihood be endangered over what had been accepted for thirty years!

On a bitter dawn in November following the tragedy at Pendleton, the gang of cattlemen galloped up the gulch toward her house. Plumes of dust flew from their horses' hooves. Their wool collars were pulled up to their chins.

The sheriff and brand inspector followed behind in their cars. They were the two who knocked on the door.

The sheriff shivered in the doorway. He wouldn't look her in the face and offered no pleasantries.

"I've brought the brand inspector with us to go through these cattle. I believe that's what's fair. To them and to you. Would you like to step out here while we sort through?"

All the cattle were close to the house so she could feed hay when the time came. The men ran them into the corral. They roped them one at a time and the brand inspector looked them over. On the first dozen animals, he ran his fingers deep into their winter hides to trace out the brand. With the wind ramping up to a gale force, the method became too slow for the men to tolerate, and they pushed him to speed up. After that, he barely looked at each animal before they dragged it away to the group of cattle they would take.

They thought they had distracted her, but she caught the vulture-eyed man trying to escape down the road leading Castor and Pollux. She grabbed the sheriff's arm. "Stop him, he's stealing my horses."

The sheriff called and the man stopped. He swung his horse round and rode back toward them, his head tucked down in his collar. Castor and Pollux whinnied, bewildered by the commotion and their separation from the other horses. They nosed one another, raised their heads, and gazed over the pastures where they'd spent most of their lives. Their eyes were warm and clear with no foreboding of what they should fear.

"Jasper," the sheriff said, "I thought we were here to pick up cattle. You didn't say anything about horses."

"These two are mine. I warned her the last time we were here."

"And I told him he was a liar, and he should take his filthy hands off of them."

The brand inspector examined them and shook his head. "No brand."

"They were young horses when I last saw them. I'd just got them broke and turned them out late in the fall. I'm sure they're the same horses. I recognized the one by a scar he's got on his knee."

"How long have they been missing?" asked the sheriff.

"September around ten years ago, I believe."

"Ten years ago!" snapped Sunny, "You don't have any idea if these are the same horses."

"Not a lot of people around here have Clydesdales and I have a Clydesdale stud."

"Mrs. Albright, do you have a bill of sale for these horses?"

"I certainly do," she said.

She left the men staring after her as she slammed the house door. She pushed open the lid on the rolltop desk and leafed through receipts, bills, newspaper cuttings. She opened each of the drawers, pulled out more papers and threw them on the floor.

There wasn't a bill of sale for the horses. There wasn't a bill of sale for any one of the animals on that ranch.

She pulled at her hair. "Clem, please, please." Please let me find some kind of paper, even if it's a lie.

She lay her head down on the desk. The gale rattled the loose shingles on the roof, roaring around the cabin. The men were out there, waiting.

Maybe if she sat there long enough, they'd freeze to death.

She heard knocking on the door. "Mrs. Albright, Mrs. Albright, can we come in?"

She wiped her eyes, buttoned her coat back up, wrapped a bandanna around her neck. She opened the door.

"No, Sheriff, you can't come in. I can't find a bill of sale for those horses, but I know Clem bought them for me as a gift. A Christmas gift. They didn't come here in the fall. They came here at Christmastime. And it wasn't ten years ago. It was Christmas 1921."

"Hear that, Jasper? You satisfied?"

She knew how they regarded her with her hair uncombed and her face doughy and lined. *Just a crazed old witch.* Some of these boys might have purchased tickets to a show where Sunny Gale had performed. One or two of them could have leapt to their feet as she'd crossed the finish line at a Roman race, or as she'd thrown her hat in the air after a winning bronc riding score.

They used to love her the way that men always love those beautiful mortals who strive with the gods, even when those gods reside deep in the hearts of wild horses.

They'd forgotten all about that. They'd forgotten that she had ever mattered.

"Tell you what, Mrs. Albright. Jasper will take these horses home and you can go up to Rawlins and file a claim at the courthouse. The judge'll sort it all out there."

"Don't take my horses."

Jasper was already back on his horse, leading the two Clydesdales away.

Sunny ran back in the house and grabbed the shotgun from the gun rack. In her mind, that old French Indian tried to hold her back. *Miz Hannah, cowgirls can't love their horses!* But Sunny brushed him aside, cocked her gun and aimed.

All the men gathered in the doorway were startled. The whites of their eyes showed, just like panicked horses. But the sheriff didn't stir. He looked hurt, as if she'd smacked him.

"Mrs. Albright, you don't want to do that."

She took one step forward and they all stepped back.

"I know what you've been through, Mrs. Albright. A lot of hard things have happened—things a lot worse than falling off a bucking horse. But this isn't how you want it to end. Put that gun down. You'll stay the champion you've always been."

The rest of the day she spent indoors crying. She didn't go to the window to see what they were doing. By nightfall, there were twenty head of cows left and four swayback horses.

She visited Clem at Christmastime. When they brought the shackled man to her, she couldn't find a trace of her frontier husband. Just a hollow-eyed wastrel, shaved bald, who licked his cracked lips, looked at the floor. After a moment, he raised his chin and smiled at her. The sun coming in the barred windows threw striped shadows across his face.

"Glad you could come."

His front teeth were missing.

This isn't my husband!

No words came to her. The feelings she once had for Clem Albright had vanished as completely as the man she once knew.

I don't know you!

Her shock registered on his face and his eyes watered.

"This isn't how I wanted it to turn out for you. For us," he croaked.

"You betrayed me. Whoever you are."

He shook his head. "I told you. I didn't do it."

"They came and took Castor and Pollux. My horses."

"I'm sorry."

"How can I get my horses back?"

The chains on the shackles jingled as he adjusted his feet. He clasped his chained hands together on the table.

"Sell the ranch, Sunny. Take the money and buy yourself some new horses. After you pay the bills, you should have enough left over to start you on the next rodeo season."

"Then where would you go home to when you get out?"

"With the years I have left, who's to say I'll come home? Eight men have died since I've been here. A couple killed in fights." He looked back down at the floor. "I see how you feel, so you're better off to let me go. Maybe you could go down to New Mexico, stay with that one-legged man. What was his name?"

"No telling if he's even alive."

"You could find out. C'mon, Sunny. Tell me

you'll do this so I know you'll be all right. No matter what happens here."

"All right. I'll do it."

"One more thing," he said as the guard called their time.

"What?"

"Don't come back."

"Don't be silly. Of course, I'll come back."

He'd read her mind. They both knew she would never return.

And then the doors clanged behind her.

At the turn of the year, the Frontier Days committee was first to announce that there would be no more women's rodeo events. No women's steer roping, no saddle bronc riding, no racing.

"We're returning to the idea of simple wholesome family entertainment," said Arthur Smithey, now president of the committee.

All the other rodeos followed suit. One after another returned her letters and entry fees.

She read that Hazel O'Malley moved to New Mexico and began a new career in movies. Other performers she knew of faded into the fabric of the West: the small towns, reservations, and ranches where husbands and children, cooking, laundry, and sewing awaited. Posters, photographs, articles, awards were tucked away.

Eleanor wrote to Sunny. "Sell the ranch and come here," she said. "You are welcome with us."

Sunny felt too emptied to plan what would come next. No costumes to sew. No tack to embellish or polish. No more days in corrals on horses, dreaming of what could be achieved. Aimlessness itself became a burden. She allowed the needs of the day to drive her. Ice on the water tanks had to be broken. Hay to feed the livestock had to be found. By February, 1931, she begged hay from the same men who'd stolen her cattle and horses. They gave it to her.

In March, the cows began to give birth. The new white faces that greeted her every morning lifted her spirits. *Here,* they said, *your life is here.* She could sell these calves in the fall and stay on. Who knew, maybe next season all the hullabaloo would blow over. Women's rodeo would return. This ranch wasn't such a bad place to wait. With no rodeo to prepare for, she could sit and enjoy the fox kits romping just beyond the corral.

Late in the spring, she took in some colts to break, but she returned them in a matter of days. She'd been out of the saddle too long. Her old neck injury ached. Pain in her hip, too. She could hardly haul herself up in the saddle. She was grateful for the swayback horses they'd left her who could barely break into a slow jog.

For the first time since she'd been a teenager, there was no money to be made with horses.

She sold the horse van and bought a motorbike. She got a job as postmistress at the Medicine Bow post office and puttered into town every day, dressed in Clem's old coat and overalls. Once at the post office, she changed into a long skirt and blouse. She hauled the coal indoors, stoked the stove and began sorting the mail that had come off the train.

Everyone—ranchers, miners, business proprietors, wives—all addressed her as "Mrs. Albright." She handed them their mail with a smile, even when she recognized the thieves who'd come to the ranch. She wouldn't be a fool. She had to keep her chin up, fit in here, if she wanted to survive until next spring. Next year—she began to believe it—rodeo would begin again. "Sunny Gale" would be back, and she'd be whisked away. These people would be faces barely glimpsed in the crowds.

She bought peppermints for the children who came in. To them, she became the "Peppermint Lady."

With her cattle proceeds in the fall, she paid off part of her bills. The property taxes weren't paid. She'd have to try and pay them next year. She kept her heifer calves, the start of a new cattle herd, branding them with a mark she registered, a "double S." No one would ever show up and claim her livestock again.

The air in September shimmered even as the sun sidled southward. When the frost melted midmorning, the smell of sage filled the air all around. Inhaling it brought her peace. The hay stashed in the barn smelled as if summer itself had been folded and tucked away while outside cows basked in the afternoon sun. Lazy clouds lit up in pumpkin shades at the close of day.

In October, the wind picked up its growl again, ripping shingles off the roof of the house.

All of this belongs to me. That's what the wind hissed. *You're nothing here. Nothing.*

SUNNY GALE

December rode in on the wind like a juggernaut. And within days, white faceless drifts closed her in.

17

February 17th

She found Zephira on the other side of the fence. The filly has turned away from her and is headed into the storm.

How did she escape? The pasture gate is closed. The fence must have fallen somewhere. Snow is blowing so hard she can't tell where the horse got out.

The wind rages and rages with that old bottomless hunger.

She tears for the barn, scoops the last oats in a can and tries to run over the drifts. They break beneath her and she flounders. Still, she manages to close the distance between her and the horse. She shakes the can.

She shouts against the wind. "Zephira!"

The filly stops to gaze at Sunny while the snow blows between them. Minutes pass.

The filly makes her decision. Her head drops as, again, she turns away.

"Zephira! No!"

Sunny chases after her. Zephira crosses the gully, lunges up the other side. When Sunny looks down, there are no tracks, no animal sign at all, other than jackrabbit footprints.

Still, Sunny wallows through the snow and when she crests the other side of the gully, she looks back. The clouds part and shafts of sunlight fall on the little ranch, the cabin and corrals, the animals huddled against the wind. Whirling snow crystals catch the light and glitter. From sky to snowbank, billions of light particles, pirouetting, riding the updraft and swooping down again.

See, Hannah, says the wind. See how lovely I can be.

Which is the path to God, she wonders. Was it the horse's way or the human way? Was it the way she had lived? Of joy, of loss, of love and family, of the pleasure in growing with one's horses, building trust with these strongest and swiftest of creatures, winning a race, winning a bronc ride, riding the crowd's exhilaration? Consciousness of all that was out there to achieve and savor, was this the path to God?

Or was it the eternal present lived by the horse? The sun on warming hides, muzzles in the streams quenching thirst, the sweep of endless rolling country, the press of bodies together in *a star-studded winter night, the sweetness of sprouts in the spring, the ecstasy in collective motion, the comfort of another muzzle against one's own. An eternal present stretching back over innumerable years to the night where the first true Americans—brown-skinned—had busted open a Spanish stockade and whispered, "Go!"*

She looks up in the blinding light and asks out loud, "Which way?"

And then the snow curtain falls between her and the ranch, obliterating it all. She raises her hand in farewell. Then she turns, following the filly who leaves no tracks behind.

SUNNY GALE

JAMIE LISA FORBES

Afterword

I was born in 1955, some twenty years after the rodeo arenas had been emptied of their women bronc riders, racers and trick riders.

I grew up on a ranch on the Little Laramie River. As a child, going to stay at my grandparents' mansion in the big city of Laramie was a treat. The house was huge, a great place to explore, to hide, and play in. I slept in the "girls' room" where my aunts used to sleep. On the walls hung two large portraits of my aunts as Laramie Jubilee Days Queens. Jubilee Days, right before Cheyenne Frontier Days, was Laramie's rodeo week.

My aunts' broad grins and sparkling eyes intimated the promise of what it meant to be a grown-up young lady. Fine cowboy hats and Western jackets and unlike the dusty, dirty, smelly riding we did at the ranch, Jubilee Queens, and their ladies-in-waiting rode prancing horses in the parade down Ivinson Avenue.

While I never aspired to being a Jubilee Days' Queen, I absorbed the message communicated to me in those portraits. Beauty, poise, manners: the essence of young womanhood. And at the Jubilee Days parades, I stood on tip-toe on my Great-Aunt Alice's stoop looking for the rodeo queens with their rhinestone crowns and their white gloves. Maybe one would glance down at me. And nod.

In my southeastern Wyoming home, brawn and bravado in the cowboy world was the province of men. Bronc riding, roping, bull riding—men's domain. Skill, agility, strength—all for men to demonstrate, while the rodeo queens and princesses from towns across the West carried their flags, checked their horses at the sidelines, and never stopped smiling.

In 1960, it would have been blasphemous for a lovely young lady to mount a bronc and try to ride that bronc for eight seconds. My town looked down on girls that were too loud, too assertive, too boisterous, too wild. They'd never find husbands.

To be honest, I have photographs of my Great-Aunt Alice during the women's bronc riding era. In her high collars, long sleeves, and ground length skirt, she wouldn't have approved of women's bronc riding in 1920, either.

And neither at Jubilee Days nor at Cheyenne Frontier Days, the "Daddy of 'em All," was there ever any sign that women's bronc riding had occurred. Every picture, painting, poster, photo, statute, every rodeo representation ever popularized and available to me were of men on broncs. The Wyoming state emblem is a silhouette of a man on a bronc.

SUNNY GALE

I was well into my sixth decade when I came across the black and white photos of Prairie Rose Henderson in her bloomers and beaded boleros, Mabel Strickland grinning ear-to-ear while riding a bronc, Bonnie McCarroll hurled from a bronc and landing in a somersault, Fanny Sperry Steele in her long split skirts on a rearing horse and dozens of other women riders. I thought these photos were gimmicks. The history of women in professional rodeo had been so obliterated that I found it incredible.

Unlike the suffragettes who were their contemporaries, the women who flocked to the arenas to ride were not advancing an agenda. They may, or may not, have cared about equal rights and the right to vote. They were there because they loved to ride—and no one thought to stop them. In the late 1890s, the newly "civilized" West was still too new and too fresh to constrain anyone's possibilities.

Prairie Rose Henderson became the cowgirl sitting on my shoulder as I wrote this book. Through her and her contemporaries, I began to envision all the challenges those cowgirls would have faced in following their passion to ride, from sewing costumes to the rivalries and resentments, to the friendships, to the challenges of family life while living this career, to the hostility and manipulation of some of their male counterparts.

Prairie Rose Henderson was one of the first to conceive of rodeo as a professional career in an era where a "career" was not to be a woman's objective. She was one of the first to insist on riding saddle broncs as part of her competitions. Her rejection of a "Mrs." appellation, her costumes, her tone, her single-minded commitment to rodeo well into her middle age—despite the rough-and-tumble of that life—lit the way for the women who followed. And they followed by the dozens over two generations, rivaling her and some of them, exceeding her.

Bonnie McCarroll, who won bronc-riding championships nationally, including at Madison Square Garden, was killed in 1929 while riding with hobbled stirrups at the Pendleton Roundup. Though for decades, rodeo performers' flirtations with danger, injury and death had sold thousands of rodeo tickets, no towns ended these popular events—only women's participation in them.

By the time Prairie Rose Henderson disappeared from her ranch in a February blizzard in 1933, there were no rodeos for her to compete in. Her body was not found until 1939 along with a leather halter and reportedly, her Cheyenne Frontier Days championship belt buckle. She is buried in Lakeview Memorial Cemetery in Cheyenne.

In 1940, the first Laramie Jubilee Days was held with the first-ever Laramie Jubilee Days Queen. Queens, princesses, ladies-in-waiting were all welcomed back in the arena, but not in roles competing in what had become men's events.

By 1960, the year I first remember studying my aunts' lovely portraits, nothing commemorated the women who, some sixty years earlier, had proven for all time that one's gender had nothing to do with skill, courage, self-sufficiency, ambition and the pursuit of glory and immortality.

Take the man's silhouette off the bronc and put a woman's there. The meaning is just as profound. And true.

Acknowledgments

I am grateful to Tage Benson for sharing the best horse story I ever heard.

Thank you, Annette Chaudet, for your tireless editing of this manuscript. I owe you more than I can ever say. For helpful comments and editing, I am also indebted to Dr. Linda Hobbs.

The American Heritage Center in Laramie, Wyoming, provided me with invaluable materials. I am grateful for their time, effort and assistance.

Heidi Thomas's historical account of women's rodeo, *Cowgirl Up!*, was the springboard for Sunny Gale. It is a superb window into the lives of these intrepid women performers.

Thank you Trish Nelson, Lauren Emily Sarraf, Susan Eastman, Jack Williams and Celia

Urion for your exhaustive editing, your love, your encouragement and your comments.

I would never have been able to write this book without my years among horses. Every horse is a new beginning. Every horse is a new education in humility, respect, and trust. Jonah, Penny, Scooter, Cody, Lizzie, the Forbes Ranch string, and many others—I cannot repay you enough for the worlds you carried me to, and the depths of awareness you brought to my life and this work.

About the Author

Jamie Lisa Forbes was raised on a ranch in the Little Laramie Valley near Laramie, Wyoming. She attended the University of Colorado where she obtained degrees in English and philosophy. After fourteen months living in Israel, she returned to her family's ranch where she lived for another fifteen years.

In 1994, she moved to Greensboro, North Carolina. In 2001, she graduated from the University of North Carolina School of Law and began her North Carolina law practice.

Her first novel, *Unbroken*, won the WILLA Literary Award for Contemporary Fiction in 2011.

Her collection of short stories, *The Widow Smalls and Other Stories,* won the High Plains Book Awards for a short story collection in 2015. Her novel about life in rural North Carolina entitled *Eden* was published in 2020.

Ms. Forbes continues to live—and write—in North Carolina.

SUNNY GALE

9 781941 052723